LORD RENWICK'S PROPOSAL

"I am nothing special," Eustacia said.

"That, my dear, sounds like your stepmother speaking!"

Eustacia was silenced for a long moment. "I suppose it does. You would say she was wrong?"

"Very wrong."

Eustacia sighed deeply. "I doubt I will ever manage to believe that."

"It will be my duty, as your husband, to spend part of each day convincing you. And you must spend an equal amount of time convincing *me* that I am not so very bad. Which will be difficult, will it not? Because it is far more obvious *I* am no prize."

She laughed as she knew she was meant to do. "Still, even if we each agree the other is wonderful, there is your aunt."

A touch of arrogance lifted his chin. "What has she to do with my marriage?"

"Surely, you agree"—Eustacia hesitated only a moment before continuing—"it would be improper to go against her wishes!"

"Do I? I think not. I know the sort of girl my aunt would wish upon me. A meek little mouse who will never learn how to say boo. You would wish such a meek creature on me? My dear, you have not thought. *Sahib* would *never* approve. And, although I can and will, if necessary, wed against my aunt's wishes, I *cannot* marry to disoblige Sahib. Impossible!"

"You would say Sahib is our Cupid?"

"An odd Cupid, wearing fur and claws, but yes. Eros, Amor, Cupid—whatever you would call him, Sahib has been and will continue to be our angel."

Books by Jeanne Savery

THE WIDOW AND THE RAKE

THE REFORMED RAKE

A CHRISTMAS TREASURE

A LADY'S DECEPTION

CUPID'S CHALLENGE

LADY STEPHANIE

A TIMELESS LOVE

A LADY'S LESSON

LORD GALVESTON AND THE GHOST

TAMING LORD RENWICK

Jeanne Savery

Zebra Books
Kensington Publishing Corp.
http://www.zebrabooks.com

ZEBRA BOOKS are published by

Kensington Publishing Corp.
850 Third Avenue
New York, NY 10022

First Printing: December, 1999
10 9 8 7 6 5 4 3 2 1

Printed in the United States of America

For my husband
who once took me to a region in India
very like the area in which
Lord Renwick loses his sight.

And with apologies
to all big cats everywhere.
Sahib is, after all, a touch of magic;
so one cannot expect him to behave exactly
as any other self-respecting tiger would do!

Prologue

India—1809

The elephant, his trunk swinging gently, lumbered in near silence through a silent jungle. No birds squawked. No rustlings suggested small game. Just silence. Unusual silence.

Eerie silence. A silence which told the most experienced hunter in the howdah, a shikari long in the maharaja's service, that the tiger lurked. Somewhere. The old hunter's disquiet grew as the day drew on and they found no trace of the killer beast.

The local maharaja, a minor despot of a region high in the hills north and east of Calcutta, sat before the shikari in the ornate hunting howdah. Also in the party was the maharaja's son, a boy of eight or nine, and Lieutenant Lord Jason Renwick.

And, more importantly, the lieutenant's modern rifle.

Thanks to an infected paw, the tiger had become a man-eater. News of her latest kill had raced like wildfire through the palace the preceding evening. It was a horrifying tale of a three-year-old, taken as she innocently played near where her mother worked. On this occasion, the snarling beast had come right into the edge of the village.

Something must be done before another tragedy occurred. Lieutenant Lord Renwick scanned the jungle in all directions. He felt loathing for the beast, the emotion roused by the vivid tale of the child's ordeal and death and deep compassion for the child's mother. He had no desire to return from the hunt before the tiger was brought down.

The lieutenant gave thanks to God that his duty had brought him to the area just when a modern gun was most needed. A detachment from his regiment had escorted a delegation of East India Company men up into the hills. Once they arrived safely, his orders said he was to act as equerry to their leader before the maharaja while the Company man negotiated a contract to build a hotel. Assuming all was settled in an amicable fashion, homes might also be constructed here in the hills where, in summer, wives and children might live, safe from the fevers of the hot season in the river land below.

Renwick had asked to be allowed to lead the difficult journey. He'd not been in India so long he was bored by new sights, sounds, and smells, and he had found the march fascinating.

Always interested, ever willing to learn, he had kept his sergeant, an old India hand and an intelligent observant man himself, busy supplying information about everything. From the oddities of flora (the wondrously delicious fruit and the amazing variety of flowers, for instance); and the fauna (the ubiquitous poisonous snakes were the least happy example); to practical everyday matters (often, how to deal most advantageously with the indigenous population), the lieutenant was learning much.

And now, today, the young officer was experiencing a tiger hunt! Such treats were not often available to lowly lieutenants but, in this case, the necessity of finding the beast and killing it quickly had the maharaja demanding that he and, more crucially, his gun, attend royalty on the hunt as they fulfilled their duty to keep their people safe.

The old shikari with silver threads in his dark hair and neat beard, had impressed Lieutenant Renwick from the moment the man quietly introduced himself as Bahadur. The old gentleman limped, maimed in a long forgotten hunt, but it slowed him not at all and, obviously, he knew his business.

Bahadur's gun was another matter entirely. The piece was so ancient Renwick wondered if it *could* be fired. It certainly explained why he himself was invited. *Ordered* might better describe it! But Renwick was glad to have the man at his side since he was unimpressed by the maharaja's variety of good sense.

The prince was worse.

The boy, Renwick discovered, would obey no one but his sire and, occasionally paid no attention to him. The eight- or nine-year-old made the crowded swaying howdah miserable, too, by climbing over the men's legs from one side to the other, leaning dangerously far out, asking innumerable, mostly unanswerable, questions and, in every way, making a nuisance of himself.

Renwick held the charitable opinion that the lad would not have grown to be quite so obnoxious had he not been the maharaja's only son. The local potentate had a plethora of daughters, it seemed, but only the one boy and, because of that, the lad was cosseted.

Lieutenant Renwick wished very much that the maharaja had *not* given in to the prince's latest whim and that the boy had *not* been allowed to come on the hunt! It was obvious to the meanest intellect that, if something happened to the boy, heads would roll. Including his own.

Especially his own?

Despite empathy for the boy's curiosity, a failing they shared, and respect for the lad's inborn intelligence which, unfortunately, was unleavened by common sense,

Renwick wanted nothing more than to grab the child by his scruff, push him into a seat, and insist he stay there. But it wouldn't do. No mere officer, a foreigner at that, would dare to lay a hand on the lad.

It was an added complication that the prince feared nothing.

Or more likely it was that lack of common sense. At one point, the child actually slipped over the side of the howdah and, holding the silken trappings, slid to the ground beside the huge beast. He'd run back along their trail for no better reason than to pull a ripe mango from a tree.

Then, of course, the elephant stopped while the boy was returned where he belonged. Once he was in the howdah, he dripped sticky juice over everything and everybody as he greedily consumed his fruit. And that was *not* a welcome addition to their progress since the juices drew insects Renwick could have done without.

And what if the tiger had lurked just there? Luckily, she was elsewhere. In fact, as the day wore on toward evening, they found no fresh sign. The spoor leading from the village had disappeared not far from it and it reappeared in none of the places Bahadur knew to look.

The maharaja grew impatient with his shikari for not locating the beast, and the boy, a pest from the beginning, indulged an obnoxiously cranky mood which soon became unbearable. Lieutenant Renwick kept his tongue between his teeth with great effort.

"Well?" demanded the maharaja.

"We will try the old water hole," said the shikari, softly giving directions to the mahout.

"If we do not find the beast there," decided the maharaja, "we must return to the palace." When his son objected he was told to be still. "You may," continued the maharaja indulgently, once the boy settled sullenly into a corner of the howdah, "go with the hunt tomorrow. Unfortunately, *I* will be occupied elsewhere."

Renwick felt muscles jump in his jaw. Stop the hunt? Allow the tiger to live another night? Give her another opportunity to kill? He hoped very much the beast had laid up at this last water hole. He couldn't bear the thought that another woman or child might die, savaged by claw and fang. Almost as horrifying, he thought, with the first touch of humor he'd felt all day, was the notion the prince would accompany them with no father to exert even minimal control over him!

The jungle's near silence deepened, grating on the lieutenant's nerves. Surely the tiger was near. The lieutenant peered into the dusky underbrush, hoping to catch a glimpse of a striped orange hide but . . .

Nothing.

The boy's volatile emotions shifted once he knew he'd not be forbidden tomorrow's treat and he chattered gaily. Since he'd been bored for several long miserable hours, Renwick wondered *why* the boy wished to repeat the uninteresting experience. But perhaps it would be unnecessary. Perhaps they'd find the tiger here, a place where many animals came to drink.

The shikari raised a hand, asking for silence, but was, of course, ignored. Jason gritted his teeth, knowing he must not interfere however irritated he became. Ah, to have control of the boy if only for a month! The lad would change his ways! *If,* thought Renwick, *I am ever so lucky as to have a son, the boy will not be allowed to grow into such a brat!*

The trees opened up slightly and there, before them, was a shallow weed-filled pool. On the far side a family of wild boar looked up, snorted, raced away, slipping and sliding in the mud. Nearer, a young gazelle-like creature looked around and then lowered her dainty head for another sip.

And *there,* lying along a half fallen tree trunk and almost hidden in the brush, was the tiger. His eyes riveted to the beast, Renwick's heart pounded. The feral beauty dried his mouth. Awe held him still.

"A chital!" exclaimed the prince, sighting the gazelle. "I want it."

Reacting a moment too late, Renwick reached for the boy, but the child slipped through his fingers like oil. The prince once again slid down the side of the elephant, instantly attracting the attention of the killer tiger.

Without thinking, Renwick dropped to the ground, positioning himself before the boy, his gun at the ready. The shikari, too, came down quickly if slightly more awkwardly, ready to give his life for his lord's son.

The tiger crouched, snarling.

The men took aim. . . . She leapt, several hundred deadly pounds of killer.

Renwick pulled his trigger before the shikari did. That first shot caught the tiger perfectly . . . and fatally. Then Bahadur's ancient piece, in quite as bad a condition as the lieutenant had feared, exploded.

The leaping beast, already dead, fell toward them. Renwick saw, and worse, *felt* the explosion instants before heavy pads, claws extended, caught him across his shoulders, pushing him down. The tiger's last twitching movements resulted in deep gouges along both arms, but for the lieutenant, the intense pain of the powder burns on the right side of his face and, to a lesser degree, the left, caused the greater misery. He was barely aware of the new pain.

But, even as his head spun, as blessed darkness engulfed him, he heard the prince complain he'd been pushed down, been hurt by the nasty red coat.

For once the maharaja gave his son no support. The "nasty" soldier had saved his heir's life by taking the brunt of the tiger's last attack!

One

England, 1811

Embarrassed, Miss Eustacia Coleson glanced warily around the inn's public room, but no one appeared to be listening to her stepmother's monotonous voice drone on and on. The old man half asleep on the settle near the fire had no interest in them. Nor the two in the far corner with their heads together. She looked around the room, but, except for a strangely marked fur someone had dropped in a pile near a high-backed chair facing the window, there was no one to embarrass her further, or be embarrassed by Mrs. Coleson's monologue.

Eustacia had lost count of the times Mrs. Coleson insisted it was Eustacia's duty to accept Mr. Weaver's suit and to do so as soon as possible. If she did *not*, she was assured yet again, it was as certain as the sun would rise they'd find themselves in the basket.

"But, Mother," whispered Eustacia, "he has not asked."

"Then it is your duty to bring him up to scratch. . . ." Mrs. Coleson inserted the words into her lecture and continued as if uninterrupted.

Eustacia closed her ears to what was, after all, a tiresome repetition of everything said for the whole of the preceding month. The lecture had echoed in her ears ever since the fat old man began haunting the house she'd inherited from her father.

What funds Mr. Coleson had, had made up Mrs. Coleson's widow's portion, leaving Eustacia with the small house and naught else but the little she inherited from her birth mother, her father's first wife. Mrs. and Miss Coleson, living from hand to mouth, eked out their frequently inadequate meals by cadging invitations.

It was not, of course, necessary that they suffer so. Together, they had sufficient income for their keep—or *would* if Eustacia's stepmother had not desired to cut a dash in the local society. Together, they might have had a comfortable if quiet life. Unfortunately, Mrs. Coleson did not wish a quiet life. She had, she insisted, quite enough of that as the wife of a vicar who was more interested in the undeserving poor than in her good self.

Eustacia, rapidly approaching a settled spinsterhood, had arranged to receive the income from her inheritance, originally set aside for a dowry. She did so in the rather futile hope they would make ends meet. But there was not enough to keep them comfortable and for Mrs. Coleson to cut a dash and, in Mrs. Coleson's opinion, cutting a dash was, by far, the more important.

Already nostalgic, Eustacia looked back over the few days which the two had spent away from home. A somewhat distant cousin had invited them to her wedding and the cousin's father obligingly sent a carriage to take them to and from the ceremony. Except for the second Mrs. Coleson's sly hints that there might soon be another wedding in the family, Eustacia had been delighted with the visit.

It was unfortunate, she felt, that her brief vacation from Mr. Weaver's attentions was nearly over. But tomorrow, if they left the inn at an early hour, they were bound to reach their own small house well before nightfall. Eustacia sighed softly at the thought.

"There is not enough to pay the butcher, you know. As I have told you and told you, there is only one solution. You must wed the man."

"Sometimes I think he comes to visit *you,*" muttered Eustacia, actually expressing the surprising thought which had, on more than one occasion, entered her head.

"Me?" The widow considered the notion for all of a blessedly silent minute. "Nonsense," she finally, if reluctantly, concluded. "Why would he court me when he could have a sweet young innocent such as yourself? Even with that awful birthmark you are not hard to look upon."

Eustacia's hand slipped up to cover the left side of her face.

"And you have been well trained. I've seen to that. You will admit I have done my duty by you, Eustacia." Mrs. Coleson glared as if expecting an objection to that. "And now," she continued when it did not come, "it is time you did yours, however reluctant you profess to be."

Mrs. Coleson continued in the same vein, one which Eustacia sometimes feared she would tire of hearing and would, for no reason other than to stop her stepmother's droning voice, agree to wed Mr. Weaver.

"He's fat," Eustacia whispered, feeling a shiver of disgust. "If things have gotten so very bad," she went on, aloud, interrupting Mrs. Coleson who just then was totting up what they owed, "then perhaps I shall look about me for a position."

"Look about you!" Shocked at such a notion, Mrs. Coleson was stunned into blessed silence for very nearly another minute. "Eustacia Coleson, that is utter nonsense. Mr. Coleson's daughter cannot take up a *position.* Why, child, think! You are the granddaughter of an earl!" She shook her head. "No, it is not to be thought on!"

"It makes little difference that I am an earl's grand-daughter if he will not acknowledge me."

Besides, she added to herself, *Mr. Weaver smells.*

"The point remains. The granddaughter of an earl must not lower herself to any sort of menial position. You will marry Mr. Weaver and . . ."

"Fat smelly old Mr. Weaver," she whispered. "No, I won't," she answered, but said it softly so her stepmother, talking inexhaustibly, did not hear.

A few minutes previously, Lord Renwick, sitting with his back to Miss and Mrs. Coleson, had lain his hand along his pet's scruff when the white tiger growled softly.

The beast subsided and Jason relaxed. Traveling with Sahib was becoming chancy. Fully grown, the tiger was far too large for anyone but Renwick himself to handle with impunity. Nearly any stranger who dared approach the beast took his skin, if not his life, in his hands. It had become something of a nuisance on those rare occasions his lordship was forced to leave the security of his own home.

Security? A wry look creased his lordship's face. More aptly, a *prison.* In the more than two years since losing very nearly all ability to see on the occasion when he'd saved the life of an east Indian princeling, Lord Renwick often felt life itself a prison.

A dungeon, perhaps, he thought with sour humor, *in which I alone am imprisoned.* He not only lived in a nearly black world, but a blackness filled his soul. Even there he could bring no light to brighten things. Or only rarely and only briefly before anguish returned to haunt him. Certainly despair filled him whenever he recalled that fateful day in the jungle-covered hills east and north of Calcutta.

After the accident he was returned, a hero, to the maharaja's palace where he, the savior of the prince's life, was treated in princely fashion himself. Not that he recalled that journey. He had, thankfully, slipped into unconsciousness.

Nor, for that matter, had he a true recollection of the days immediately following. The pain from the infected wounds was extreme and Renwick was heavily medicated with opiates and, for the first weeks, drifted in a dream-world which was part poppy-induced delight, but equally a nightmare. In fact, he'd been dosed to the point he later found it a problem to do without the boon—or perhaps *bane*, once the need for the drug was done.

At the time, however, he welcomed the relief. Besides, at that time the future hadn't mattered a jot. With the pain blunted so he could think, he had concluded it was unlikely he'd survive. When much to his surprise he had, he was unconvinced it was a blessing. In fact, he very much wished he had not. Still, he was alive and the grateful maharaja had rewarded the savior of his only son in a variety of ways.

There was, first, a welcome if embarrassing monetary reward. Once Renwick recovered from his wounds, he was made to stand in a basket so large it rose to his waist. The basket was filled with gold coins, gems of every color and size, and gold and silver chains formed of intricate links and bangles.

Lord Renwick had joined the army out of necessity. His father, an inveterate but ineffectual gambler, had run through his fortune, leaving Renwick nothing but a heavily mortgaged estate which, only because of an entail, had not been sold. The maharaja's generosity had made it possible to redeem the mortgages and, that done, Jason was, much to his surprise, still comfortably well off. When the estate again produced as it should, he'd be *more* than comfortable. Not that it mattered. Not when he could never enjoy it.

Besides the wealth that had been literally poured around him until he was half buried, a title was bestowed on him. He could never remember exactly what it was although, somewhere, an ornate parchment detailed it. Written in the local dialect, Bengali, and English, it was something along the lines of Savior and Keeper, the Prince's Earthly Guardian, Forever and Ever. Whatever it was, it meant nothing now that he was in England. Thank the Lord. He wanted nothing to do with the boy who was the irresponsible cause of his blindness.

But it was the *last* gift which had very likely saved his sanity. When he accepted that, blind, he was fated to survive, Renwick tumbled into a bottomless well of despair, his anguish nearly drowning him. The maharaja's hunter, Bahadur, understood the feelings of an active independent male who suddenly found himself helpless. And he'd known how to help.

The shikari spoke to his maharaja of the special one among the tiger's kits. Unweaned when the mother died, her kits were carried back to the palace. Among the three rescued was a white cub, thought to have magical powers, and it was to this one the shikari referred. Once the hunter had his maharaja's reluctant consent, he dumped the kit into Renwick's lap, a soft, tumbling, playful ball of fur which adopted the man far sooner than the man adopted it.

Lord Renwick was not so far lost he did not understand that, now the kit was his, the creature was dependent for its life on what he did or did not do. And, as time passed, he accepted that caring for the tiger prevented him from turning into a raving lunatic. He'd hand-fed the cub, played with it, trained it, and kept it content in its new circumstances. The cub, in exchange, gave him back an interest in life.

But *life? Some life.* Bitterness flooded his lordship, as it had over and over since the accident.

Not that he was *fully* blind. Merely nearly so. That he could make out shapes with his left eye did not amuse him. That he could, in good light, find his way without too much stumbling, contributed a trifling bit of confidence. At least it did in his own home, which he'd memorized and where the staff had orders they were never *ever* to move any piece of furniture from where it stood.

But elsewhere? It was stressful to go into the world as he'd done this past week. Exhausting. A misery to be avoided.

Unfortunately, in this case, he'd felt it his duty to his godfather, an aging relative who was dying and had asked to see him. Renwick, having fond memories of his mother's older cousin, had forced himself to make the effort. When he was young and his father's failings a burden, his cousin had done his best to help. The man's excellent example, too, had kept the boy he'd been from following in his father's footsteps! But now the ordeal was nearly over. Tomorrow he'd be home and far less lost and helpless.

And speaking of helpless!

Jason raised his head and, using his remaining senses, which were, he'd discovered, far more sensitive than before, turned his face from side to side. Irritably, he wondered where his aunt had gotten to. Still more irritably he wondered when she'd return. Without her guidance he dared not rise from this chair, dared not try to locate his room where he wished he were. Where he could stretch out on the bed and doze away the hour or so until dinner. He was tired. So very tired. Travel did that to anyone but in his condition it was worse.

He remained alert, awaiting his aunt's return. He would hear the rustle of silken skirts or smell her perfume, a distinctive scent which, years earlier, she'd adopted as her own. Now it was so faint he knew she'd been gone for some time.

But what he really awaited was a sound. If his aunt came anywhere near, if she moved at all, he'd hear the faint tinkle of delicate gold chains, each bearing an abundance of still more dainty shapes. He'd presented them to her when he recalled the musical sounds surrounding young Indian maidens whenever they moved, carefully selecting that one particular set from the maharaja's hoard with which he'd returned to England.

Renwick had not told her *why* he wished her to wear them. He suspected she had guessed, however, since she did so at all times.

Once again Sahib growled the soft rumbling growl, more felt than heard, and again he laid his hand on the beast's head. It occurred to him to wonder what roused the tiger's irritation. Jason perked up his ears when he heard a soft lilting voice, a soothing voice, a voice he felt he could listen to for hours—which was unusual since most voices grated on him very quickly.

But what was the girl saying? That perhaps she should find a position?

Lord Renwick winced at the sound of the second voice, one he realized he'd been doing his best to avoid hearing. He wished that second voice would stop its ceaseless prattling and that the first would speak again.

But what was the older voice suggesting? *Ordering?* It ordered the girl with the beautiful voice to wed? *Could* that girl be old enough to wed? Wed a Mr. Weaver?

Jason heard: "Fat smelly old Mr. Weaver. *No, I won't.*" He smiled slightly. The chit had gumption. He hoped she kept to her resolution. This Mr. Weaver sounded like a man who would have no respect for such a wonderfully comforting voice.

"Jason, a private parlor has been prepared for us," said Lady Blackburne, interrupting his thoughts. She approached briskly, only to stop short a little way from where Sahib lay. "We will have privacy."

Her ladyship sniffed a ladylike little sniff, a sound which told Jason his aunt disliked their surroundings, which, as he recalled from long ago, were clean and decent but rather bare and dark.

Obediently, Renwick rose to his feet. Extending his hand into nothingness, he felt his aunt's wrist come up under it. He grasped her firmly. When ready to move, he spoke softly. "Sahib. Up. Come."

The tiger rose and stepped to Jason's side. The beast was fully grown now and Jason could touch the top of the animal's head with his fingers. He did so now, his signal the beast was to walk beside him.

As they left the room, Jason heard an indrawn breath, a soft sound of startled amazement and joyous awe. Very quietly, under the drone of the second voice, he heard:

> "Tyger, tyger burning bright
> In the forests of the night,
> What immortal hand or eye
> Dare frame thy fearful symmetry?"

Renwick paused. The chit knew Blake? Surely not. Surely no parent would allow a young woman to read the works of William Blake! The changed timber of her voice as she recited suggested she was older than he'd first thought, but, still! Old enough to peruse *that* particular poet's work? Blake's thoughts were far too blasphemous for a female to have studied!

But, oh! That voice! Jason Renwick craved that voice. He could not believe the lovely things it did to his nerve endings. Jason firmly put *that* particular observation from his mind!

Because he was an observant man, he had, while in India, recorded anything and everything which had caught his eye. Once, when in a more hopeful humor, he'd considered the possibility of writing a book, using his notes, but how could he when he could not read? He needed a secretary, someone who could decipher the voluminous entries written into the fat journals, someone to read passages to him in a voice he could tolerate for more than brief periods.

But the voice *must* be right. Unfortunately, since returning to England he'd heard none which did not quickly annoy. Until now. And now that he'd found one, it did him no good. Jason sighed, wishing the girl really were looking for a position.

It was well over two years since the accident. Yet, whenever he allowed himself to think of India, his mind teemed with pictures of busy markets, garish clashing colors, and impossibly bright flowers under a sun burnished to the color of copper. He saw the ubiquitous white bodies of holy cows wandering wherever they chose, the lithe hardened brown bodies of workmen dressed for a minimum of decency, the gently swaying hips of sari-clad women who revealed skin properly brought up Englishwomen would be embarrassed to show.

And, above all, the hot sun glaring over everything.

But those inconceivably hot daylight hours were followed by lovely long evenings lit by lanterns and torches. The brilliant colors so tasteless by daylight were muted, seeming proper, by torchlight. Everywhere one looked was a kaleidoscope of movement, of *life*. Ah! An Eastern night, after the sun set, when a heat-dulled people quickened and life was at its most exuberant.

Despairing of ever again experiencing anything half so exciting, Renwick sighed deeply. His life was over and now he could only endure until it ended. Except someone like that girl might make it a trifle more tolerable.

Perhaps?

Yes, it *would* be nice to have that angelic voice there whenever he wished to hear it. Someone with whom he would work, hands which would set down the impressions retained in his mind before time erased them, as time eventually would. He sighed still again at the irony of finding the voice of which he'd dreamed and being unable to acquire it for his own use.

"Has it been horrible, Jason?" Lady Blackburne cast her nephew a sympathetic glance.

"No more than usual. Oh. You refer to my sighing and moaning, do you not?" He grimaced. "It is merely that, having finally heard a voice I'd like to employ, it is, unfortunately, in the body of a person whom I cannot hire!"

"A *voice*?" Lady Blackburne closed her gaping mouth. "Jason, whatever do you mean?"

He grasped the back of the chair to which his aunt guided his hand. Moving around it somewhat awkwardly, he seated himself and rested his head against the high back. He smiled in the general direction of the sound of his aunt's rustling skirts and tinkling chains.

"It is a girl in the common room along with another lady. The older one speaks in a style better suited to a long-winded parson. The other? My *voice*? An angel, perhaps, with"—Jason acquired a dreamy look he'd have denigrated had he known of it—"the sweetest of tones which are akin to the purest music."

He made a sound in his throat which was very much like Sahib's rumbling purr. He sighed for the fourth time, his face revealing a momentary despair.

"Ah, well," he said after a moment, "there is no sense in repining."

"The *voice*?" persisted Lady Blackburne.

A wry smile twisted his mouth. "I could listen to her for hours, Aunt. At one point she suggested she find herself a position, but I think it was a jest. The other said she is the granddaughter of an earl, so it is unlikely it could be anything more, do you not agree?" Jason, before he could stop himself, sighed yet again. His eyes closed.

The conversation was more than a little disturbing and he wished that his aunt would be still or would go away.

"A girl, you say," persevered his aunt, drawing him back from the dreamworld into which he drifted far too much of the time. "Did you hear a name?" she asked.

"Hmm? Coleman? Coleson? Coleson, I think. Yes, the droning crone used the name Eustacia Coleson. Not that it makes the least difference. You must ignore my nonsense, Aunt Luce. It is a silly notion, that she might help me. It is to be instantly forgotten."

Jason dropped his hand to Sahib's shoulders. The big cat shifted slightly under his fingers and Jason idly scratched the massive shoulder and neck. He loved the feel of the soft silky pelt, the movement of skin over hard muscle.

"Aunt?" he asked a trifle sharply when he heard her move away.

"I forgot something."

Jason would have been shocked by the mulish look on his aunt's face.

"I'll return soon."

The parlor door shut with a snap. Jason grimaced. His aunt was given to erratic comings and goings which made no sense to a mere male. Besides, already half dozing, he was content that he no longer needed to pretend to be alert.

Lady Blackburne reentered the inn's common room and looked toward where she had a vague recollection two women were seated. They were not there! Had they gone on? She glanced around, wondering how she'd find them.

"Ah!"

The women had *not* departed. The one, a female of uncertain age, and the other, much the younger, had merely moved nearer the fire. The older woman's gown was far more ornately decorated than was acceptable in proper travel attire. The girl, to the contrary, wore a proper gown, but out-of-fashion and showing more wear than one could like. Lady Blackburne's eyes narrowed. She studied them and schemed. How should one approach them?

The younger looked up, met her ladyship's eyes, and Lady Blackburne was pleased by what she saw. The woman, for she was a woman rather than a girl, had reached her mid-twenties. At the least. That meant she was well beyond that awkward age when a girl blushed and tittered and, generally, was more a nuisance than a help to anyone—including, quite often, herself.

But Coleson? Lady Blackburne's mouth compressed into a line. Years ago . . . a scandal enjoyed by the *ton* for several weeks, was it not?

Yes. It was coming back. A spinster well beyond her last prayers, Lady Esther had eloped with a man in religious orders, of all things. A man her ladyship's father thought beneath his daughter. The *ton* was both horrified and titillated by the discovery that, in a temper, his lordship had disinherited his offspring!

Lady Blackburne's eyes gleamed as plans rampaged through her head, considered, discarded, then new ones made. Perhaps? Lady Blackburne nodded.

"My dear child!" exclaimed her ladyship as she moved forward. "I have stared quite rudely, I know, but surely," she gushed in a manner quite unlike her normal manner, "oh, *surely*, you are Lady Esther's daughter?"

The young woman rose slowly to her feet. "She was my mother. Did you know her?"

"My *dearest* friend," lied Lady Blackburne with nary a qualm. "You've the look of her, have you not?" Her ladyship thought furiously, recalling family traits. "Especially," she said triumphantly, "about the eyes!"

"My father used to say I had her eyes."

Miss Coleson stared at the matron holding out her hands. Slowly she raised her own and put them into the stranger's firm clasp.

"My dear child, come over here and talk to me." Rudely ignoring the older woman and refusing to allow the chit to escape her, Lady Blackburne led the way across the room toward a bench.

"I cannot believe I've found you, my old friend's daughter!"

Eustacia, allowing herself to be pulled along, glanced back at her stepmother, who, impressed by the stranger's up-to-the-knocker travel attire to say nothing of the gold around her neck, made encouraging shooing motions. Eustacia, bemused, seated herself. For long moments she answered impertinent questions put to her by the overbearing woman who had accosted her. Finally she even admitted she was being pressured into an undesirable marriage.

"But, my dear!" Lady Blackburne allowed her eyes to widen. "You must not. My dear Esther's daughter? Intolerable!" Her ladyship frowned, pursing her lips and pretended to think. "I know! You will come to me for a visit." She gave a slow conspiratorial smile and the merest hint of a wink. "A *long* visit!"

Eustacia blinked. She glanced toward her stepmother. "Oh, but . . ." Embarrassed color stained her cheeks. She looked everywhere but at the lady facing her.

Lady Blackburne chuckled. "You would say you do not know me, would you not? Very sensible. What can we do?" Again her ladyship gave a problem hasty consideration. "Ah, the *landlord* knows me. I have stopped here often over the years. *He* will vouch for me, if I call him in. Shall we?"

Eustacia stared for a moment and then, her lips rather tightly compressed, nodded.

"No flies on you, are there, my dear?" Lady Blackburne laughed gaily. "Very well." A hand bell sat on a nearby table. Her ladyship gestured. "Do ring for him, child," she said. "You will find me perfectly respectable."

The scowling landlord entered, outraged that impertinent nobodies would bother him when he was rushed off his feet helping to prepare a dinner fit for the baron who rested in his best private parlor. The host's demeanor changed instantly when he saw who had summoned him.

"Yes, Lady Blackburne?" He bowed obsequiously low. "What may I do for you, my lady?"

"You will, my good man, tell this young woman I am a respectable soul and that she is not to fear I wish to abduct her."

"Lady Blackburne!" Then the astounded man relaxed and chuckled. "Ah! I see. It is a jest, perhaps?" He looked from one to the other, a rather insecure grin flickering across his plump face. "Do give over, my lady!"

"Are you satisfied, my dear?" her ladyship asked.

Eustacia, blushing still more rosily, nodded.

"That will be all," said her ladyship, nodding graciously. "Thank you."

The bemused landlord disappeared. Thinking it over, he very nearly salted the escallops of veal a second time as he wondered what mischief Lady Blackburne, who had a bit of a reputation as a managing soul, was up to now.

It was quite true, of course, that Lady Blackburne meant mischief. In fact, she did her best, which was always more than adequate, to convince Miss Coleson to join her nephew's party immediately. She urged that her young friend not return home, wherever that might be, but that she come along when their carriage departed in the morning for Tiger's Lair.

"Tiger's Lair?"

"Renwick Towers, I *should* say. The locals renamed Jason's estate Tiger's Lair," she explained, "as soon as the presence of his pet became known."

The odd name had been picked up by the surrounding gentry and even Jason sometimes referred to his estate that way rather than as Renwick Towers, its legal name. Her ladyship, who had thought herself above succumbing to vulgar nicknames, grimaced in a very ladylike way.

Lady Blackburne laid a hand on the chit's arm. "You *will* come, will you not?" she coaxed.

"I do not know if my stepmother will allow it," said Miss Coleson.

"My dear!" Her ladyship's eyes widened. "I do not wish to offend, of course, but surely you are of age?"

Eustacia, who had suffered through her twenty-fourth birthday only a month previously, blushed furiously. She nodded.

"Then it is unnecessary to ask permission. It will be sufficient if you *inform* her you mean to join me for a visit. A long visit."

Again Eustacia hesitated. "You travel with the tiger?"

"Oh, yes. The beast is my nephew's pet. Jason is blind," added her ladyship carelessly. "Or very nearly so."

"Blind?"

"He doesn't care to have it mentioned, of course, and he is exceedingly bitter. I best admit immediately that, if you come, you will need patience."

"But that extraordinary tiger which attended him? Surely such beasts are dangerous?" asked Eustacia a trifle hesitantly. "Is it always allowed to walk free?"

Lady Blackburne's own fear that the tiger would revert to a feral state was one her ladyship did her best to suppress. Once again ignoring the deep instinctive dread of which she could not rid herself, she spoke firmly. "The animal has shown no sign of wishing to maul anyone. Certainly not when Jason is near."

"But surely Lord Renwick cannot be near at all times?"

A trifle defensively, Lady Blackburne said, "There was a bit of a problem once. A new footman entered a room in which the tiger was napping after a large feed. The servants know to stay out of a room when a dog's collar is placed on the door handle. They know it means the beast is alone and must not be disturbed.

"This new man either forgot or did not understand." Her ladyship compressed her lips. Then she sighed and shrugged. "Jason's pet roared at him. Unfortunately that was sufficient to frighten the fellow half out of his wits. Such a nuisance. He refused to stay, you see, although he was an excellent match for another of my footmen. It has been impossible to find another of proper size and shape. As I said, a nuisance."

"I see."

"You don't, of course." Her ladyship chuckled. "But you wish to know about the beast. From bits of information my nephew has allowed past his guard, I believe the creature saved his sanity. I will tell you the whole at some future date. But now"—Lady Blackburne rose to her feet—"I must inform your stepmother you leave with us in the morning. We will, of course, see you are returned home when the visit ends."

Lady Blackburne swept across the room. All agog that such a great lady not only accosted Eustacia, but kept her in close conversation for so long, Mrs. Coleson rose and bobbed a deep and rather awkward curtsy.

"My lady," she breathed.

"Mrs. Coleson, you've a delightful stepdaughter."

Mrs. Coleson blinked. "Hmmm . . . thaaank you."

"In fact, she is so delightful I have decided to steal her away from you and keep her to myself for a long visit."

Mrs. Coleson's vicarious pleasure in Eustacia's coup of drawing a great lady's interest faded. This wouldn't do. Mrs. Coleson shook her head and adopted a stubborn look. This wouldn't do at all. Her stance firm, she frowned and said, "I don't understand."

"An old friend's daughter, you know," said her ladyship carelessly. "I will take this opportunity to know the child. I should never have lost track of them," lied Lady Blackburne once again and without turning a hair.

"But, my lady, she has a—"

"A pet?" interrupted Lady Blackburne, wanting to hear nothing of the unsuitable suitor. "I should send a footman to retrieve the creature?"

"Pet?" Diverted, Mrs. Coleson exclaimed, "Good heavens *no*. Dirty smelly beasts. I'll not have one in the house. Far more important, Mr. Wea—"

"Never had a pet?" interrupted Lady Blackburne still again. "Not even a *kitten?"* Her ladyship tut-tutted. "That *poor* child," she said in a suitably shocked undertone.

And rather wondered at herself that she was such an accomplished actress. She watched with hidden delight as embarrassed color came into Mrs. Coleson's cheeks at the feigned disapproval. Lady Blackburne had taken the overdressed woman in dislike and setting her down a peg gave great pleasure.

"Ah, well," continued Lady Blackburne as the overly plump Mrs. Coleson was about to speak. She glanced at the lady's badly trimmed hat which was an insult to all who must look upon it and winced. "If dear Eustacia has no pet, then we needn't send a footman, need we?" She turned as if all was settled. "Miss Coleson, we mean to leave at sunrise. You'll not keep us waiting, will you, child? Perhaps I shall order a maid to knock you up in good time?"

"Yes, please," said Eustacia, keeping a firm straight back turned in such a way she could not see her stepmother who gobbled objections. She twitched her skirts from Mrs. Coleson's grip when the woman jerked at them in an urgent fashion.

"Until morning then."

Lady Blackburne nodded to the women and, turning, swept from the room.

"Why, that . . . that . . . that is outside of enough!" said Mrs. Coleson, staring at the closed door. "Such arrogance! Such thoughtlessness! Such . . . oh, dear. Oh, dear. *Eustacia, whatever am I to tell Mr. Weaver?*"

"If Mr. Weaver is truly interested," said Eustacia, experiencing a burgeoning glee, "which I do not believe for a moment, then he will still be interested when I return. Unfortunately."

"Unfortunately!" screeched the purple-faced woman. "You ungrateful child! You snake in my bosom, you . . ."

Mrs. Coleson, once started in this vein, would not soon subside, as Eustacia knew to her sorrow. Her stepmother had a large stock of such phrases at her fingertips and would, before she finished, draw out every one. Luckily the woman never required a response when ranting on about Eustacia's multitude of failings so Eustacia, as was her habit, went into her head.

She sifted through the store of poetry there, looking for something to provide nuances for thoughtful consideration and the enjoyment of the mental vistas painted by words on her mind's eye. Why she chose a passage from Byron's "The Corsair" she hadn't a notion. Surely it had nothing whatsoever to do with the tall dark man with the enigmatic look, a rather haunted look. On the other hand, the startlingly Oriental touch of a full-grown tiger padding silently at his side might have suggested the poem.

But then, most likely it was merely that "The Corsair" was the latest work from which she'd committed long passages to memory.

Two

In the gray-brown, nearly colorless time of dawn's earliest light, the Renwick carriage stood waiting in the inn yard, the baron's servants loitering here and there, talking softly or drinking a last mug of the innkeeper's home brew. They looked up, alert, when Lady Blackburne appeared, a young lady in tow, then relaxed when ignored.

The women strolled toward the high gate. "I asked you to walk with me for a reason," said her ladyship.

"Aunt?" called Lord Renwick from behind them. His hand grasped his valet's wrist and his tone was sharp enough to rouse Sahib who growled.

Lady Blackburne looked back. "Put the beast in the carriage, Jason. We will return in less than ten minutes."

"But it was you who wished an early start." He grimaced and the tiger, which traveled in a special bed built where the forward seat should be, opened his mouth in an unvoiced snarl. "Quiet, Sahib," said Jason, touching the animal's head.

One eye on the creature, Lady Blackburne said, "Truly, Jason, you must not concern yourself. It is necessary for me to speak with Miss Coleson for a few moments only and, frankly," she added crossly, "I've no desire to do so in your presence. Come along, Miss Coleson. This requires only a moment."

A footman opened the carriage door and Sahib, knowing they were to enter it, led his blind master toward it. Lady Blackburne watched silently until Jason put a hand on the side of the carriage, a foot on the iron step. The tiger waited, the great head turned toward them, his eyes afire in a ray of sunlight which found its way into the yard.

Lady Blackburne turned away sharply. She could not like that tiger! "We will stroll to that stone bridge where we may look at the water as we converse."

Sahib continued to stare through slitted lids. Miss Coleson, after a nervous but simultaneously entranced glance, hurriedly followed her ladyship. "My lady?"

"Come along, please."

Bemused, Eustacia followed to where a gently humped bridge crossed a narrow stream which chuckled over and around the stones in its bed. "My lady?" she asked again when her ladyship stopped and put her gloved finger tips, all ten of them, on the dew wet wall at the side of the bridge, ignoring the damage which would be done to them.

Lady Blackburne sighed. "I've a confession. If, when I've explained, you wish to return to your stepmother, I'll not stop you. But, if you wish to avoid wedding that truly awful man, then you will agree to come with us."

When her ladyship didn't continue, Eustacia frowned. "It would be better if you explain instantly. I've an overly active imagination, you see, and I am thinking all sorts of odd thoughts."

Lady Blackburne chuckled softly. "Perhaps you imagine my nephew adopted some strange Eastern superstition which requires that a young woman be offered as virgin sacrifice to that dratted tiger? No," she said quickly, "I should not say that. It is far too likely the tiger's existence saved the dear boy from self-destruction! I should *not* think bad thoughts about the beast!" She sighed. "In any case, my dear, I have plotted nothing so very extraordinary." She sighed again, this time in irritation. "The truth is, I did *not* know your mother."

"I did not think you had."

Lady Blackburne's spine straightened. Slowly she turned. Stared.

Eustacia laughed softly. "You see, my lady, my mother was not young when she married. I was born rather late in her life. You are too young yourself, I think, to have been her friend."

Lady Blackburne's startled expression changed to respect.

Eustacia grinned mischievously. "I, too, can plot!" A stern expression made her appear more her age. "You see," she said gently, "I would do very nearly anything to avoid wedding Mr. Weaver. Even impose on a stranger."

"Ah! Now *that* I understand. Anyone with sense would feel as you do. Well, then . . ." She fell silent.

"My lady, I prefer frank speaking," said Eustacia firmly. "Do not attempt to find the ideal words. Simply open your budget and explain."

Again her ladyship turned to look at Miss Coleson who stood straight as an arrow beside her, pale hair pulled back and mostly hidden beneath her bonnet. "Very well. I came with the invitation when my nephew admitted that you have a voice he could not merely tolerate but would enjoy. He has become overly sensitive to voice tones. He is too polite to say so, but even mine rubs on him after a time. He called yours the voice of an angel. He likes to be read to. And he might work on a travel book, writing about his stay in India, you know, if there was someone who could decipher his journals—his hand is truly atrocious! He needs someone to help with the writing of it, too. And finally," she finished, her tone one of minor triumph, "he said you spoke of finding a position."

"Only half seriously, but yes, the thought has crossed my mind." Eustacia thought of the money owed everywhere in her village and knew she might more accurately say it was *often* in her mind.

"Then will you join our household?" Her ladyship held up a hand. "I would prefer that you pretend to be my guest and only gradually work into helping Jason. I will pay you a salary from the beginning, however, and will provide you with a wardrobe"—she eyed Miss Coleson's gown which was only a trifle better than that worn the previous evening—"proper to a stay as our houseguest. Your room and board would, of course be suppl—"

"It is too much." Eustacia ran the tone of that through her mind, realized she'd sounded more than a trifle rude and added, "My lady?" She bit her lip, casting a look toward the older woman from the side of her eyes.

Lady Blackburne smiled. "We will see. We may, of course, discuss the details at our leisure if only you will agree to come?"

Eustacia hesitated. Then, vivid in her mind, she saw a picture of fat smelly *old* Mr. Weaver. Mr. Weaver with his little piggy eyes that watched her speculatively. Greedy Mr. Weaver who ate up everything in sight, leaving her, all too often, hungry for her tea. She nodded her agreement after only a fraction of a second's consideration that *that* was what she must endure as the alternative to going with her ladyship.

"Excellent. Come, then. Jason has lost all patience along with his sight and when Jason is upset the beast becomes nervous. I would very much rather," she said in a dry voice, "not travel with a nervous tiger stretched out across from me!"

The two returned to the specially designed traveling carriage.

"Jason."

Her nephew leaned toward the open door.

"We are to have company. You must slide well over to make room."

The two women were helped in.

"Miss Coleson, my nephew, Lord Renwick. Jason, Miss Eustacia Coleson."

There was no hint of it in her voice, but Eustacia could see Lady Blackburne was a trifle nervous. "My lord?" She touched his hand, was offered it, and grasped it. "I'm very pleased to meet you."

Only then did Eustacia admit, to herself, that that was nothing more nor less than the truth. She'd been intrigued the night before, seeing him leave the room with the tiger at his side. She was entranced when the two came out of the inn into the early morning light and she had seen the white pelt of the tiger magically disappearing against the whitewashed side of the inn.

And then when the tiger stared at her. . . .

What had she felt then? Awe? Yes. Excitement? Oh, yes. And the oddest feeling of expectation, as if the future held something special for her. Something exceptional.

"My lord, will you introduce me to your feline friend?" she asked.

Jason, who had been struck dumb by the sound of his angel's voice, cleared his throat. "My feline fr—? Ah. Sahib."

The tiger opened his mouth in a nearly silent roar.

"Sahib," said Jason, forcing his voice to steady, "this is Miss Coleson. She will be visiting. You will treat her as a friend."

"Hello, Sahib," said Eustacia softly. "I hope we *will* be friends."

The steps were put up as they spoke, and the equipage moved forward. For just a moment Eustacia wondered if she had done the right thing, but it was too late for such thoughts now. She put aside her concern for what the future might hold and, rather fearfully, studied the tiger.

"I wonder," she murmured after a thoughtful moment,

"where the poet, Blake, you know, experienced a tiger. His poem. So accurate, is it not?"

"Miss Coleson, would you recite it? If it pleases you?" Renwick spoke harshly, always unhappy when asking a favor of someone. "You began it last night and I have wished to hear the whole ever since," he added a trifle more naturally.

After a glance toward Lady Blackburne who nodded, Eustacia complied, speaking softly but with those delightfully light and melodic tones which had first caught Lord Renwick's notice. And then, when finished with Blake's verses, she cast a mischievous glance toward the man seated beside her and asked, "Do you know Leigh Hunt's 'To a Fish'?"

He shook his head, bemused, so she began:

"You strange, astonished-looking, angle-faced
Dreary-mouthed, gaping wretches of the sea,
Gulping salt water everlastingly . . ."

Lord Renwick, after only a few lines, barked a sharp laugh. "No, no," he said, "do not stop. I have not heard that before. Do you think it was written as a parody of Blake's? No, do not answer. Go on, please do!"

She did and followed *that* poem with Hunt's "A Fish Answers."

"Amazing monster! that, for aught I know,
With the first sight of thee didst make our race
For ever stare! O flat and shocking face,
Grimly divided from the breast below!"

Which, when she finished, drew another laugh from Lord Renwick.

Giving him pleasure made her feel happy, so Miss Coleson continued with other verses, sometimes choosing herself and sometimes obliging, if she knew it, with something the others requested. It was some time later when the carriage pulled up to an inn where they were to eat a nuncheon and rest the horses.

"Have we arrived at Hawkhurst already?" asked Jason, startled. "Miss Coleson, you have been a jewel to make our drive so pleasurable."

His lordship opened the door on his side and, when his valet's wrist pressed up under his extended palm, stepped down into the inn yard. Sahib rose, stretched, seemed to move in flowing pieces which awed Eustacia all over again as she watched the great beast make its way down to Lord Renwick's side.

"Beautiful," she whispered.

Jason, hearing, turned and smiled.

Eustacia, observing that particularly sweet smile, felt her heart lurch. Beside her, she heard Lady Blackburne gasp softly and turned to find her ladyship staring, unmoving, after her nephew. Eustacia turned back to watch the tiger and its master, who was, she was surprised to discover, even *more* intriguing.

When they disappeared beyond hearing, Eustacia turned a questioning look on her hostess. Assuming, of course, that under the circumstances, one could call her that! Her employer? Except she was not to think of her ladyship as employer but, untruth that it was, as her mother's friend. It was, decided Eustacia a trifle crossly, going to be very difficult to know exactly how to go on, how to behave in a proper way.

Lady Blackburne remained in the same rigid posture, staring after her nephew. The woman's eyes appeared painfully wide.

"My lady?" asked Eustacia softly, drawing her ladyship's attention. "What is it? What is the matter?"

"I haven't," said her ladyship in a bemused tone, "seen that particular smile on Jason's face since before he left for India. It is not only that you have the voice of an angel, my dear. I begin to think you *are* an angel!"

Miss Coleson thought of her own base motives for hoping she'd please his lordship, that they would discover they could work together and that it would be unnecessary to return home any time soon. After all, this odd chance, if it succeeded, was her escape not only from the financial chaos her stepmama provoked, but also from her even more unpleasant suitor!

Eustacia chuckled softly. "Oh, no, my lady," she said. "Definitely not. I doubt I could ever aspire to an angel's halo!"

Very likely, she thought, *it is his lordship who is the angel. My guardian angel, who will, I pray, protect me from the fate my ever-so-slightly wicked stepmother persistently and insistently wishes on me! Well, whatever else may happen, I need not think of Mr. Weaver again. He is not the sort who will sit around waiting for a bride . . . especially since he was never certain he could stomach wedding me in any case!*

Her fingers crept up to cover the disfigurement marring the side of her face. She had known the smallish birthmark was an unforgivable blemish, but for so many years she had no longer thought of it. Except that, where Mr. Weaver was concerned, she was very glad to have it!

Three

The following day, from the moment Lady Blackburne
swept into her room to see if she was yet awake, Eustacia
found the hours full to bursting. First there was the wonderful luxury of a bath. She reveled in that.

She was not so pleased by her ladyship's somewhat tactless gift of a gown, a gown which, her ladyship assured
Eustacia, did not suit and was no loss to her wardrobe.
It didn't particularly suit Eustacia either, but since her
own clothing had disappeared, she'd no choice but to
don the new gown which, she felt, revealed a great deal
too much of her chest.

She stared into the mirror, wondering if she dared
asked the maid for a chemisette or, if that was unavailable,
a bit of lace she might tack into the edges of the neckline.
But, Lord Renwick was blind and one was, she'd heard,
expected to ignore the existence of the servants. Therefore, she supposed it didn't matter.

She sighed. Because it *did* matter. To her. Nevertheless
she followed the maid to the breakfast room where she
stopped just inside the door, surprised to find his lordship
there.

And the tiger.

Sahib rose to his feet and growled, a surprisingly deep
and not unpleasant rumble of sound.

"Who is there?" asked Lord Renwick sharply. He dropped a hand to the tiger's ruff.

"Just me. Miss Coleson," she added, fearing his lordship would not know her voice. "Should I go away?"

"No, of course not. And don't hover," he ordered crossly, surprising her that he sensed her indecision. "Sahib doesn't approve. You must always act as if it were the most normal thing in the world that Sahib is near." His lips twitched. "Then, of course, *he* thinks so as well."

Eustacia chuckled. If she didn't quite believe it, she did realize the sense of not showing the fear she could not quite rid herself of feeling. "Good morning, Sahib," she said softly. She was rather startled to receive a wide-jawed nearly silent roar in response. The tiger then resettled himself beside Lord Renwick's chair.

Renwick smiled. "He likes you, I think. He greets me that way when I tell him good morning."

"I sincerely hope he likes me," said Eustacia ruefully but with a touch of humor.

Keeping an eye on the beast, she served herself two rashers of bacon and a boiled egg from the sideboard. It was a delightful change from the thin and often tasteless gruel which was her usual breakfast in the Coleson household.

Eustacia took her plate to the table and saw that his lordship, taking great care, had poured her a cup of tea from his own pot. It would be unnecessary to ask a servant to provide her fresh, something she rather dreaded. She did not feel she'd a right to importune the servants. Not when she herself was no more than an employee. However much she was to pretend she was a guest, she knew she was not. As she had feared, it would be difficult to know exactly how to go on.

"I must, I believe, do for you what I did for my aunt," said Lord Renwick. He felt for the fork he'd laid down before pouring the tea, then touched his food lightly, checking where everything was.

Eustacia had been doing her best not to stare. Now she turned from her teacup and looked down the table. His aunt's immaculate place setting awaited her. "Excuse me?" How had he done anything for his aunt if she had not yet come to breakfast. "What you did . . . ?"

"Those chains she wears." He cast a questioning look in her general direction and she murmured a response. "I chose them from the hoard a maharaja wished on me. The dangling bits make a jingly noise and I know when she is about. I recall another chain which sports tiny bells. Silver, Aunt Luce said. I believe it would be suitable for a guest's use. If you would be kind enough to wear it during your visit, I will know when you enter a room."

"An excellent plan," she agreed. She whacked the top off her egg and spooned the innards onto her plate before reaching toward the toast which stood near his lordship. Immediately, she pulled back her hand. Perhaps the toast was all his? She resigned herself to a toastless breakfast.

"You sigh. Something is the matter?" Almost absently Lord Renwick felt for the toast stand and pushed it toward her.

Eustacia chuckled. "Not now. I hesitated, you see—" The maladroitness of the phrase dismayed her and she couldn't go on. "Oh, dear," she muttered.

He stared. "What is it? What happened?"

Sahib rose to his feet, a low muttering growl issuing from his throat, molten eyes staring up at her.

She stared back, appalled at what she'd wrought. "I . . ."

"Come now, it cannot be so very bad." His lordship relaxed and his hand fell to the tiger's ruff. "Did you spill something, perhaps? Should I ring for a footman?"

When the tiger subsided, Eustacia relaxed as well. "It

is nothing like that. Just ridiculously embarrassing. But, given Sahib's sensitive nature, perhaps we had best have it out. I cannot go about frightening your pet and I know I will forget and do it again, and then I will embarrass myself, startle you, and rouse the beast all over again!"

A rusty laugh issued from Jason's throat which startled him almost as much as had Miss Coleson's odd comments. "I think you must explain."

"If I upset you in any way will you tell me? I have never dealt with anyone with your problem. I made a terrible blunder—and yet you did not seem to react to my *error* so much as to my *concern* about it."

"You have yet to explain, Miss Coleson," he said. "I had thought you intelligent," he added, his tone verging on rudeness. Then he was rude. *Quite* rude. "I begin to alter that assessment!"

Eustacia grimaced but put the hurt of the insult from her mind. "I no longer remember what I said to begin with, but I ended with the words 'you see' which, of course you could *not*. I will try not to say such a thing again. It must be the ultimate in insensitivity," she finished reflectively.

Again he laughed, but, this time, not with humor. "Nonsense. Merely a manner of speaking and not a reference to sight. You meant, *did I understand.* I am not so sensitive to my blindness that *that* bothers me, Miss Coleson, so do not change your way of speaking. I order you to forget any sensitivity you feel and go on as if I were a perfectly normal male and not suffering from a ridiculous handicap."

"It is not ridiculous and, come to that," she continued, faintly aggressively, "I cannot think it all that much of a handicap. You have compensated for the loss of sight by becoming far more sensitive to sound, to touch, and, I suspect, to smell."

He looked startled.

"You sniffed," she explained, "as I entered the room. But," she added, when she saw a muscle tensing in the side of his jaw, "those other senses can do only so much, of course."

"My greatest hardship is the loss of the ability to read." He was, he discovered, rather cross she took him seriously when he said he was not sensitive to his blindness.

Eustacia jumped on the opportunity handed her on the proverbial platter. "I enjoy reading aloud. Will you, perhaps, allow me to read to you on occasion?" *Did I do that smoothly enough?* She decided more was warranted. "I have had few opportunities to do so since my father died. My stepmother has no interest in books and considers reading a waste of time better used elsewhere." Eustacia grimaced. "What *she* considers a better use, of course!"

"Good morning, Jason," said Lady Blackburne, entering the room just then. She, too, kept one eye on Sahib as she served herself her breakfast. Before she turned from the sideboard, she lifted a hand bell and rang it.

Almost immediately a footman appeared at the door. "Yes, my lady?" he asked. Eustacia noticed he glanced toward the tiger, but Sahib ignored him after lifting one eyelid to see who was there.

"A fresh pot of tea," her ladyship ordered. "And one for Miss Coleson. Jason? Will you have fresh? Oh, more toast or, if Cook made them this morning, scones," she finished.

She sat at her place which was as far from Sahib as possible. "My dear, did I hear you say you like to read aloud? Will you read to me of an evening? I used to enjoy it of all things and cannot think why I no longer indulge in the delightful pastime."

"Perhaps, Aunt," suggested her nephew, with the faintest hint of acid, "because you have had no one who professes to enjoy the more active half of the pursuit!"

"It is true I myself do not care to read aloud." She

ignored his pique. "Have you plans for today, Jason? I wish to take Miss Coleson into Lewes for a few trifles. You will go on all right without me?"

"Aunt, I am home and feel at ease." He waved a hand. "Go with my blessing."

"I will check in at the lending library. Given the boon of Miss Coleson's offer, we must not waste it! Have you finished, dear? Then run up for your bonnet. I shall meet you in the hall at half past the hour."

But half past passed and her ladyship did not appear. Another ten minutes dragged by as well. Eustacia had just nerved herself to ask the footman to discover if she erred as to where she was to wait when Lady Blackburne, deep lines of irritation marring her wide brow, stalked toward her. Her ladyship motioned to Eustacia to follow and continued on out the door, hastily opened by a footman. The carriage turned into the main road before Eustacia nerved herself to ask what was wrong.

"I am distressed to discover you are utterly cruel and tactless," said her ladyship bitingly. "I had not thought it of you."

Eustacia stilled. "Cruel?"

"Did you actually refer to my nephew's blindness? Did you speak of it? How could you be so rude, Miss Coleson? You must know we do *not* speak of it, that, of all things, he dislikes talking about it. I simply cannot believe it of you!"

Eustacia's eyes narrowed and her lips pursed. Very carefully, using all her self-control, she refrained from saying any of the things which popped into her head.

"Explain to me, *if you can*," demanded her hostess, "how you came to do it."

"Quite simply." Eustacia described what had happened in a few terse sentences. "He claimed I was not to concern myself," she continued when her hostess appeared unappeased. "He said he was not so sensitive as all that.

I complimented him on the greater sensitivity of his hearing. He complained his greatest loss was the ability to read so I made my offer, which you heard. My lady, if that is not explanation enough of something which has, once this morning, embarrassed me half to death, then I do not know what else to say."

Somewhere in what Eustacia feared had become a tirade—a mild tirade, but nevertheless a tirade—Lady Blackburne not only relaxed but smiled.

"I apologize," said her ladyship. "Jason made a comment after you left us to the effect that you are a very outspoken young woman. I expressed interest and he told me much the same tale, but I interpreted it differently. I tend, you see, to be excessively protective of my nephew." Her ladyship smiled a sweet sad smile. "He is very special to me."

"You would, I think," said Eustacia slowly, "like to pretend he is not blind."

"If there were any possible way to do so, yes, I suppose I would."

"But he is blind."

"I," said Lady Blackburne, her voice once again taking on a chill, "surely know that better than do you."

"Yessss."

"You would say something."

"I would," said Eustacia, her disastrous frankness came again to the fore, "but I do not know you well and I've no wish to give my head for washing yet again this morning. When you disapprove. Which you will."

A sharp laugh escaped her ladyship. "You, my dear, have a way of disarming one which is quite delightful. Do you always get your way?"

"Get my way?" Eustacia thought of her stepmother's uncontrolled spending of what was no more than the barest competence. She sighed. "Rarely, actually."

"Then enjoy a small victory. I would hear what it is that I will disapprove."

"Simply this. Ignoring a problem will not make it go away."

"One can hardly ignore this problem," said her ladyship dryly but a touch bitingly as well.

"Pretend, then." *One might as well be hanged for a sheep as a goat,* thought Eustacia, and continued. "It always seems to me that one should alleviate a problem rather than pretend it does not exist."

"I have done everything I could think of." Lady Blackburne frowned, her lower lip pushing up against her upper. "How more *can* one help? He is *blind,* my girl! There *is* no cure."

"But surely there are ways to make his life more enjoyable. And surely he is wealthy enough he might pay for his enjoyments. Instead he appears to hide from the world, keeping to a narrow little life. He is an intelligent man, I think. Why has he not set that mind to discovering what he *can* do?"

"Miss Coleson," asked Lady Blackburne again, gently but insistently, "what *can* a blind person do?"

Eustacia grimaced. "He must be *too well protected* by his wealth!" She sighed still again and decided she had sighed far too often that morning. "My lady, there is an old blind woman in our village. *By herself,* she raised four children. Her husband died in the explosion which blinded her. He made fireworks and she helped him. Until the explosion."

"Raised four children!" Lady Blackburne's mouth gaped. She closed it with a snap. "You jest."

"She had a small income from her husband's savings but not so much she could hire someone to care for them all. She taught herself to cook and clean and how to tell if her children were presentable. Each boy went to the dame school for as long as that good lady had something

48 *Jeanne Savery*

to teach them. They grew into good men who, as she grew elderly, took excellent care of her." Eustacia shrugged. "Even now she demands and achieves an independence of a sort."

"Are you saying that woman is a better woman than my nephew is man?"

Eustacia had had enough. "The moral I wished you to draw is that mollycoddling someone does him no good!"

For an instant Lady Blackburne bridled. "I think of him as my son."

"Yes. You love him." Eustacia bit her tongue. It didn't suffice to stop her and, against her better judgment, she added, "But you must mother, not *smother,* him."

Lady Blackburne frowned. She was unused to having her actions questioned, yet could see the sense of what Miss Coleson said. It had never occurred to her that someone who was blind *could* do what that woman had done out of necessity. She would have said it was impossible.

Her ladyship cast a quick glance toward Miss Coleson who sat with her eyes on the passing countryside. Surely the chit had not made that story up out of whole cloth! Lady Blackburne shook her head slightly. No. Miss Coleson did not lie. It was, after all, her appalling honesty which roused this tempest!

And tempest it was. Lady Blackburne's mind roiled. Had she, in her desire to help, actually harmed her nephew? By surrounding him with aid for every step he took had she made him dependent? Had she killed in him any notion he might have had that he could care for himself, killed that thing in him which would give him a good opinion of himself?

She thought of her nephew's character and decided it had not gone so far as that. But very likely only because he did not allow her to wrap him up in cotton wool so completely as she would like! Lady Blackburne bit her lip. Was it too late? Could she undo any damage that, inadvertently, she had done him?

Ancient castle ruins made jagged points against the sky. Lewes. They had nearly arrived, so she'd no more time to think now. Now there were other things to which she must tend. Lady Blackburne straightened in her seat, her hands going to her exceedingly smart bonnet which she also straightened.

"We have arrived, Miss Coleson. Georgie will drive to the inn where the horses will be baited. Depending on when we finish, we may indulge in a bite or two ourselves before the team is put to. Now, I've a list here. A basic wardrobe for going on with. See if you think of anything I have forgotten."

The list consisted of clothing for Eustacia that began next to her skin and included everything from head to toe. "But, my lady!"

"You are my best friend's daughter"—Lady Blackburne's eyes twinkled at that mild bit of humor—"so you must not object if I wish to give you a present. My dear child, *not a word!* I can easily afford these bits and pieces and it will give me great delight! Do not say I may not," she finished in a pleading tone. Again her lower lip pressed into the upper. Then she sighed softly. "You see, my dear, it was not given to me to have children of my own. I wanted a son for my husband's sake, but, oh, my dear, I wanted a daughter for my own! Do let me pretend, while you visit, that you are that daughter."

"I . . . don't know if I can."

"My dear"—Lady Blackburne scowled in a theatrical fashion—"we must rid you of this tendency to absolute frankness! It is exceedingly disconcerting. Especially when one was raised in the *ton* and knows only the ways of the polite disclaimer. The misleading innuendo. The tactful lie. The . . ." She shrugged. "You understand me. What you *should* say is, 'Thank you very much. I will enjoy that.' "

"Even if I won't?"

"Will you not?"

Eustacia grimaced. "How could I not? Even when my father lived I owned less than half of what you call a basic wardrobe—"

"Which I will augment as time goes on."

"And anyone enjoys new clothes. But I've this inconvenient conscience! I cannot see how to repay you for such generosity. And do not"—she held up a hand and her ladyship closed her mouth—"suggest it is part of my salary. I *might* be paid the exorbitant amount of twenty pounds a year for what you suggest I do for his lordship, but I doubt anyone would offer so much when I've no experience. And that is not a tenth of what you would spend on my back!"

"You forget Jason's pet," said Lady Blackburne. "Surely you deserve something extra for the stress of working so closely with that fearsome beast." Involuntarily, she shuddered. "I have known the animal for nearly two years now and have yet to become used to him. I doubt I ever will. Even after all this time, whenever he opens his mouth in that odiously silent roar, I think I shall scream."

"He *is* fearful . . . but Sahib is also a beautiful creature, is he not?"

"Beautiful?" Lady Blackburne looked thoughtful. "I suppose he must be, but all I see are claws and horribly sharp fangs! *They* are not beautiful! Ah. We have stopped. Thank you, Marcus," she said to the liveried footman who helped them from the carriage. "You will attend us about town. I warn you, you will have a great many packages to carry before we are through! Come, Miss Coleson. We've a busy day ahead of us."

Eustacia compressed her lips, shrugged slightly, and then, only half convinced she did the right thing, fol-

lowed. She was chagrined to realize she did so mostly
because she would have to go home if she did not and
would leave behind this wonderful new world. Leave Sahib . . . and, of course, his lordship.

Lady Blackburne flattered, bullied, cajoled, and otherwise manipulated shopkeepers and the modiste so that
they returned to Tiger's Lair with so much Eustacia rather
wondered how she would have use for all the *other* things
her ladyship had ordered! Lady Blackburne had asked
her if she did not get her own way more often than not?
Lady Blackburne herself, it seemed, *did*.

While putting on her old slippers that evening, Eustacia
ruefully recalled the one occasion her ladyship failed.
There was nothing in the cobbler's dim and dusty shop
which fit Eustacia's narrow high-arched foot. Eustacia herself had refused the one pair of slippers which her ladyship insisted could be kept on if only she were to tie
ribbons around them, holding them to her feet.

Now, dressed in a gown she suspected the modiste took
from another's order, Eustacia started for the salon where
the family met before dinner. Eustacia chuckled at the
memory and at Lady Blackburne's irritation that, for
once and a way, she failed. She was startled when her
chuckle was answered by a rumble of sound. One hand
on the bannister, Eustacia halted her descent of the stairs
as Sahib came into view in the hallway leading into his
lordship's ground floor apartments.

Eustacia drew in a deep breath, decided she had best
begin as she meant to go on and, softly said, "Good evening, Sahib." Again she was rewarded by his nearly silent
response. Then his lordship appeared as well.

"Miss Coleson?" he called, his hand dropping to rest
on the tiger who moved slightly to press against his leg.

"Yes, my lord. It is I. And a good evening to you, too. Have you had a good day?"

Lord Renwick grimaced. "As good as can be, I suppose. I made my next move in a chess game I play with my old tutor," he recited as if he had practiced his response to that very question. "We post each other our moves, you see." He smiled then and turned his face toward where he thought her to be. *"You see,* Miss Coleson, even I use the expression. You must not concern yourself." He touched Sahib's ears and laid his fingers between them. "Will you come down? I will escort you to the salon if you will trust me."

"And why should I not? You know your home far better than I. In fact," she said as they started off, "I had the wrong room in mind."

For half a second Lord Renwick hesitated, wondering if he had, while talking with his aunt's guest, become disoriented. But Sahib moved forward, drawing him on, so he continued, hoping his pet knew what he was doing. It seemed he did, since, moments later double doors were flung open.

A footman, who was trained, as were all the servants, to tactfully inform his lordship of where he was, said, "Lady Blackburne's compliments, my lord, and she will join you here in the blue salon in twenty minutes."

"Twenty minutes? Am I so early?"

"No, my lord. Her ladyship's apologies. She is delayed."

The door closed and Lord Renwick chuckled. "Apologies? That must be her maid's addition. Aunt Luce is not given to making apologies."

Eustacia fought down the conviction she should not remain alone with his lordship in a room to which the doors were closed. Still she was, when all was said and done, no more than a servant, even if her position was concealed by the charade she was a guest. Such niceties of behavior were wasted on a mere employee, were they not? So, since she was no more than a hireling, should she not ignore the proprieties instilled into her from an early age?

Taking her courage in her hands, she moved farther into the room, his lordship and Sahib moving with her. "It looks very pleasant over by the windows, my lord. Shall we await her ladyship there?"

Since he habitually sat near the hearth his lordship hesitated. He turned his head and, rather surprised since he rarely bothered, half saw and half felt the glow of sunlight streaming in. He turned Sahib's head and they moved toward it.

Eustacia stopped. Gently, she moved his lordship's arm forward until he felt the chair they'd reached. She moved away from him and seated herself in the one across from it. As he moved around the chair, feeling his way, she said, "The sun is setting, my lord, and the light is playing tricks with the flowers. Shall I describe them?"

"Please do."

He spoke politely with little hope of enjoying hearing about what he could no longer see. But then, slowly, word by word, she built for him such a picture of shape and color and play of light and shadow he found he could visualize the scene. When she finished he was silent for a long moment.

"Thank you," he said finally. He wondered if she not only had an angel's voice, but also, perhaps, the mind of one that she could see beauty and then describe it so well. "I had forgotten how very lovely an English garden could be," he said, a hint of apology in his tone. He added an explanation to what he feared would be considered mere complaining. "I still have India in my head, those last months of my seeing experience."

"Can you tell me?" she asked diffidently, uncertain whether it would upset him or not. "I have read about

India, travel books, you know, but never met someone who lived there, who saw it and lived with it."

His head laid against the chair back, his fingers lazily scratching Sahib's head and ears, his lordship spoke of one of the gardens he'd known well, describing amazing flowers and then he went on to wildflowers seen in his travels. He spoke fluently, his words building pictures at least as clear as any Miss Coleson had drawn.

His aunt, arriving in her usual brisk fashion, stopped the instant she heard his voice. She was astonished at his fluency.

Lady Blackburne knew that, when a schoolboy, Jason wrote more than adequate poetry and that some of his essays had been published. That had been her main reason for encouraging him to write of his India experience. But if this was an example of what he had to say, then she must do more than encourage him. She must insist! She moved near when he paused for a moment.

"Aunt?" He turned his head toward the sound of her jewelry.

"I wish you might go on, Jason, since I find it fascinating, but Cook will have a spasm if we do not go into dinner. And you know what happens when Cook has a spasm! We might as well leave home until she recovers, for her cooking will be inedible!"

Jason rose to his feet, color high across his cheekbones. "I think I have run on forever. I apologize to Miss Coleson"—he bowed slightly—"for being such a bore."

"Please don't. Don't apologize, I mean. I found it fascinating. May I try to write your words down?" she asked even more diffidently than she'd originally requested that he speak of India. "I've an odd memory, as you know from the poetry I spouted while traveling here. I believe I may do something close to justice to your words."

"If you wish," he said offhandedly.

The two women glanced at each other. Eustacia smiled

broadly. Lady Blackburne clasped her hands and raised them high. She shook them as a pugilist would do.

Her ladyship, if seen by someone knowledgeable, would have been chagrined she'd used a sign she'd no business knowing. But her plans had fallen into place with such ease she found it difficult to believe her luck in bringing Miss Coleson into her household. Miss Coleson, of course, had no notion of the meaning of the gesture, but it seemed apt.

And now. Now, if nothing went wrong! If nothing upset what was set in motion! Her ladyship put it from her mind as they entered the dining room. What would be, would, after all, be.

The long dinner proceeded to its end and her ladyship rose to her feet. Miss Coleson reluctantly followed suit since she had enjoyed hearing more of his lordship's memories.

"We will be in the blue salon, Jason. I found a work by that Scotsman who wrote *Marmion,* which I hope may be, at the least, half so exciting. Although I cannot tell you how we'll manage," she teased, "we will wait for you to come to us."

"Please, my lord," added Miss Coleson quickly, "do *not* rush your cigar which I see you mean to enjoy. I must write out your words before they fade from my mind and are lost."

Eustacia was still seated at the gate-legged table Lady Blackburne suggested she use for her writing when his lordship, with Sahib at his side, entered the room. Lady Blackburne twisted the fragile chains around her neck with their burden of tiny trinkets, making it tinkle softly. Lord Renwick moved toward her, hesitating as he approached his usual chair.

"Your usual place is empty, Jason. Miss Coleson is still writing, if it is that which you are trying to determine."

Jason's color rose for the second time that day. "You

will admit it would be more than a trifle rude of me if I were to try to sit in a chair she already occupied."

"Miss Coleson is not stupid, Jason. She will learn to give you a hint as to her location and what she does."

"My location," said Eustacia, "is right beside you, my lord. I have finished and hope I've not done too badly in my attempt to capture your words. Perhaps tomorrow I might read it to you? You will tell me if I have left something out and you may adjust my words where I recalled only the sense of yours. I will be glad to rewrite those passages you wish to shape more to your desire. But for now, my lord," she said as she seated herself, "perhaps we could read? It is a volume which has not come my way and I am eager to begin."

With more ease of manner than Lady Blackburne had developed in all her months with Jason, Eustacia led him to his chair. Then, still speaking, she adjusted the Argand lamp which hung from a fancy stand beside the chair between aunt and nephew. When the oil reservoir would not shadow her page, she seated herself. Opening *The Lady of the Lake,* she began to read.

Eustacia continued reading until the tea tray arrived. Since it was more than an hour later, her voice was becoming a trifle raspy. She was ready for refreshment. It had been so long and tiring a day she was also ready for her bed and excused herself almost as soon as she finished her tea.

Preoccupied, she took herself up the stairs. It had been an interesting day, of course. Or some parts were. Breakfast with a tiger, for instance! But then the shopping, that very embarrassing shopping trip, when she felt more a doll her ladyship was determined to dress in the very latest style than a real person. Still, there was that second meeting with his lordship before dinner and his fascinating descriptions . . . and the tiger, of course.

Eustacia allowed herself a few moments to consider her

fear of Sahib. The beast was huge, weighing far more than she did herself. Sleek muscles were delineated by his every movement. That glowing pelt of softly striped whitish fur only emphasized each and every one. He was awesome.

Awesome. Fascinating. And fearsome.

She must learn to deal with Sahib. *But how,* she wondered, *does one make friends with a tiger?* Time would—or would not—provide an answer to that particular problem, so she went on to a second question she had tucked away to ponder. The tiger's master!

When speaking in that amazingly fluent and fascinating manner of Indian flora, Lord Renwick had became another man. A vibrantly alive man. As he was not when he sat isolated and alone in his blindness, lost in a dark silent place in his soul. Yes, when he spoke of India he was very much alive. Lady Blackburne had been remiss in not encouraging him to speak of his experiences!

And that, decided Eustacia, *is something I can do and—I will.*

She would do most anything to keep that excitement, that enthusiasm, that . . . well, whatever it was which seemed to make of his lordship a different man. He even *looked* different, the very skin over the bones on his face taking on a better color, a firmer tone.

Frowning ever so slightly, Eustacia wondered at the strength of her determination to do her best to make life more interesting for the morose, sometimes testy, man she had seen for the first time little more than forty-eight hours earlier.

Oh, well, of course, she contradicted herself, *Sahib was the first thing to catch my interest.*

But the man was as intriguing. More intriguing, perhaps, because his was a problem which could be solved. She knew he could make an interesting life for himself if he were only helped to do so.

Could she help?

Somehow, soothing thoughts of behaving generously toward another did not satisfy Eustacia's niggling concern that something had given *her* a new feeling for life, a quickening in herself similar to that which *he* had acquired when speaking of India. An annoying foreboding pricked at her, insisting she should instantly return to her home.

But dark humor filled Eustacia at that thought. Her lips compressed and her eyes narrowed. Whatever it was which bothered her about remaining near his lordship, *nothing* could be worse than returning to face her stepmother's constant nagging that she wed her fat, old, *and smelly*, suitor.

Assuming, of course, Mr. Weaver *was* her suitor.

Surely *nothing* was worse than returning home. But if the thing skittering around the edges of her mind, not *quite* coming into consciousness, was what she suspected . . . then perhaps she should.

Four

Lord Renwick awoke the next morning experiencing an unexpected willingness to rise and dress and get on with his day. Surprised, he tried to determine what was different, what made this day special.

And then he remembered. His angel had read to him. She had, although he'd yet to hear her version, written down his words describing an Indian garden. And, on top of all else, she had Sahib's approval! That last thought made his lordship chuckle, a sound his valet heard upon opening the door.

"My lord?" asked his man a trifle sharply.

"Eric? Very good. I bathe this morning if it will not put you out too much."

"Very well. My lord?"

"What is it, Eric?"

"Well, my lord, it is just that you were laughing."

"Is there something wrong with that?" asked Lord Renwick testily.

"But you never laugh."

"You are looking about you, are you not?"

"Er, yes, my lord." As usual a touch of superstitious awe rippled up the valet's spine. Just how, he always wondered, could a blind man know such things?

"*Why* are you looking about you?"

"Well, my lord, whom were you laughing *with*?"

The obviously perplexed valet set Renwick to chuckling all over again. It felt good and he wondered why he did *not* laugh more because it was quite true he did not.

"Eric, have you never enjoyed a private joke?"

"Hmm, a private joke, my lord?"

"Yes. Some thought which tickles your funny bone."

"Funny bone? Er, no, my lord. I do not believe I know where this bone is located so how could I know if it were tickled?"

Renwick burst out laughing. He controlled himself only to have the laughter return when he repeated his valet's comment. "This will never do," he said when he could speak. "I am the most sober of gentlemen and such caprice"—he chuckled again—"so early in the day is surely bad for me."

"Er . . . for your health, you mean?"

"You would not agree it is bad?" Lord Renwick put his hands behind his head, locking his fingers. He felt his lips stretch in a wide grin. "Well, Eric, *so do I.*"

Sahib put both paws on the bed and breathed his heavy breath into his master's face. Jason pushed him away and the tiger returned to the floor but continued to stare in what might, by a sighted person, have been called puzzlement.

"My bath, Eric."

Jason threw back his covers and immediately heard his valet approaching. The man would hold his robe for him and guide his arms into the holes. For reasons he did not understand, Jason found this, their usual proceeding, repugnant.

He walked toward the window, his hand extended so he'd not bump into the pane, and told Eric to lay the robe aside and see to the bath.

"My lord!" said the valet, alarmed.

Jason paused. "Yes?"

"The window is open, my lord!"

Jason swung his arm and his wrist connected sharply with the frame. "Hmm. That was a near thing, was it not? In future when a window in this house is left open something must be set before it. See that Reeves is told. He will find a solution."

The valet gulped. *"Yes,* my lord."

"You are feeling some trifling panic, Eric? A fear you might be blamed if I tumbled head first on to the lawn?"

"Er, yes, my lord."

"Oh, go get the damn bath," said Jason harshly, angry at the man's honesty.

In this particular situation a tumble of a few feet was unlikely to harm him, but his blasted blindness was, one day, going to cause him serious problems unless he found a way of dealing with it. It was ridiculous to go on as he had, allowing others to guide his every step, doing everything for him.

He must, somehow, become safely independent. Jason felt a muscle jump in his jaw as he wondered how to accomplish such a thing. What *could* a blind man do? A picture arose in his mind of an Indian fakir, a man who, for religious reasons, had stared directly at the sun until it blinded him. Considered holy by those around him, he had had a boy with him, a servant of sorts, but the fakir walked alone, carrying an overly long cane-like implement which he'd swung before him, tapping it against the ground. Jason pursed his lips, wondering where he could order such a thing.

His valet quietly entered the room, directing the footmen who carried water and the bath. Jason waited until the others departed and then turned.

"Eric, who supplies my canes?"

"Jones and Johnson, my lord."

Jason repeated the names. "Where are they located?" he asked.

"Why, number 4, the Marine Parade. That's in Brighton, my lord."

"Thank you," said Jason dryly. As if anyone did not know where to find the Marine Parade! *Why,* he wondered, bitterly, *do people think I lost my memory along with my sight?* "Is that bath ready?"

His valet had moved into the dressing room to choose his lordship's clothing. He called out that it was and that he'd be right out to help Lord Renwick into it.

Jason crossed the room, stopping when his skin felt the warm moist air rising from the hot bath. He stripped off his nightgown and felt for the tub with his toe. Finding it, he pressed nearer and, with care, climbed in. Releasing a sigh of satisfaction at winning what was, after all, a very minor battle, he relaxed. "Wonderful," he said, sighing still again. "Truly delightful."

Eric, returning, stared. His lordship always had allowed him to help him at such times. How odd. Actually, decided the valet, his lordship had been acting in a distinctly singular fashion from the moment he'd opened the door and heard his lordship chuckling with no one there to share the joke.

Should her ladyship be informed? Eric dithered, then decided to wait. If Lord Renwick continued to behave oddly, *then* he'd inform her ladyship.

"Eric, Sahib was on short rations while traveling. He must be fed extra today. Send a message that fresh meat be prepared for him."

Eric shuddered. *That blasted tiger.* If he were not so very well paid he'd leave! One day that animal would savage someone. The valet prayed, often, that it would not be himself!

Miss Coleson entered the breakfast room a trifle hesitantly. The day before a maid had asked if she would prefer to dine in her room of a morning and she had said she would not. On the other hand, she found sitting in the same room in such near proximity to a tiger somewhat detrimental to her appetite. Therefore she was pleased to discover no one there. It did not, of course, remain that way. Lord Renwick entered, felt for the chair standing a yard or two into the room at that end of the table and, carefully, made his way to the window end where he seated himself.

As Eustacia wondered if she should say something, his lordship looked around sharply. "Someone is here," he said, upset he didn't know who it was.

"Just me, my lord. Miss Coleson. Where is Sahib?"

"He had a large meal and will now sleep it off. I suggest you not enter the room next to the music room which is considered his boudoir at such times. Marcus," he finished, raising his voice. "Where the devil are you?"

"I believe he was sent off by Lady Blackburne with a note to one of your neighbors," said Miss Coleson in her most soothing voice. "Tell me what I may do for you."

Jason frowned. Feeling about on the table before him, his hand encountered a hand bell which he rang furiously. A footman came running, sliding to a stop just within the door. "Yes, my lord?"

"Tea, damn and blast it. And toast." Jason drummed his fingers. "When you have returned you may tell me what Cook supplied for breakfast."

"Jenkins," said Eustacia softly, "I, too, would like tea. Please."

"Yes, miss."

Jason glared at nothing at all. Where had all his good feelings gone? Where were his elation and that embryonic hope for the future? Lost in a single moment of uncertainty!

"Are you in pain, my lord?" asked Eustacia after a moment.

"What?" He turned in her direction. "Pain? Why should I feel pain?"

"You frown so. I just wondered . . ."

"Well, *don't.*"

Silence fell. The tea and toast arrived and Jenkins proceeded to serve his lordship. Silence persisted. It bothered Miss Coleson, but she was determined she would not open her mouth except to put food in it until his lordship apologized. Well, not perhaps that, but she would not, herself, start a conversation.

Jason finished and rose to his feet. He stopped at the doorway, turning. "You will come to my study, Miss Coleson, and read to me what you wrote last evening." He stepped into the hall and paused again. "At your convenience, of course."

"Yes, sir. I'll see that it is convenient immediately I finish my breakfast."

Jason had taken another step but, at that, stopped. Had the chit actually dared reprimand him? Surely not? He stood there, indecisive. Had he, perhaps, been too abrupt? Then he heard her laugh softly. The sound made him smile. "You were teasing me, were you not? And laughing, perhaps, at my bad humor?"

"I fear I was, my lord. But surely you will agree you are a trifle twitty this morning."

"Twitty!" Jason opened his mouth. *"Twitty,"* he repeated. Again he heard that soft ripple of laughter and again it brought a smile to his lips. "Very well. If you insist, I suppose I may have been a touch *twitty.*"

"If you prefer," she continued, slyly, *"you* might say you are in a bad skin."

His lordship's mouth dropped open. Quickly he closed it. "My dear Miss Coleson! It has been some time since I last went into society, but I doubt very much that *that* has become an acceptable phrase on the lips of a lady!"

"No. Which is why I thought you'd prefer it. Because

I should *not* suggest such a thing, whereas I may, with propriety, accuse you of feeling twitty."

"Ah! I much prefer it that I am in bad skin so you may not comment on it. Except now," he added, surprised, "I am not." He bowed. "If you please, Miss Coleson, I would appreciate it, if you could see your way clear to join me in my study once you have finished breakfast. There is no hurry."

"I will be no more than twenty minutes, my lord, assuming your aunt has nothing she wishes me to do."

"Ah, yes. My aunt." He frowned. "I will have her informed you are helping me for a few minutes."

The few minutes stretched to very nearly two hours.

The long paragraphs Eustacia transcribed the evening before were dealt with quickly. Lord Renwick approved nearly all of it, asking that she expand on only two points. He gave her the words with which to do so and could feel how attentively she listened. Once he'd finished he heard her arrange an inkwell and paper. The scratching of a pen in need of mending was, then, the only sound in the room.

Jason occupied himself with wondering what his angel looked like. Was she tall? Not so very tall, he decided, remembering where her voice came from when she'd walked beside him the previous evening. Was she thin? Fat? She seemed to have no more than a normal interest in her food and was light on her feet, so perhaps she was of reasonably normal shape?

But her coloring? He'd no clue to that and could imagine her any way he liked! Whether she was light-skinned or dark, her hair flaxen or brown, her lips like cherries or thin and unpleasant. With a hint of a smile hovering around his lips, Jason designed several women and finally chose one he labeled "Miss Coleson."

Very likely it bore no resemblance to his angel, but he liked the woman he had created and called by her name.

His imaginary woman was of medium height and had heavy brown hair which, held back by a ribbon, hung loose down her back. She had eyes the blue of the gentian and a rosy tone to cheeks and lips and perhaps that nice peach tone to her skin which darkened in the sun if she were not very careful to avoid it. She was graceful in her carriage and smiled often.

At least, he thought, *I can be reasonably certain of the smile!*

"My lord," Miss Coleson broke into his thoughts. "I have finished. Shall I read it again?"

His lordship tucked away his portrait not caring whether it held any resemblance to reality. It was a new game. A very pleasant game. He would play it again soon and come up with a different picture, another woman. Why, Miss Coleson could be a whole regiment of women all by herself!

"My lord?"

"Hmm? Read it again? Please do."

He listened, made two corrections which he asked her to pencil in rather than take the time to rewrite the whole. "I wonder," he said when she finished, "if we might occasionally do this again? If it is not too much an imposition?"

"I would enjoy that, my lord."

"Excellent. Now I wonder where I might find a folder in which to keep those bits you write out for me."

"I could make a cloth-covered folder, my lord."

"Nonsense," he said testily. "There must be such a thing among my supplies." He frowned, his hands clenching. "It is merely that I have forgotten where they are kept."

"And why, my lord, *should* you keep such facts in your head?"

"Hmm?" His scowl deepened.

"Why should you," she repeated patiently, "remember such details? I am certain that before you were blinded it would never have occurred to you to know the location of every little thing you might need. You would ring for a servant and deman—er, *request*—that the thing be produced."

His brows rose the instant she broke off one word and substituted the other. His lips twitched. He chuckled. "Miss Coleson, you are a minx!"

"Minx, my lord?" She was exceedingly glad he could not see her heated cheeks.

"You are not at all intimidated by me are you?"

"Should I be, my lord?"

He heard surprise in her tone and smiled again. "No. I know of no reason why you should."

"When will you tell me more about India, my lord?"

"Hmm. So you may write it down for me?"

"My lord, I believe your observations should not be lost, when they are phrased so . . ." It was her turn to frown. "I would say poetically, but I think that that is not quite right. Your words build pictures and one sees what you describe. You have a great talent, my lord, and should use it, not hide it."

"Again she dares to reprimand me!"

But he obliged her curiosity, describing more of the flora he had encountered, breaking off now and again for her to transcribe his words. A sound interrupted his train of thought. Irritated, he turned his head at a second light tap-tap at his door.

"Yes," he called.

The door opened and Reeves cleared his throat.

"Yes, Reeves?"

"The beast, my lord. He seems restless . . . ?"

"You wish me to release Sahib?"

"Yes, my lord. I believe the creature wishes to go out."

"What time is it?"

"Very nearly twenty minutes to two, my lord."

Jason's brows arched. "So late? How can that be? But,

of course, Sahib must have a run. I'll see to it immediately, Reeves." Almost as an afterthought he added, "Thank you for reminding me."

"I will leave you, then," said Miss Coleson, ruing her flushed cheeks. *Reeves gave me a very odd look,* she thought. *He must find my being behind a closed door alone with his lordship quite odd. Unacceptable, even. Oh, dear.*

"One moment." Lord Renwick rose, his fingertips pressed lightly to the bare desk. "I am about to make what will seem an impertinent request, Miss Coleson. I kept journals while in India. I wonder if you might look at the first and see if, by some magic, you find yourself able to decipher my writing. If you can, perhaps you could, occasionally, read sections to me, reminding me of my days in India? My aunt has encouraged me to write a memoir or travel book. Something of the sort. Perhaps, with your help, I might do—er, might make a beginning for her?"

"You might do it, my lord, for yourself as well, and for all those readers who will, I am certain, enjoy your writing."

"You, my dear," he said only a trifle tartly, "are an abominable chit. The way you have of mixing encouragement with reprimands is an art of which not many are capable. Thank goodness. Now, if Sahib is not to be very angry with me, I must go."

Lord Renwick felt along the edge of his desk and, finding the corner, oriented himself to the door. He walked firmly toward it. As he extended his hands just before reaching it, checking for its exact position, he was reminded of his need for that specially designed cane which must be ordered. Immediately. He would have Reeves do so as soon as he returned from taking Sahib to his pen.

"My lord."

He didn't turn. "Yes?"

"Where might I find your journal?"

"Journals. There are several. Aunt Luce put them on the shelves behind the desk. Gray bound books, a foot high and ridiculously awkward to carry about India with me. They have stiff covers and fall open easily so were exceptionally easy books in which to write. They are numbered, Miss Coleson. Start with the first and we will consult about anything you manage to decipher." He opened the door. "Ah! I almost forgot. I used abbreviations and symbols which I must explain. Assuming you do not find the writing impossibly boring, of course."

She laughed.

"You find that amusing." His head snapped up and his eyes narrowed. "Why?" he demanded.

"My lord, if you write of India with anything like the enthusiasm with which you speak of it, then I can only be fascinated. As you know. You were jesting."

"I did not jest."

He exited and shut the door behind him with that extra caution which denotes anger or some other strong emotion. Blankly, Eustacia stared at it.

The man is an enigma, she thought. *He makes no sense at all, speaking, one moment in a reasonable fashion, and more or less politely, and then,* for no reason, *he becomes another man, arrogant, sharp of tongue, harsh voiced . . . in short,* she thought, *a tyrant. No reason I can see,* she amended. Then, accepting that his rudeness was most likely a result of the frustrations roused by his blindness, she excused him.

Eustacia found the journals, but *not* the first one. She plucked number two from the shelf and went in search of Lady Blackburne.

Eustacia explained her problem and her ladyship was equally mystified. "I haven't a notion where the first volume might be," said her ladyship. She frowned. "I tried to read one, but found it too difficult. I was curious," she added a trifle diffidently, when Eustacia frowned, "about his tour of duty and who he might have met that I know."

When the girl's frown did not lighten her ladyship's lips tightened. "You need not look disapproving. You've no notion what it was like when my nephew first returned," she said. "I hoped his journal might reveal a friendship with someone who had also returned to England, someone I might invite here, someone with whom he could reminisce. I now see that for foolishness, but at the time . . . Oh, why do I try to explain what is no business of yours?"

Eustacia nodded. "If I somehow communicated my"— she discarded the word "shock" and quickly substituted another, which wasn't much better—"distress—I am sorry for it."

"I read *disapproval*, Miss Coleson," said her ladyship, coldly.

Eustacia nodded. "Very likely. I could never read another's private words unless I'd his or her permission and somehow, I'd the notion, you had not. But it is, as you say, not my business."

"You do not believe one is occasionally justified in behaving in an underhanded manner?"

Eustacia chuckled. "How can I not? Were we both not more than a trifle deceitful in our first dealings with each other? You claimed friendship with my mother. I knew it for a lie, but I did not contradict you. It is human nature to use others for one's own ends, but not an admirable trait. You agree, do you not?"

Lady Blackburne, who knew herself to be a master at manipulation, did *not* agree. One used others. One hoped it was to the advantage of all, but, if a choice were necessary, she would advantage those she cared for over the needs of a stranger.

And, however disarming, Miss Coleson was very much a stranger.

"I've no time for a discussion of the ethics of such behavior," said her ladyship. "I must discover the where-

abouts of that missing journal!" She turned on her heel
and left the room in search of Reeves.

Reeves knew no more than she. He offered to make
inquiries.

Most of the household servants would not admit to having seen the journals. Those who had, maids who dusted
the study for instance, could not read and found it ex-
quisitely humorous that they were suspected of taking it.
Everyone was told to look for it.

Three days passed and the book remained lost. Then,
after their evening meal, Lord Renwick declined his usual
cigar and followed his aunt and Miss Coleson into the
blue salon, impatient to hear the next part of Scott's
work. It was not, perhaps, a book he himself would have
chosen, but he was starved for the written word and drank
in every line.

Later, when the tea tray arrived, he asked the question
Eustacia had dreaded hearing. "How, Miss Coleson, do
you progress with my journal? Since you do not mention
it, I fear you are as bored as I predicted."

"I am more than a third of the way through the second
volume, my lord."

His brows arched. "Amazing. Aunt, you are wrong."

"Wrong?" asked Lady Blackburne, exchanging a worried glance with Miss Coleson.

"My writing cannot be so very bad after all. Miss Coleson has managed in only a few days, to progress well into
the second volume of my poor efforts. But she has yet to
tell me what she thinks of any of it."

Eustacia bit her lip. She stared at Lady Blackburne who
shook her head, making her chains dance and tinkle. Too
late, her hand came up to cover them.

"Aunt?"

She didn't respond.

"Something is . . . not right." His hands clutched the

arms of his chair and his head swung, looking blindly
from one to the other. "Tell me. Instantly."

"It is nothing serious, my lord," said Eustacia quickly,
glancing at Sahib who rose to his feet at his master's agitation. She, too, rose and went to his lordship—his other
side—and lay her hand against his arm. She was shocked
when he covered hers, the warmth of his hand very nearly
making her forget what she meant to say. Despite a rapidly beating heart, she managed, "The thing is, I have
not read your first journal. My lord, we cannot find it."

"Cannot . . ." A scowl formed and he dropped her
hand.

Eustacia put her other hand over the warm flesh his
had abandoned and wondered why, exactly, she felt such
a sense of loss.

"Damned and blast!" he continued, unaware of the
bleak thoughts and bleaker emotions roiling through Eustacia. "Of course you cannot find it. Aunt, ring for Eric."
His fingers drummed on the chair arm until the door
open. "Eric?"

"Yes, my lord?"

"Go instantly to my private sitting room. Lift the lid
on the game table. You will find a gray-colored book
there. Bring it to me."

"Yes, my lord."

Lady Blackburne's mouth dropped open. Amusement
cut through the emotions Miss Coleson *didn't* wish to feel
and she covered her mouth to keep back the giggles.

"Well!" said her ladyship sharply. "But why?"

"Why did I take it to my room? When I cannot see,
cannot read?" Lord Renwick's scowl deepened. "I cannot
explain it for the very good reason I don't *know*. Why
then did I not return it to the study? That I can answer.
I deliberately put it from my mind because it was such a
stupid thing to have done in the first place."

"Not stupid," said Eustacia softly. "Merely that you

wanted some reminder of happier times and your months in India *were* happy, were they not, my lord?"

A muscle jumped in his jaw. "I enjoyed them immensely. Despite the heat and the dirt and the—the . . . ugliness one saw along with the beauty."

"Ugliness, my lord?"

"If I had lived there a decade I would not have understood some native beliefs. In my first week I saw a woman lying by the side of the road. She was starving but was considered a sort of pariah and no one would touch her. Then I saw others, people suffering from the last stages of leprosy, for instance, people *we* would hide away and try to forget, who were carefully tended, fed, given alms. I could not understand it. Why the one, I wonder, and not the other?" He shook his head and lay it back against his chair.

Eric knocked and, given permission, entered. "I have brought the book, my lord."

Lord Renwick gestured tiredly. "Give it to Miss Coleson."

"At last," she breathed.

"At last, Miss Coleson?" he asked, his eyes still closed and his hand ruffling the fur at the back of Sahib's neck.

"We tried to find it, my lord. I think we feared to upset you by mentioning it. We even accused the servants, suggesting that one of them had taken it."

"Nonsense. The servants, except for Reeves, Eric, and my housekeeper, cannot read. Certainly not something so badly written as my journal!"

"Yes. That finally occurred to me as we sat here. We should have asked you immediately, my lord."

"Yes, you should have."

"But you see—" She chuckled. "Oh! There are those words again, my lord, but *you see you cannot see*, so it did not occur to us that you might have it."

She heard Lady Blackburne gasp softly and wondered

if she had gone too far. She cast a worried look toward his lordship and relaxed when she saw that his lips were curved upward in a bit of a smile.

"I am so glad to have it," she continued. "There are several shortened words I've not deciphered. They will be clarified in the first volume."

"Umm? Oh, yes. On first usage, I used both the full spelling of the abbreviation and the short, did I not?"

"I am making a list, my lord," she said. "I consult it when I forget."

His lordship never opened his eyes. His hand strayed again to his side, found Sahib's head and scruff. Sitting with his head laid back, his eyes deep sunk and dark ringed, he fingered the creature who rumbled contentedly.

Eustacia felt concern. Or perhaps it was pity? He looked so tired, so discouraged. And yet . . . why should she pity him? He was a strong healthy male. An intelligent man.

But he was haunted, unhappy. Lacking . . . something.

Eustacia turned to Lady Blackburne who set stitches in a long strip of needlepoint which, once finished, would recover the bench in the hall where footmen sat when on duty there. In many households, Eustacia knew, they would not be allowed to sit but were forced to stand for hours in a hall or outside a room, with nothing to do, no way of amusing themselves.

Is it any wonder, she mused, *that footmen have a reputation for wildness? Their life must be excessively boring. Anyone might be excused for kicking over the traces when freed from duty for a time!*

"What are you thinking?" asked Lord Renwick, speaking with no warning.

"Me?" asked his aunt, surprised. She glanced up, saw her nephew's head turning toward her voice and realized he'd spoken to Miss Coleson. She pretended not to notice. "I am planing the meals for the remainder of the week. And you, Miss Coleson? What is on your mind?" Lady Blackburne chuckled. "She blushed, Jason. Just what," her ladyship said in teasing tones, "could bring such color to her delightfully creamy cheeks?"

"You will think it odd, my lady, but I had just concluded it is not surprising, with the long boring hours they spend doing nothing, that footmen have a tendency to wildness on their days off."

Lady Blackburne did not hide her surprise. "But, Miss Coleson, when they are not on hall duty, they have wood to polish, floors to wax, silver to clean. They are *always* busy, are they not?"

"I was thinking of hall duty, my lady," explained Eustacia. "In your household they are allowed to sit, but in some homes they are not. I can barely imagine how awful it must be to stand for hours doing nothing as those men are required to do."

"Like a soldier on guard duty," said Lord Renwick. "When I was in India, I tried to arrange it so no one under me suffered such duty more than another. Not that one could be entirely fair, of course."

He sighed and then rose to his feet. Orienting himself by the soft sound of his aunt's tinkling chains, he stepped toward her. She lifted her hand to touch his and he leaned forward. She presented her cheek for his kiss, moving against his lips. As he straightened, she squeezed his hand.

Turning, his lordship said, "Until tomorrow, Miss Coleson. Sahib? Bed?"

The tiger came to Lord Renwick's side. He pressed slightly against the man's leg and Renwick's fingers moved to rest on his pet's head. The two padded, equally silent, toward the door. Sahib paused for Lord Renwick to search out the latch and press it and then they disappeared through the opened door. Eustacia thought of the two together, the man militarily straight, the tiger sleek and regal. They looked so right.

Lady Blackburne interrupted thoughts which Eustacia reluctantly put aside. "Do you think," her ladyship asked, "that you can help Jason to write that book about his stay in India?"

"I'm certain of it, assuming we can decide how to organize the book."

"Organize?"

"One could begin with day one of journal one and go on, day by day, to the end, but his lordship has jumbled together so many different observations about so many different things that that might be overly confusing to a reader. At least, I have found it so. I have wondered if it might not be best to choose a subject for each chapter? Perhaps he might wish to write more than one book."

"More than one?" repeated Lady Blackburne.

"Yes. One might be about the people and the customs." Eustacia shrugged. "In another he could concentrate on the flora and fauna which he found fascinating."

Lady Blackburne's eyes narrowed. She stared at the young woman seated across from her. "It sounds," she said slowly, "like a far more ambitious project than I had conceived. I merely thought it a means of bringing Jason out of the mopes and hoped he might develop an interest in things again."

"You have not read his journals, my lady. You cannot know how detailed they are. Not only the things he described, but his comments on them are of interest even to one such as I who knows so little."

"Just how much *have* you deciphered?" asked Lady Blackburne abruptly.

"Of volume two? Did I not say? More than a third."

"And you already think there is so much of interest that my nephew might produce more than one book?"

"Oh, yes. For instance—"

Eustacia opened journal one at random. Stumbling, since she had not previously seen the passage, she read out Lord Renwick's description of a wedding party.

"That is half a page in volume one. If he has not forgotten, and I'd guess he has not, he could very likely produce a chapter on that alone!"

Lady Blackburne stared at the young woman. She had, she decided, not thought through the ramifications of her decision to hire the chit. Although it was true that Jason was far more outgoing, far more talkative, far *less* apt to fall into those long black silences she dreaded, there was something happening. Something which bothered her a great deal!

There was, she concluded, no use denying it. Miss Coleson might become a danger to her own position in her nephew's household. Jason might grow dependent on the young woman. He might decide he could not get along without her.

The pace of Lady Blackburne's heartbeat increased uncomfortably.

Jason might decide to wed Miss Coleson!

Five

Wed her? And why should he not? Not a brilliant match, of course, the daughter of a vicar, but what could a blind man expect? Besides, she was the granddaughter of an earl, even if the earl had disowned her mother.

Still, Lady Blackburne was unhappy with the notion.

Eustacia broke into her ladyship's rampaging thoughts. "My lady?"

"Hmm? Oh. I was thinking that you must be correct, Miss Coleson," she said with the faintest chill to her tone. "I have been remiss. I did *not* know how interesting he could be nor how deeply my nephew had thought of these things. Perhaps you are also correct that there is more than one book locked up in his journals. And now"—her ladyship set aside her stitching—"I believe I, too, feel in need of my bed. Perhaps it is the weather? There is a heavy sort of day which tires one even when one does nothing. Have you never noticed it?"

Lady Blackburne decided she was blathering on merely to cover up the perturbed emotions her vexatious thoughts roused. The notion Jason would ever wed was nonsense and she would put it from her mind. He was not the sort to inflict his problems on another. He would not want pity and what else could a young and active woman feel for him *but* pity?

Lady Blackburne heaved a relieved sigh. Jason would

not send her away. He would continue to need his aunt. Which was what she wanted. She was a woman who knew herself well, and she knew she needed to be needed.

Left alone in the blue salon, Eustacia stared for a seemingly endless moment at the chair in which Lady Blackburne had sat. "She lied," muttered the younger woman. "I've no notion know why she lied or about what, but she lied."

A frown marred Miss Coleson's usually placid brow as she worried about what had upset her hostess . . . or her employer, depending on how one looked at it. She sighed. Deeply. This living in another's house was, as she had feared, not easy. Or was it that she had not had time to think ahead and was, therefore, confused by each and every little difficulty?

Still, she wasn't required to maintain peace with her stepmother and suffer the woman's constant nagging, and she was free, for a time, from her suitor's importunities. Too, she was earning money with which to pay off debts in her village. So, difficult as it might sometimes be, she was, she decided, far better off here in the Tiger's Lair!

With that decision made, Eustacia adjusted the lamp, opened journal one, and lost herself in the formidable detail of Lord Renwick's observations upon first arriving in India. When, finally, she could not read for the jaw-cracking yawns interrupting her, she glanced at the clock. Shocked, she rose to her feet and moved nearer. Could it possibly be after three in the morning?

"Oh dear," she muttered. "I'll never wake at a proper hour!"

She turned off the lamp, noting as she did so that the level of the oil was reduced until little more than a scum wetted the bottom of the reservoir. That bothered her, too. For the whole of her life she had been imbued with notions of economy and to have wasted so much of the best quality winter grade whale oil caused her conscience several distinct twinges.

Her conscience received still another jolt when she went into the hall and discovered a footman there, waiting for her to go to bed. Or, at least he must have been supposed to wait up. She stared at the young man asleep on the bench set there for the footmen's use. But surely, not for this use! Eustacia lit her bed candle. Better light revealed it was Marcus. She called his name softly. He snored softly, snorted, and snored again.

"Marcus!" she said a trifle more sharply.

Another snort and the man lifted his head from his arm. He looked around, realized where he was and rose to his feet. Eustacia put out a hand to steady him, but drew it back as he found his balance.

"Miss Coleson," he said. "Sorry." He yawned, muscles tightening in his jaw and face as he tried to muffle it. "Didn't know . . ." The footman rubbed sleep from his eyes.

Eustacia chuckled softly. "Go to bed, Marcus. I will try, in future, to avoid putting you to such trouble!"

Eustacia was watching him move toward the back of the house when Sahib's roar turned her head toward Lord Renwick's part of the house. A shiver ran up her spine and, shielding her candle, she hurried up the stairs, stopping at the top to lean over the railing and listen intently. But Sahib appeared to have settled himself and no one came to see what the trouble might be. She relaxed, heaved a relieved sigh, and hurried on.

Arriving at her room, she rubbed her eyes which were gritty from so much reading. Then she yawned. Widely. She was asleep very nearly before she had the covers up and over her shoulders.

* * *

For most of a week Lord Renwick and Miss Coleson discussed the form a book might take. Occasionally Lady Blackburne sat with them, sewing, but more often they were alone in the study.

Alone except for Sahib.

The tiger developed several new habits which disturbed Lord Renwick. For instance, the beast growled softly whenever Miss Coleson approached. But then, when she actually arrived and spoke to him which she invariably did, he gave that nearly silent greeting which Lord Renwick thought signified acceptance.

Also, whenever Miss Coleson was near, Sahib placed himself closer to Jason than was usual and always between his master and the intruder. When Miss Coleson walked with them, the tiger nosed between them. Still, once he *was* between them, Sahib allowed Miss Coleson to touch him. Jason knew that because he once encountered her fingers when he reached for Sahib with his own!

His lordship found his pet's behavior confusing. "Sahib, what has gotten into you?" he asked one afternoon when the tiger followed a departing Miss Coleson to the door and then returned to Jason's side to lean against his legs. Jason found the beast's head. He put his hands around the great jaw and lifted it until the animal looked up at him. "Do you like her," he asked, "or do you not? I cannot allow you to be a danger to her, you know."

The response was that silent open-mouthed roar, the hot oddly smelling breath of a healthy carnivore rising into Jason's face.

"I wish I understood you, Sahib. I wish I didn't fear you will someday realize you are a beast and hurt someone."

The tiger nudged his leg and Jason scratched his neck.

"Still, as yet you've shown no signs that might happen." Jason sighed and leaned back in his chair. His nearly blind eye caught the sunlight pouring into the room through a tall window. Again he sighed.

Then, recalling Miss Coleson's description of a lad working among the roses, he smiled. Miss Coleson had noticed a pup come trotting up to the gardener's boy, a stick in its mouth. The terrier's tail wagged so hard the animal's whole rear end shook from side to side but the lad, scowling, pushed him away and continued to work rich compost in around a bush.

The dog persisted and the boy looked around in a surreptitious manner. Then, standing, he glanced around, guiltily. A motion of his hand brought the dog near. The stick dropped at his feet and the pup backed off, his tail again wagging in excited anticipation. The boy threw the stick as far as he could and, hands on hips and a wide grin on his face, awaited the pup's return.

He continued the game until, suddenly, a fierce voice interrupted it. Tail between his legs, the dog ran off. Figuratively tail-between-legs, the boy returned to his work, enduring a lecture. Finished with his lecture, certain the boy was well cowed, the gardener, too, moved on. The boy's face, however, split into a grin, and, whistling softly, happily, he went on with his work.

Jason played with a portion of the long leash on which he let Sahib out his window. The boy, according to Miss Coleson, had not been cowed. Still, he *had* gone on with his work and with a will. Was there a lesson here?

Making an unusually impulsive decision, Jason rose to his feet. He must speak with his estate agent who, he recalled, meant to spend the afternoon taking inventory in the carriage house.

"Come, Sahib," he said. Renwick's extra long cane had arrived and, surprising himself as well as others, he'd quickly adapted to its use, finding the knowledge there was nothing in his way, nothing over which he might stumble, gave him confidence. So, with it in one hand

and Sahib's head under the other, Jason strolled to the tiger's run; from there, a trifle more hesitantly since it was not a place he often went, he made his way to the carriage house where he found his agent.

After a spirited argument the man agreed to try Lord Renwick's plan. "But just a trial, my lord," he insisted. "If it does not work as you expect, we revert to the old way." Obviously he thought the plan would *not* function. "I'll pass along your lordship's orders that every child in your employee under the age of fourteen is to be given, morning and afternoon, twenty minutes free time. But, my lord, if the privilege is abused, I'll rescind it."

Jason retrieved Sahib and returned to the house. He had meant to sit in the garden room where the combination of scents and, when it was generous enough to show itself, the sun through the windows, were good to his senses. To occupy his time, he intended to add a new Miss Coleson to his regiment of Miss Colesons, replacing his current Miss Coleson, who had short, pale-colored, fly-away hair, a cute little snub nose and the narrowest of gaps between her front teeth.

For a time he had placed a small mole above her lip, but decided that was too much. Miss Coleson had been fair of skin and hair for long enough—although he rather liked the turned up nose! Perhaps this time she could have brown hair so dark it appeared black?

As he walked toward the entrance hall the sound of strange voices accosted his lordship's ears, interrupting his agreeable thoughts. He stopped. Sahib, at his side, tensed and the hair of his ruff stiffened under Jason's fingers. He heard the low warning growl which told him that, indeed, strangers were about. Someone had arrived.

The tiger was not alone in disliking strangers. Since his blindness made it impossible for him to size up new acquaintances quickly, Jason avoided them as much as possible. Now, certain he was still hidden from view, he

waited, his hand on the tiger's head, listening to the low
murmuring voices. His hand tightened when he heard
another growl from Sahib.

Then his aunt's heels click-clacked in their brisk fashion across the hall. "I understand," he heard Lady Blackburne say, "that you wish to see Miss Coleson?"

"My stepdaughter," said a sugary sweet voice Jason instantly disliked. He realized it was a new and even less
pleasing version of the droning voice at the inn where
he'd first heard Miss Coleson's far more lovely tones.
Then the woman's voice had nagged and nagged. Now
it pretended to some more positive emotion . . . but what
and why pretend?

"Marcus," ordered Lady Blackburne, "take Mrs. Coleson—"

"Mrs. Weaver, I'm proud to say," interrupted the voice.
It was sharper and reminded Jason more of the woman
he'd taken in dislike at first hearing.

"Take Mrs. Weaver," Lady Blackburne corrected herself, "and her husband to the morning room. Supply
them with refreshment, whatever they will, while I locate
Miss Coleson."

"You must *find* her? You have *lost* her?" The voice was
still sharper. "Surely she has not gone off *alone*?"

Jason, sensitive to the emotions revealed by voices,
knew the woman only pretended outrage. His dislike
deepened.

"How can you allow it!" continued the stranger.

"She is not alone," lied her ladyship smoothly. "Not
that there would be a thing wrong with roaming the estate
whenever and wherever she pleased. Marcus, the morning
room," she ordered, giving Mrs. Weaver no time in which
to respond and again Jason heard the distinctive sound
of his aunt's brisk steps, the tinkle of chains.

Lady Blackburne turned into Jason's wing of the house

and found her nephew and Sahib. "Jason, you heard?" she whispered. "That awful woman!"

"You do not like Mrs. Col—hmm, *Weaver*, did she say?"

"Like her?" His aunt chuckled. "Why I believe I must! After all, she up and married her daughter's unsuitable suitor. I had not thought of that possibility. I am sure our Miss Coleson will be much relieved to hear it." Her ladyship added, "Jason, he is *exactly* as Miss Coleson described him. Old, fat, and quite smelly!" She lowered her voice. "And a distinctive odor it is. Addicted to blue ruin, or I miss my guess."

Jason felt a twinge of mild shock. "Miss Coleson's suitor is a gin drinker? She has had a lucky escape, has she not?"

"She has. Now I must go to her."

"If she is not out walking, which I assume she is not, or you'd have gone in another direction, then where is she?"

"Poor dear. She has become enthralled with your scribblings, Jason. She adopted the small room beyond your study as her own and is to be found there more often than not."

"If she is to act my scribe so assiduously, Aunt, we must see to giving her a salary."

"I believe you will find she is doing it as much for her own sake as for yours, Jason, but we will see. It is a good suggestion if she would agree." Lady Blackburne felt not one scruple as she, once again, lied without pause—this time by omission. She had no wish that Jason know the truth of Miss Coleson's *visit*. "Unfortunately, I must tell her of her stepmother's arrival. It would be outside of enough if I did not."

"I suppose she must, for propriety's sake, present herself." Jason had another thought and his features sharpened into horror. "Aunt! Must I suffer an introduction?"

"Not unless I have difficulty ridding us of them." Lady

Blackburne laughed gaily. *"Then,* Jason, you will not only present *yourself* but also *that animal!* I am often amazed at how quickly people take the hint they are not wanted when growled at! In this case, the more quickly, the better."

"Mushrooms?" he asked, his brows rising.

"Exceedingly pushy mushrooms who will attempt to grow just where they are not wanted and with nary an excuse. I do not like pushy people, Jason. This couple will not find a foothold in society through us which, I believe, is what they intend." She sobered. "Unfortunately in this case, they have some slight excuse for coming here. And, unfortunately, I am forced to take Miss Coleson to them."

"I will be in my study if I am needed," said Jason, changing his own plans. Once he was settled there, he wondered how Miss Coleson would deal with the Weavers and allowed his imagination to play with several vignettes.

"Mother?" said Eustacia perhaps ten minutes later. Somewhat hesitantly, she entered the small room in which the couple waited. "Mr. Weaver?"

"There you are, dearie. Did Lady Blackburne tell you our secret?" asked the new Mrs. Weaver, beaming.

"Indeed she did. Best wishes, Mother. Congratulations, Mr. Weaver."

"You will have to call me 'Papa' now I've up and married your mama," said the man, his insinuating tones grating on Eustacia's ears.

"Yes, sir," said Eustacia and hoped she hid her distaste for the notion. It had been difficult learning to call her stepmother "Mother" although she had been quite young at the time. She would *never* call Mr. Weaver "Papa." And, indeed, there was no reason why she should. He was merely the husband of her father's second wife!

"We have come to take you home," said Mrs. Weaver, interrupting Eustacia's thoughts. "You just run along now and pack up your things. Quickly, girl."

"Now?" Eustacia thought of the journal she had abandoned to come to her stepmother. With a touch of panic, she also thought of abandoning Lord Renwick. Something deep inside tightened in denial. "I do not see how I can." When Mrs. Weaver's lips tightened, she added, "Not just yet."

"Got a family, now. Must see that," said Mr. Weaver, wheedling. He and Mrs. Weaver exchanged a quick look. "Family should be together."

"I was invited for a long visit and, frankly, I am enjoying myself."

"See that," said Mr. Weaver. "Got a new gown which was very generous of her ladyship and a fine place to live, which, missy, you must enjoy. But," he finished with less patience, "you belong to home."

"I will return when my visit has ended," said Eustacia, beginning to feel a touch of panic. "I am happy to learn of your marriage, Mother, but"—she had a sudden happy thought—"due to your new status, I cannot think but that I would be in the way. Newly married couples, I understand, wish privacy. For quite some time, I know." Actually, she didn't *know*, but she *hoped*.

"Nonsense," said Mrs. Weaver. But a touch of color gave her pasty complexion a more healthy look.

"Want you home," insisted Mr. Weaver.

Although she couldn't comprehend why, they appeared to mean it. Still, Eustacia had good reason to remain. She stiffened her spine. "I cannot come."

" 'Course you can. Your mama wants you. We both want you. *You will come.*"

Was there something just a trifle dangerous in the

man's tone there at the last? Eustacia stared at him, blankly. She'd always believed Mr. Weaver something of a doormat, a greedy, piggy, dirty man . . . when he wasn't a wheedling, whining pup. Or perhaps so fat a man could not be considered puppyish? But if so, then why did she feel a sudden wariness?

"You pack your things," repeated her stepmother, "and we'll be off. Although one would think," she continued pettishly, her multiple chins pressed into prominence, "that such a great ladyship could see her way to inviting us to stay the night." She waved a pudgy hand. "All this room and we've so far to go and all?" Mrs. Weaver pouted, an expression which did nothing to improve her looks.

"You do not understand," said Miss Coleson, struggling to remain firm. "I cannot go just yet."

"Will not, more like," sneered Mr. Weaver. "Well, missy, your mama wants you, so you will come, like it or not."

"Come?" said Lady Blackburne, opening the door just then. She swept into the room and, having found a quizzing glass among unused possessions in a drawer she rarely opened, raised it to her eye and glared. "Come?" She turned toward Miss Coleson. "My dearest Eustacia? Where are you to come?"

"Come *home* where she belongs," said Mr. Weaver belligerently. But there was more than a touch of his old whine to his tone and he did not or could not meet her ladyship's gaze.

"No," said Lady Blackburne sweetly. "I think not. I cannot do without the dear child. When I am done with her, then we will deliver her to her home. Come along, Eustacia." She extended an imperious hand. "I will send for your carriage." Her ladyship's hand firmed around Eustacia's elbow and, very nearly, she pushed the younger woman from the room. "And I will send Marcus to guide you to the front door."

"Here now." The door clicked shut and only the tone, not the sense, of angry voices filtered through.

"I think, my dear"—Lady Blackburne pretended to wipe sweat from her forehead—"it would be best if we were to find somewhere to hide? Just until they've gone? The blue salon perhaps?"

Eustacia, walking beside her ladyship, discovered she was more than a trifle overset. "He is more awful than I remembered."

"Yes. The worst sort of mushroom."

Eustacia smiled at the cant term. "I did not like him before, but now he seems worse."

"In what way?"

Eustacia hesitated. Then, still hesitantly, she said, "He is changed somehow. It was, I suppose, foolish of me, but, for a moment there, I felt a touch of *fear.*"

"As one does with Jason's pet?"

"Oh, no. Nothing like that. With Sahib the fear one feels is so confused with admiration, that it is very nearly a positive emotion. What I felt for Mr. Weaver was just—" She paused then shrugged. "I cannot say what it was."

"Fear. I wonder . . ." Lady Blackburne paced along thoughtfully until they reached the blue salon, her favorite room. Once they were safe inside, the door closed, she glanced with narrowed eyes at her young friend. "Why," she asked, "just now when they are newly married, would they want you with them?"

"I asked that," admitted Eustacia. "They didn't answer the point but merely said my place was with them."

"It seems strange. Ah, well. They will go and we may forget them again. In fact, my dear, it seems to me you should put them from your mind altogether. I can think of no reason why you should not forget they exist!"

"That might be difficult," objected Eustacia in a dry voice. "They live in my house and the time will come, of course, when I *must* return there." She frowned. "I do not think I want that awful man living with me." She sighed. "I don't know what I can do, however."

Lady Blackburne smiled quizzically. "Are you required, then, by your father's will, to house your stepmother? Even if she remarries?"

Eustacia had been so very unhappy, striving to retain emotional control while the will was read, that she found she'd no recollection of the details. "I don't know," she admitted.

"We must find out," said her ladyship soothingly. "I lied when I said I was a friend of your mother's, Miss Coleson, but I have come to feel for you as I would if you *were* an old friend's only daughter. I've a very good solicitor who will contact yours. It is quite possible that, now the woman has remarried, all sorts of changes should be made."

"I *would* like to know how things should be," Eustacia said. "It is terrible to be so ignorant." Her chin rose a notch. "I do know that now I am of age that she cannot order me about as she did when I was young, but still—" Eustacia paused. "Oh, she must have *some* rights. She was the only mother I knew from a young age."

In an exceedingly dry tone, Lady Blackburne said, "Why do I have trouble believing she was a good mother?"

Eustacia smiled weakly. "It is sad," she said, "that I have never felt at all close to her. My father realized, soon after he married her, that he was mistaken in her and spent a great deal of time with me. As an apology, he once said, when something she did made him angry." Her smile waned. "I was very happy to have it so, that closeness with him."

They heard the sound of hooves and looked toward the windows. A hired carriage could be seen bowling down the long drive. The Weavers had departed.

Each woman felt relief. Lady Blackburne's was motivated by the fact she had not had to involve her nephew or the beast.

Eustacia was relieved because, this time, she had managed to avoid leaving Tiger's Lair. But what would Lady Blackburne's solicitor discover? Could she possibly be rid of the Weavers? Forever? Eustacia remembered the years her stepmother was married to her father.

It is far more likely, she concluded, *that they will forever be a burden to me.*

Six

A few days later a new disturbance broke the peace of their small world. Eustacia had occupied most of an hour reading to Lord Renwick some passages she'd previously marked in his journals. Now she laid them aside to allow his lordship time to think about what he'd heard and organize the bits and pieces in his mind. She rose from her place and strolled to the window and was, therefore, looking down the long drive when the cavalcade—it could be called no less—appeared, the unheralded arrival of an obviously important visitor!

"My goodness!" she gasped. "Who can *this* be?"

Jason turned his head. "What do you see?"

His lordship had discovered he didn't at all mind asking Miss Coleson to describe to him what she observed. In fact, it was often a great relief, that freedom to ask, to discover what went on around him. It was, he'd decided, because she was so good at it. He wouldn't allow himself to think it might be something more.

"The first carriage," she responded, "is the largest and most ornate I have ever seen. There are pictures painted on the sides, a ridiculous amount of gilding, and a number of pennants. It is pulled by six matched horses, all white, with manes and tails braided with ribbons and plumes on their heads. Following it is a second carriage. It is somewhat less elaborate and has only four horses.

Black horses. Beyond that are three more vehicles, the everyday kind anyone might own. Two of those are piled high with trunks and bales and boxes and crates and, oh dear, every sort of container one can imagine."

Eustacia drew in a breath, "Riding beside each carriage are outriders. There are three along each side of the first carriage, two on either side of the second but only one on either side of each of the others."

As she spoke Jason rose to his feet. He leaned forward as he listened as if he would see for himself.

"The outriders, my lord," she continued, "are dark-skinned men dressed in ornate uniforms. The jackets—or should one call them tunics—anyway, they are a silvery blue color and criss-crossed with gold."

"It can't be!" Jason exclaimed, remembering the maharaja's colors.

"There are plumes in their hats which are similar to a dowager's turban, although far larger. They've swords hanging from jeweled belts. At least, they *sparkle* as if they were jeweled. And each carries a rifle in one hand while controlling his mount with the other. Oh! Their trousers are rather baggy and their shoes! My lord, now they've come nearer, I can see their shoes are red and have *points—*"

"Baggy trou . . . ?" He sat with a thump. "By God, *no.*"

"No?"

He drew in a deep breath. "Miss Coleson, it sounds very much as if a personage from India visits us." His lordship fought his negative response to the notion. "Do you suppose they invaded England and no one bothered to inform us?" he asked quizzically.

"India?" she asked, ignoring his obviously forced jocularity.

Jason heard the interest in her voice and chuckled. "Yes. The trousers are a clue, if all that gilding and the blue and silver livery had not already made me wonder."

A muscle worked in his jaw. "Come along, Miss Coleson. We must see who has arrived."

As they entered the front hall Eustacia giggled.

"Miss Coleson?" asked Lord Renwick.

"You should see the footmen," she whispered. "Their mouths gape open. Even Reeves looks more than a trifle nonplussed."

Lord Renwick grinned.

Lady Blackburne, arriving just then, observed his smile with that odd mixture of gladness and jealousy she often felt for the young woman she had introduced into their household. It chagrined her mightily that Miss Coleson could bring such looks to her nephew's face where she could not.

The jealousy never lasted long. Lady Blackburne's love for her nephew and her desire to do her best for him always restored her proper sense of things. And *now* was no time to think of all that. Not when the forecourt was a milling mass of humanity and horses and carriages.

"Jason!" she called. Drawing near, she added, in a hushed tone, "If you'd any notion of this—this *invasion* and did not tell me, I will have words to say to you! Who is it?"

"I had no warning, Aunt Luce, but from Miss Coleson's description, I've the great honor of hosting an Indian dignitary. Although *why* we had no warning of the invas—er *visit*—I know not. There are protocols. Someone should have been sent ahead, *should* have warned us." A muscle jumped in his jaw and he dropped his hand to Sahib's head. "Although we are taken by surprise, my lady Aunt, we must do things as properly as possible."

His lordship raised his voice. "Reeves," he called bringing the gaping butler back to a sense of his own dignity. "Line our footmen up facing each other across the steps. When you've done that return."

The four footmen were soon in place and Reeves, mopping his forehead came to ask anxiously what he must do next.

"Next," said Lord Renwick, "you place yourself, at strict attention, on the landing outside the doors. My aunt and I will appear as soon as you have done so."

"Jason, what do I *do?*" asked his aunt in a hurried undertone.

"We are in England, my dear. We will do no more and no less than we would when greeting some English personage who has unexpectedly arrived. A curtsy and a welcome. That is sufficient on your part."

"I don't wish to insult—"

"You are English, Aunt."

The reminder put a stiffening in Lady Blackburne's spine. She forgot Eustacia and all else in her curiosity to see who had arrived.

After a moment's hesitation and experiencing a great deal of reluctance that she'd miss what promised to be a rare show, Miss Coleson took herself off to find the housekeeper. As she hurried toward Mrs. Climpson's rooms, she mentally totted up what she'd seen. There were five drivers and a guard on each carriage. The outriders made twenty-six. Very likely personal servants rode in the second and perhaps the other carriages but how many she couldn't say.

Oh, dear, what would they do with them all?

Even as she calculated, Eustacia felt further twinges of regret that she must remove from the hall. She would miss the most exciting thing ever to happen near her! Nevertheless, knowing preparations must begin at once, she carried on.

As Eustacia left the hall, the door to the second carriage opened. Stiffly, old joints unhappy from the jolting ride over badly repaired roads, the shikari descended. His gun, exploding, had blinded Lieutenant Lord Renwick, and he stared up the handful of steps to where his lordship himself awaited the arrival of his guests. The old man saw the long cane and sighed. The blindness had not healed itself and if it *had* not, *would* not. How would his lordship feel when required to house the man responsible?

Squaring his shoulders, the shikari moved toward the first carriage. At a nearly imperceptible motion of his hand, several of the mounted outriders lined up in two rows. Their horses, facing each other, formed an aisle leading to the steps. When that was done, he opened the carriage door. Very softly he spoke to the occupant.

"I don't want to." It was a high-pitched, clear-toned voice speaking only slightly accented English.

Lord Renwick's eyebrows arched and his nostrils flared slightly.

Again the shikari spoke too softly for those waiting to hear. "I have said it," was the response. "I do not wish to get out. I desire to go *home*. I *will* go home!"

Jason heard a touch of desperation in the young voice. His growing anger was diminished by a mixture of pity and exasperation. "Damn," he said very softly. "Why me?"

Carefully, Jason made his way down his front steps, a mystified Lady Blackburne following. At the bottom she guided him toward the carriage.

Jason bowed. "I have, I think"—he spoke in the boy's own language, hesitating over certain words—"the great honor of receiving the Kumar Ravi to my home." It was nearly two years since he'd last spoken the boy's language which was not the dialect he'd spoken most while in India. He'd had a far greater facility in Bengali.

Later, Lady Blackburne described what happened next to Eustacia. "Just a child, my dear. I felt so sorry for him! The boy poked his head out of the carriage like a rabbit from a hutch and then drew it back in again. More slowly, he appeared a second time."

"Just appeared? He didn't step down?"

"No. He stood there, bent because of the door, and asked, 'My Lord Renwick?' Jason nodded and the poor lad drew in a deep breath, cast a despairing glance toward that terribly stern old man who appears to be his keeper, and began an exceedingly long and exceedingly formal piece he'd obviously learned by heart."

"In English?" asked Eustacia.

"In English. Oh, he used his own language whenever he named Jason. Some long, important-sounding, title which made Jason wince whenever he heard it." Lady Blackburne grinned. "It was most amusing, although I would never tell Jason so. My nephew, not surprisingly, is suffering from shock."

"So is the household. They haven't a notion how to deal with so many people who cannot speak English. My lady! Not a word!"

Horrified, Lady Blackburne's eyes widened. "Oh dear, I have not had a moment to think! Someone, I hope, is deciding how they are all to be housed, are they not? Poor Mrs. Climpson. How will she cope!"

"There is room with the grooms for the prince's private army and with the male house servants bundled together there is room for the boy's indoor servants. Except for his cook and his helpers!" Eustacia shook her head. "He's terribly fierce! After stalking all over, angering *your* cook by poking his nose in everywhere, he chose a room—a storeroom actually, but it has a fireplace—and gave orders to two youngsters who trotted at his heels. They ran to bring in equipment and supplies and what appear to be bedrolls."

Eustacia drew breath. "The cook," she continued, "prepared the *smelliest* food." Eustacia grinned. "I doubt, if they remain long, you will *ever* rid that room of the odor! They ignored your servants who, with no excuse at all I'm sad to say, manage to come and stare at them.

There were always two to six standing about watching."
Eustacia shook her head at the chaos the arrival of the
prince had caused in Lord Renwick's well-run home.

"I hope you had words with them about ignoring their
duties."

"*I* did not, but *Reeves* did." Eustacia grinned at the
memory of the butler's biting comments. "When the food
was cooked," she continued, "I managed to ask for a
taste."

Lady Blackburne chuckled at the look on Eustacia's
face.

"Be warned, my lady," said the younger woman, half
laughing and half seriously. "If your curiosity leads you
to try it, have a pitcher of ale handy! A *second* glass took
most of the bite away."

"*Two* glasses of Reeves's homebrew?" Shock and humor
fought for supremacy within Lady Blackburne. "My dear,
you must be reeling! Myself, I think he has a rather heavy
hand with the hops, but the men seem to like it."

Eustacia grinned, a faint rosiness to her cheeks, but
didn't comment. "I watched the Indians dine," she continued. "They didn't eat at a table, Lady Blackburne, but
squatted in a circle and ate with their fingers. I discovered
they eat great quantities of rice with that spicy food. Perhaps the rice alleviates the burning but I hadn't the courage to find out."

She smiled and then, drawing in another breath,
added, "Later, as I was about to return to this part of the
house, I saw Lord Renwick following his nose. He spoke
their language and must have asked for food." Eustacia
looked as puzzled as she felt. "My lady, he ate in the same
messy way, squatting as the Indians did, and seemed to
relish every bite."

"I hope it does not make him ill!" Then her ladyship
sighed. "I do not know what to do. I am told the prince
will mostly eat the food his cook prepares for him, al-

though, as part of his education, he is, sometimes, to eat our food in our Western fashion." Lady Blackburne grimaced. "From what you say, I cannot imagine how he will go on at the table."

"His *education?*"

"Yes. Had you not wondered at the reason for his arrival? His father sent him," she said, her voice astringent, "so that Jason might teach him English ways and the proper behavior for an English prince. And to improve his English, of course, which is good but rather limited. I cannot help but feel sorry for him. He is so alone."

"He is, from the little I saw, a brat," said Eustacia sharply, remembering when she'd been introduced to him and virtually ignored.

"Oh, yes, definitely," said Lady Blackburne who had had far more to do with the boy. "The Kumar Ravi, or, as we are to call him, Prince Ravi, has been allowed his own way from babyhood. He is, however, intelligent. With a bit of care, it is possible Jason can bring the boy about."

Eustacia knew her irritation with the boy was mostly because Lord Renwick was so obviously upset. She sighed. "I know the prince is not happy," she said after a moment in which she berated herself for a lack of sensitivity. She must remember it was a child with whom they dealt. "I didn't hear his speech when he arrived, of course, but the footmen spoke of it. Is he really expected to put himself in Lord Renwick's hands in all ways and submit to him no matter what is asked of him?"

The door had opened during Eustacia's question. Lord Renwick, looking both harassed and bemused joined them. Sahib, who had been banished to his enclosure for most of the day, pressed near to him.

"The boy will obey," said Lord Renwick. "His father has the power of life and death, even over his son and heir. Although I doubt very much the old man would order the lad executed, it is all too conceivable that he would take delight in making his son's life a misery if he were to fail in what he has been set to do. The boy knows that."

"Then you do not fear rebellion?"

"Rebellion?" Jason grimaced. "Oh, yes. Every day in every possible way! He will drive me mad."

After a moment when he did not go on, Lady Blackburne asked, "Do you *have* to do this?"

Renwick shrugged. "Aunt Luce, I accepted the honor of becoming the lad's savior, his lord and protector now and forever, or however it should be translated. At the time I'd no notion what it meant, but it seems I, too, have the power of life and death over that poor boy. At least he believes I could kill him and no one, I hope, will disabuse him! It may, on occasion, be my only hold over him. Oh, yes, it is quite true," he added when Eustacia gasped a denial. "I could order Bahadur to strangle him and the old man would do it! Can you imagine the horror I feel at having such power? I must watch my tongue every moment! If I were to become angry and make some thoughtless remark!" Jason took a handkerchief from a slit pocket in his coat and mopped his forehead. "Well, I suppose it will be good for me as well as the boy to learn self-control, will it not?" he asked.

"Where is the prince now?"

"He and Bahadur"—he glanced up—"that's that very proud old man who feared I would throw him out bodily. It was his gun which exploded, you see? In any case, they are making themselves a temple in a room cleared for it. Or I suppose one should say they are giving the orders which will result in a place of worship."

"Will they join us here?" asked Lady Blackburne.

"Not this evening. I informed Prince Ravi that, if he is *not* tired, he *should* be. He will retire when he has finished his devotions." Jason yawned. "Perhaps I merely meant that *I* am tired." He rose and excused himself.

"Oh," he said, turning at the door, "he will join us at breakfast, my lady Aunt. Just so you are warned."

"He will eat our food?" she asked sharply.

"Not tomorrow. Bahadur will serve him, but the boy must sit at our table." Lord Renwick grinned, his expression lightening. "Merely sitting at a table is lesson enough. He has, all of his life, squatted or laid on cushions next to a table a mere eight inches high. Can you imagine how uncomfortable he will be?" He told Sahib to come. "Good night."

A wistful thought flitted through his lordship's mind as he crossed the hall. When, he wondered, would he again have time to spend with Miss Coleson? He instantly amended that. *When will we next have time to work on my book?*

It *was* that, was it not, which concerned him?

Seven

"Things were going so well," complained Eustacia a few days later when she sat with Lady Blackburne in the lady's favorite salon.

"In what way?"

"We had decided the form of Lord Renwick's book. I had much of the material ready for the first chapter. And now we may do nothing. *Nothing.*"

"I don't know how you managed so much so quickly, Miss Coleson," soothed Lady Blackburne. "Here you tell me you have already settled what you will do, when I thought it might be a month or more before you knew each other well enough to begin."

"So much as a month?" asked Eustacia. "I wonder . . ."

When Eustacia paused, Lady Blackburne prodded, "Wonder . . . ?"

"I wonder if we would *ever* have begun if we had not fallen into the way of it immediately. Or have managed it only by more formal means. As it is, I am merely his aunt's friend and our discussions were part of getting to know each other. I was not, you see, helping him so much as acquiring knowledge. If we *suggested* I act as his secretary, then, assuming he did not demur, he would have insisted I be hired in the regular way."

"And now?"

Eustacia sighed. "Now there is Prince Ravi."

Eustacia felt guilty for feeling jealous of the boy who kept her from Lord Renwick's side, from their *work*, of course. Still, no matter how she derided herself for a fool, the feeling, although mixed with pity, would not go away. It was most confusing!

And, nearly two weeks later the prince *still* kept Lord Renwick from the work both Lady Blackburne and Miss Coleson would have preferred to see him do. Worse, Lord Renwick appeared overly tired. All the time. There were marks of strain about his eyes, and his mouth was most often seen to be pressed into a harsh line.

One evening, perhaps so much as an hour before the tea tray was to arrive, Renwick entered the salon and walked toward his chair. The new cane swung in a rhythmic tap-tap before him. The changing sound it produced, moving from wood to carpet, gave him another clue to his location and his hand came out to grasp the chair firmly. As he had in the past, but with far less caution than previously, he moved around it and sat. He sighed.

Eustacia jiggled her bells, making them sing their silvery song. His lips twisted in the very slightest of acknowledging smiles and, knowing he knew she was there, she was satisfied. Without speaking, she returned to the parish sewing she was doing for Lady Blackburne, which, at the moment, consisted of a new shift for a woman in the workhouse.

The work proceeded less quickly than it had, since she could not prevent herself from glancing at his lordship every so often and wishing he did not look so exhausted.

"You should," said Lady Blackburne firmly, "send him home." She set another stitch in her tapestry.

"Along with everything else his father gave me? The title? That I would happily relinquish! I would give a great deal to rid myself of the responsibility which goes with *that*. But Sahib? How could I? And the gold and jewels?

My dear Aunt, how can I return what I no longer possess?"

"You would feel honor bound to do so?" asked Eustacia.

"Yes. As would anyone. The wealth he showered on me saved this estate. With it, I redeemed the estate before it achieved utter ruin. Pouring every cent into mortgages is not good. One cannot, year after year, take every penny out of the land and put nothing back, you know."

Eustacia heard herself sigh and glanced quickly toward his lordship. He heard and again she saw that ghost of a smile. Lady Blackburne, however, frowned at her work, setting two more stitches before asking, "Have you made any progress with the boy?"

"Very little. And Sahib is unhappy, left, as he is, in his run so many hours of the day."

"Perhaps," said Eustacia slowly, "you need to keep Sahib with you as you did before his highness arrived."

"I would do so, but Sahib frightens the boy." Lord Renwick frowned, his blind eyes staring at nothing at all. "When Sahib is there he does nothing at all. Not that he cooperates when he isn't!"

"Then, definitely, he should see you handle Sahib," insisted Eustacia.

"Why?"

"I have talked, a little, with the shikari"—she said the strange word carefully—"who tells me the tiger's color gives it special distinction. Sahib is magic in a way I didn't understand and the prince's men are very much in awe of him. I wonder if the boy is not equally impressed? If he were to see that Sahib obeys you, then would not some of that awe rub off onto you?"

Lady Blackburne's work lay in her lap. She stared at Eustacia, her mouth very slightly opened. Even as Eustacia noticed, her ladyship closed it with a snap. His lordship, she found, had straightened in his chair. Very slowly a grin spread across his tired features. He nodded and rose to his feet.

"Miss Coleson, once again you come to my rescue! Sahib will return to my side, which is his natural place." Lord Renwick bowed slightly in her direction and ruefully wished he could have *her* at his side as well. "Aunt? I am sorry, since I know he disturbs you, but I must bring Sahib back into the house. I need him."

"I see that."

"I hope Miss Coleson's notion succeeds since I am reluctant to use the physical power I have over the boy. I cannot see him, cannot judge for myself when he tries to put something over on me and when he is truly confused or, as I believe all too often the case, simply so unhappy he is rebellious for that reason alone. Homesick, you know. I can understand that last feeling and, as he adjusts to our life, that will ease. Children are amazingly resilient."

"My lord," said Eustacia when it looked as if he would leave, "when you discussed with the prince the things he must learn, did you include any—any, well, amusements?"

Lord Renwick paused, manifesting that special stillness of one who has had a new thought. "You suggest that perhaps he would more willingly do the things he does not want to do if he were allowed time to do things he *would* enjoy? If he knew there would be rewards?"

"Well, if he is to learn the ways of Englishmen, then should he not learn to ride and fish and perhaps, assuming you've a gun light enough for his use, to shoot? What about archery? Or tennis?"

"Miss Coleson!" said Lady Blackburne sharply. She glared at her guest. "Please have the good taste to change the subject!"

Lord Renwick smiled. "Please avoid mentioning sports in which I may no longer participate? And why should she not? The rest of the world has not ceased to exist merely because I can no longer do things I once enjoyed." He returned to his chair. "There is also lawn croquet, which is something you ladies might teach the boy. It will be necessary to find him an instructor for the other things, I fear."

"I enjoy fishing, my lord," said Eustacia hesitantly. "Perhaps if we were to take a pick-nick out along the river one day?"

A muscle jumped in Lord Renwick's jaw at the thought of open land with no neatly graveled paths. Rough ground over which he'd stumble. Still, it was a good notion and he could order a footman to help him.

It was strange how it bothered him less these days to admit he occasionally needed more help than his aunt provided. A feeling which had grown since Eustacia's arrival. *Eustacia.* He no longer thought of her as Miss Coleson! When had that impertinence occurred? And why?

He firmly set aside such speculation which he feared would lead to an admission he didn't wish to make. "That," he said, "is one jaunt on which I could not take Sahib—which would be reason enough for the prince to enjoy it! Did your father teach you to fish, Miss Coleson?"

They discussed fishing, relating some of their triumphs and tales of wary fish that had eluded them. Lady Blackburne settled to her stitchery and all three were surprised when evening tea was brought in.

"Is it so late?" asked Lady Blackburne, putting away her work. "It has been a very pleasant evening."

"Very pleasant," repeated Lord Renwick. He relaxed back into his chair and smiled slightly.

Eustacia, studying him, was pleased to see some of the worry lines had been erased, that he was far less tense. Ignoring the question of *why* she felt pleased, she accepted a cup and saucer from Reeves, nodding her thanks, and sipped warily at the hot beverage. "My lord," she asked, "will you go out for Sahib when you have had your tea?"

"Yes. He and I will return to our old ways. We will see if that mends matters with the prince."

"Your tea, my lord," said Reeves softly and, when his lordship lifted his hand, gently placed the saucer against Lord Renwick's palm in such a way his master could safely grasp it.

It was a move the butler and Lady Blackburne had practiced. Once Reeves was comfortable with his part, her ladyship taught Jason how to accept his tea. No one mentioned Lady Blackburne's role in this or a number of other things she did, but everyone knew she'd thought carefully about the most mundane of daily practices, finding ways of dealing with many of them.

Her ladyship realized that she had stopped thinking of ways to make her nephew's life easier some months before Miss Coleson arrived. Their days had seemed to go along so smoothly, but now she wondered if she had believed she had done all she could toward making Jason's life normal. It had never crossed her mind to wonder what things other than the normal her nephew might do. She sighed softly.

"Aunt? Is something wrong?"

"Hmm? Wrong? Nothing except that the arrival of the brat has disrupted our peace in so many ways. Jason, how long are we to house not only him but all those men with him?"

"Is there a problem of which I know nothing?"

"Well, there is the cost of it all, of course. Over thirty extra mouths! You will say I am not to concern myself with that, but Jason, they have nothing to do. They will grow bored and then restless. I cannot imagine the mischief they will get up to. Or perhaps," she amended in an overly dry tone, "the problem is that I *can.*"

Jason shouted with laughter. "Aunt, you will never cease to amaze me."

Reeves cleared his throat and his lordship's smile faded.

"You, agree, Reeves?" he asked. "It is a problem? I will discuss it with Bahadur. Perhaps the shikari will suggest how we may occupy their time productively. There must be something. . . ."

They finished their evening drink and Lord Renwick rose again. Eustacia did so as well. "My lord," she said as he oriented himself toward the door.

"Yes?"

"May I walk with you? I stayed in earlier because of the rain, and now it is too late to go alone."

"Of course you may come. Aunt?" he asked. "Would you, too, like the exercise?"

"I have just thought of something and must have a word with Mrs. Climpson." She rose. "Reeves, we will not return to the salon."

Eustacia, who had had every intention of returning and reading for an hour or two, gathered up her book and put it on the hall table. "Will it," she asked hesitantly, once she and Lord Renwick left the house by the door at the end of his hallway, "embarrass you if I say there has been a positive result of the arrival of the prince? At least one?"

"What is that, Miss Coleson?" He closed the door.

"You are far more sure of yourself. You do things more easily."

Lord Renwick smiled. She could see his teeth gleaming in the dim light through the amber-colored panes siding the lamp which hung outside the door. "We may thank Prince Ravi for that. You see, I realized very quickly the boy had no natural respect for me. I am blind. In his eyes that makes me far less a man than those who can see. I was forced to act, as far as possible, as if I were *not* blind."

He offered his arm and Eustacia laid her fingertips on it, feeling a strange tingling along her arm. She forced her hand to remain steady. Why, she wondered, did touching his lordship make her feel so warm, both happy and oddly tense?

"I had already begun to feel somewhat more secure thanks to my new cane, but the boy's arrival pushed me to a far greater effort than I'd have otherwise expended."

Sahib, hearing their approach, roared, and Jason extended his stride slightly. "Poor beast. He must be even more confused by the changes than is the prince. Well, enough of that. You have pointed out, and rightly, that Sahib's place is at my side. The prince must adapt!"

Eustacia felt a warm glow at his praise. The warmth grew to an embarrassed heat when, for just a moment, he shifted his cane under his arm, freeing that hand to pat hers. Then he pressed it against his arm. His exceedingly muscular arm . . .

Sahib roared again and then made odd grunting noises—a sort of pleading sound, thought Eustacia—and bumped his head against the gate. Lord Renwick soon had the beast freed and the tiger very nearly pushed his lordship off his feet, rubbing against his legs first on one side and then the other. Eustacia chuckled and the tiger turned to her, rubbing very briefly and very gently against her as well, pushing her skirts against her legs. Then he turned back to Lord Renwick.

"Come, Sahib."

The tiger, still pressing too close for comfort, walked beside Jason toward the house. The path was too narrow for three and his lordship apologized that Miss Coleson could no longer walk beside him.

"I mind it not at all, my lord. I *like* watching Sahib

move. There is something exceptional in the grace and strength and beauty of him."

"You make me wish I could see him myself."

"Oh, my lord, I am sorry!"

"Never apologize! Your descriptions bring life into my mind, drawing up memories I'd not recall on my own. I am blessed, Miss Coleson. If it was fated that I be blind, then at least I'd years in which to find the world a fascinating place. Think of those who are born blind, or are blinded so young they've yet to see much of anything. I've a great deal in my mind to help me understand what I hear or smell or feel, making it easier to deal with."

"I had not thought of that."

"Have you walked enough? Or would you care to stroll through this rose garden before we go in?"

They had arrived at one of Lady Blackburne's many gardens. The scent of night-blooming nicotania drifted around them. Although suspecting she should not extend their walk, Eustacia was drawn into temptation. There had been so little time with his lordship since the boy's arrival, none of the interesting conversation, none of the excitement of discussing the book, and no way to fulfill her compelling desire to make his life easier, more interesting, more exciting, and worth living.

"I would like that," she said, made shy by her thoughts, "if *you* do not mind?"

Lord Renwick found the narrower path with his cane and turned Sahib into it. "We still cannot walk side by side," he said ruefully after touching both sides of the path with the cane.

"I am happy merely to be out. It is such a wonderful night, my lord. There is no moon, but you would be surprised by how light it is from the stars alone. There is a great hazy stretch of milky color all across the sky which I was once told is made up of distant and uncountable stars. And the constellations are very clear tonight. The great bear . . . and there, I think, is Cassiopeia. . . . I fear," she said apologetically, "that I am unfamiliar with the others." Eustacia passed her gaze over the starlit garden and described it as well.

"You have a remarkable way with words," Lord Renwick said quietly when she fell silent. How he had missed listening to her make him "see" the world around them! "I have an amazing clear picture in my head of what you see."

"Perhaps it is just that I enjoy hearing myself talk and this is an excuse to do more of it?"

"Perhaps so, but I like your *seeing* the world for me." He sighed and dropped a hand to Sahib's head when the tiger nudged him. "I wish we had time to work on the book. I enjoyed our discussions about it and almost thought we might manage, together, to come up with something not too displeasing."

"We still can."

"Hmm. Perhaps. But, it is difficult."

"Perhaps once the prince can be set real lessons, or when he is out doing boy things?"

"Riding and fishing? Aha!" Lord Renwick chuckled. "You had an ulterior motive for suggesting he do those things!"

Eustacia felt herself blushing. Was the thought in her mind that, with the boy outside, Lord Renwick and she might work? Together? Just the two of them?

Alone. As now, here in the gardens, they were alone?

"I may have had something of the sort in my mind, my lord," she said, pushing the wayward thought from her mind, "but if so, I did not realize it. Still, you should not have to give up the whole of your life to the boy! It is not fair."

Lord Renwick sighed. His cane touched the grass at the end of the path and he swung it around, exploring with it. "The path turns here?"

"We can go either right or left, my lord."

"Sahib appears to have decided that we go to the left."
They turned down the new path, a broader path bordered on one side by a brick wall and a flower-filled bed and, on the other, by grass which stretched up toward the house. "I have thought more about our chapter on strange practices which caught my eye and about which I asked questions. I need, I think, some sort of introductory paragraphs which will set the scene as it were."

"Have you something in mind, my lord?"

"Yes. It is so frustrating that I cannot write down my ideas as I think of them."

Even knowing she should *not*, now that her emotions had become dangerously warm, Eustacia suggested they might spend the next hour doing just that. Why, she wondered, when they had worked in his study quite often, did it seem so different, so daring, to do so late at night? But he could dictate and she take notes. Later she would write up what he said in a clear hand and read it back to him as time allowed so that they could make necessary changes.

"If changes are necessary," she said aloud as an afterthought.

He laughed. "A great number of changes will likely be necessary. Miss Coleson, it must be late. We had our tea and my aunt has gone up to bed."

"Yes, but not to sleep. I would not." Eustacia raised her eyes to where a pale pink glow showed behind the rose-colored drapery covering Lady Blackburne's windows. "I would normally spend an hour or two reading, my lord. It is a luxury I shall miss when I return to my home."

"A luxury?"

She grimaced. "The whale oil, my lord. I've wasted a great deal of it."

He chuckled. "If you have enjoyed yourself, my dear,

we will not call it wasted." Then he stopped and made a sound of self-disgust. "Miss Coleson, since I became blind I have had a great dread of becoming lost. I've an even greater dread of admitting it, on those rare occasions it happens—"

"You wish to know how to get back to the house?"

"Exactly," he said, his voice dry as dust. Then there was a touch of surprise when he added, "I don't know why it is, but I seem to mind it less when I ask *you* to help me."

"Perhaps it is because it is my fault you don't know where you are. We were talking, were we not? There is a cross path a few feet on," she added quickly. "We return by it to another which takes us to the door."

"Lead the way, Miss Coleson."

He said it with no emotion she could hear and she hoped that meant he was not upset she must guide him. Fortunately, these paths were wider and they could, all three, pace side by side. Eustacia was glad. She liked having her hand on his lordship's arm. Occasionally, when she allowed herself to think about it, it worried her how much she liked being near him. Actually *touching* him . . . well, that was something about which she would *not* think.

They enjoyed their stolen hour. Sahib lay at Jason's feet while he talked and Eustacia, concentrating on his every word, now and again put down brief notes so she would not forget some new topic.

Finally she was forced to ask him to stop. "I fear I can remember no more, my lord," she said apologetically.

"Perhaps we might do this again soon," he said, hesitating. "One gets very tired of talking to no one but a child for hours on end."

Eustacia smiled. "I have often wondered at the patience shown by teachers of the young. Of course there must also be those who have no patience at all or there would be, I think, fewer canings."

"Now there's a thought. Do you suppose the prince would be better for a beating now and again?"

Eustacia heard gentle humor behind the comment but replied seriously. "At this point in his life? No. A spanking in the nursery has always seemed to me a far different thing than a caning from a schoolmaster."

"Yes. And I may occasionally feel as if I were in the nursery when dealing with the lad, but I am far more the schoolmaster, am I not?"

Eustacia agreed and could think of nothing to say. Nor could his lordship. Neither, however, could make the necessary decision that the evening end.

Finally Sahib rose and moved to the door. Looking back at Jason, he growled softly and returned to nudge his lordship's knee.

Eustacia chuckled. "I believe Sahib has more sense than either of us, my lord. He is telling us it is time to retire." She gathered up her notes along with ink, a pen, and extra paper. "Good night, my lord." She moved to the door. "Good night, Sahib," she said softly and was given that silent openmouthed roar.

Eustacia let herself into the hall. Once returned to her room she set to work. More than once she yawned widely before she finally put down her pen and glanced toward the mantle clock. The face of the thing was hidden among such ornate porcelain decoration it was difficult to read.

She rose and went to peer at it and tut-tutted. So late! She strolled back across the room to the desk at which she'd written industriously for over an hour. The finished prose was satisfying. She had, she thought, managed to remember everything up to the last two notes which still awaited her attention. Should she?

No. She could do no more tonight. She flexed her hand, her fingers hurting from the intensity of her effort. She glanced again at the neat pile of finished pages and smiled. Perhaps she ached, but it was for a good cause! In fact, she thought, it was a very good beginning toward an introduction to this section of Lord Renwick's book!

Eustacia went to bed feeling reasonably satisfied but so tired she could not fall into a truly restful sleep. She woke the next morning remembering a jumbled sort of dream which included Lord Renwick, Sahib, and the prince and, if the state of her bedding were an indication, must have been distressing.

Nor did she feel rested, although someone had allowed her to sleep in. And that bothered her. His lordship would have finished breakfast and she would have missed him. Somehow, on those days when she did not break her fast with him, she found something unsatisfactory in being up and around, would find herself unable to settle to anything.

Eustacia dressed quickly. She ran down the hall to the stairs where, fortuitously hearing a footman in the hall below, she continued at a far more decorous pace. She was in time to meet Lord Renwick as, frowning, he left the breakfast room, Sahib at his side.

"My lord! Sahib, good morning."

The tiger opened his mouth at her and his lordship's frown smoothed out. "Miss Coleson. You are very late."

"Last night I wrote out much of what you said. I feared I would forget if I let it go."

"Hmm." He bit his lip and heaved a deep sharp sigh. "I have no idea when we may continue. I will be occupied with the boy all the morning and I've an appointment with my agent after dinner. I doubt we will finish going over the accounts before I must check that Prince Ravi has accomplished what I set him to do." He shook his head. "Miss Coleson, I must find a sporting tutor for the boy." With a perfectly straight face he added, "It is time and more that his highness learned our games and other outdoor activities."

"Yes, my lord," she responded, equally soberly. "I have heard growing boys require a great deal of strenuous activity. It is good, I believe, for their health." Then, reprehensibly, she giggled.

Lord Renwick smiled one of his warm smiles. "I will see that something is done about it today. The sooner there is someone else to work with the lad, the sooner life will become tolerable."

"I am a burden to you," screamed the boy running up to beat on Lord Renwick.

He appeared so quickly Eustacia wondered from where he'd come! And then, mentally, kicked herself for speaking so freely where he could overhear even if they hadn't known he was near.

"You do not like me!" continued the tirade. "You do not want me!"

Sahib roared, pushing between the boy and Lord Renwick. The prince backed away, coming up against Miss Coleson who put her arms about him. She felt the youth trembling.

"It is not that his lordship does not want you, Prince Ravi," said Eustacia in her most soothing tones. "It is that he has his own work to do and, as things are, he has no time for it. You do not cooperate, which makes extra work for him. For so long as you resist learning what your father sent you to learn, his lordship will have this difficulty. You are an intelligent boy. You must see that people have other responsibilities, other interests, and must have time for them."

"He wants to push me off on a mere teacher," said the lad sullenly. "He is Savior, Lord and Protector Now and Forever. It is his duty to see to me. I will not listen to a nobody who is unworthy of the position."

"*Will* not?" asked Eustacia firmly, and then, blushing at her temerity in reprimanding the boy, glanced at Lord Renwick who stood, still and silent, his hand on Sahib's

head. His lordship's mouth was tipped into the faintest
of approving smiles so, taking a deep breath, she added,
sternly, "Is it not *your* duty to do what you are told? But
you have not, have you?"

"I can do as I please." But the prince dug his toe into
the carpet. "I *can,*" he added, looking up but not at her.
Haughtily, he added, "I am my father's heir!"

"I am very sorry for you," said Eustacia.

The prince's head came around sharply. He glared.
"What can you mean?"

"As heir you have far less freedom than a poor boy
who must only learn to earn his bread each day"—she
heard the boy say "rice" but didn't pause—"whereas *you*
must learn to care for your people, all of them, see they
have what is necessary so that they may earn their living.
You must protect them and will have the duty to judge
them when they have transgressed—"

"And when they disagree," interrupted the prince
again, but this time with less belligerence and more interest.

"Yes," she said, "you will also adjudicate"—she saw the
boy mouth the new word and repressed a smile—"between people when *both* feel they are right and, in many
cases, where each has *some* right on his side! It will be a
burden all your life. As now," she said, "it is your burden
to learn what your father sent you to learn. But some of
what you must learn will be fun, you know."

The pout on the prince's face, firmed into a frown.
"Fun?"

"Yes. Riding and fishing and archery and oh, all sorts
of things as well as learning English. To read it and write
it as well as speak it, and your maths—"

"But there are those other things? When?"

"When his lordship has found a proper teacher for you
and once you show a willingness to work at the hard
things," she said. When he grinned, she added, "But it

is *most* important that his lordship find someone who will see you do nothing foolish, nothing to endanger yourself. It must be someone who will *make* you do the proper thing even when you tell him you are the prince and he cannot order you about and that you can do exactly as you please!" Eustacia took the prince's chin in her hand much to the boy's surprise. "Because, my fine Prince, *it is not true*. You cannot always do exactly as you please."

"When I am maharaja, I can," he responded, jerking his chin from her fingers. Again he scowled.

"I doubt if even your father can always do exactly as he wishes. Not if he wishes to be a *good* maharaja and not merely a tyrant."

Prince Ravi's head tipped to an arrogant angle. "He *always* does as he pleases. Exactly as he pleases."

"Does it always please him to listen to his advisors, to learn that something must be done or something changed?" asked Lord Renwick.

The comment obviously brought to mind a definite situation since the prince's scowl deepened still more.

"You frown," said Eustacia, tactfully telling his lordship the boy's response to his words. "You have thought of something."

The lad sighed. "I will learn my reading and writing, but I wish it were not so hard."

"You find the math far more interesting, do you not?" asked his lordship.

"That makes sense," said the boy. "I don't see *why* I must know English. When I return home who will speak it? Who will *know* I know?"

Lord Renwick said, "When the English finish their hotel which you said was begun just before you left and when they come to your land each hot season, there will be parties. They will marvel that you speak English so well. More importantly, as you grow older, there will be business. You will need to know how to read contracts.

The Englishmen in India are shrewd and do their best to have things to their advantage. You must not cheat them, but you must also know enough that they do not cheat you."

"I had not thought of that, and my father will do business while I am not there to see to this fairness of which you speak." A touch of panic widened his eyes.

"Then perhaps you might *politely* write to him and request that he make no *long-term* contracts until you have returned since, someday, those contracts may affect your rule. You may say that you wish to learn much English so that you can see that all is done properly, fairly?"

The boy frowned. "There is a problem."

"Yes?"

"My father is very stubborn. He always thinks he knows best. He thinks me still a child."

"Has he a favored advisor?" asked Eustacia.

A grin crossed the lad's face and he nodded. "I will write to his dewan. *He* will know how best to explain things to my father!"

"What or who is a dewan?" asked Eustacia.

The prince glanced at Lord Renwick. "I do not know the words," he grumbled.

His lordship answered. "The maharaja's financial advisor and, assuming it is the same man who was there when I visited, then he is a good choice on your part, Prince!"

The lad preened himself at the compliment. "I will write immediately."

"We will remove to my study, then," said his lordship. "Come, Sahib."

Eustacia saw the prince flinch. He had forgotten the animal and now went on ahead of Lord Renwick. Once he looked back over his shoulder and observed that his lordship's hand rested on the tiger's head. His eyes widened before he turned and ran on.

Eustacia smiled and, quietly, as Lord Renwick passed

her, she said, "I think the boy finds Sahib as inhibiting as I predicted. Use Sahib carefully, my lord, so that you don't give the beast bestial thoughts!"

"Yes, I must keep Sahib from rushing to my defense, must I not, as he did a bit ago?" He grinned and walked on, Sahib a strong, silent, *intimidating* presence at his side.

Eight

With help, Lord Renwick managed three things. With Reeves's writing them, he got letters off to a couple of old friends concerning the whereabouts of a properly strong-minded sporting tutor. Thanks to Sahib now and again warning the Prince, his lordship convinced the boy there were things he could *not* do and, on the other hand, things he *must* do.

Best of all, from his point of view, he finally contrived a schedule which allowed him several hours each afternoon with Miss Coleson. The solution was not ideal, since Prince Ravi remained in the study with them and the boy had *not* yet learned that he should not interrupt. Still, it was far better than the long days when he saw Miss Coleson only at breakfast and occasionally in the evening.

That was another change he was determined to make: He would join his aunt and Miss Coleson in the blue salon each evening.

Even so the work went frustratingly slow. Then came a day when Lord Renwick described a flower so exotic Eustacia was startled into exclaiming that surely such a thing could not exist.

"But, Miss Coleson," interrupted the prince, "it *does*. That and many, many more which grow in the same way. Some are very small and have a sweet scent. Some are huge and gaudy and very nearly ugly. I will tell my father to send you a collection—and a man to care for them since you will not know how."

The prince bent his head back to the book Lord Renwick had told him to peruse, a collection of prints delineating architectural details in the Gothic style. Lord Renwick and Miss Coleman stared, or rather his lordship stared in the boy's direction. Then they turned toward each other.

"There are already a few orchid collections in England, Miss Coleson," said Jason after a moment. "Thank you for supporting me, Prince Ravi. Have you heard anything with which you *disagree?*" asked Lord Renwick.

The prince sat up, a frown making faint lines in his smooth brow. "About the mango. Like the orchid, there are many kinds. Some much better eating than others." He cast a sly look at Lord Renwick. "You will remember that I found one of the very best when we hunted the man-eater. The juiciest kind. The most . . . most meaty?" He frowned. "Can one say meat when it is fruit?"

Lord Renwick's lips compressed. It was one of the few times the prince had dared refer to the hunt during which he was blinded.

"You can say meaty," said Eustacia, with a quick, rather worried, glance toward his lordship. "We also speak of nut meats, the kernel inside a nut's shell."

"But, my lord," insisted the prince, "you must recall that day. The pink-skinned fruit I found? In the jungle? It is quite rare and—"

Lord Renwick spoke sharply. "I remember it was when you were a mere child and did not care that others might be harmed by your lack of discipline."

The boy flushed, cast a glance at his lordship's blind eyes, and muttered, "As you say, my lord." He bent back to his book, hunching over it.

"I have found the passage about the mango," said Eustacia after a glance toward the chagrined prince. "Will you add to what you said?"

Lord Renwick made changes. He cocked his head, listening, but the boy had not turned a page. Compassion led him to say, "Miss Coleson, I believe that was an excellent correction our prince made. He will be a help to us, will he not, when my memory fails me or I am ignorant of something about which he knows a great deal."

"I am sure the prince will help whenever he can, my lord," said Eustacia and smiled when the boy's hunched shoulder relaxed and he rattled a stiff page as he turned to the next. *The boy was not stupid. He would learn.*

The two adults went on with a paragraph describing still another exotic plant. This time it was the banana about which Lord Renwick had questioned not only his sergeant but farmers who grew the odd fruit, planting the stalks on hillsides so steep one wondered how the heavy hands of ripening fruit could ever be harvested.

The days passed and, as Prince Ravi settled in and his lordship's work grew more organized, Lord Renwick and Miss Coleson also ended each day together, making it a habit to walk in the garden with Sahib once the tray was removed from the blue salon.

For the whole of each day Lord Renwick looked forward to that half hour. Only then was he alone with Miss Coleson. Only then could he talk freely, unworried that she would criticize when he complained of the boy's behavior, knowing, too, that if she made a suggestion it would be sensible. He treasured the feeling she liked him, was comfortable with him as he with her.

The knowledge his aunt's guest would eventually end her stay, that she would inevitably leave, was a lump of dross among the silver of their days. It sank into him. A heavy weight, a dark anguished pall, would pull him down whenever it occurred to him. He had to admit, if only to himself, that only when he was with the woman with the molten-gold voice did he feel as if life might, after all, hold some hope.

It was the thought that his light-on-the-world might so easily disappear rather than the blindness itself, which now sent him tumbling into despair! The acknowledgment of his need for her was frightening. During the black days before she came, he had convinced himself he needed no one, but now, walking beside him, was a person, a pert red-haired, slim-limbed, freckle-faced angel—or that was how he thought of her tonight—the loss of whom would leave his world darker than ever.

Compelled by a need to hang on to her, to keep her close, to prevent her escape, he tucked his cane under his arm and laid his hand over hers where it rested on his arm. He had forgotten to wear his gloves and hers were short, barely coming to her wrist so that he came into contact with her skin with his thumb.

The unexpected contact set his heart to racing. Suddenly, outrageously, he wanted to stop. Wanted to turn her into his arms. Wanted to find her lips with his and kiss her. And kiss her.

And kiss her again.

But he could not. Dared not. This was not a woman with whom one could freely, idly, disport oneself. And—the old blackness filled his soul—he was not a man with whom a woman would consider linking her life.

"My lord?" she asked, sensing the tension in him.

He ignored the question implied in her tone. "Where are we?"

"Along the north garden wall, my lord, and nearing the path which leads to the side door."

"Take it."

Hurt by his gruff tone she hesitated only a moment. "Yes, my lord."

Had she, she wondered, said something? Something wrong? Had she done something? She could think of nothing. So why, between one moment and another was his lordship angry? His anger hurt far more than it might normally have done because only an instant earlier she had felt his thumb caressing her skin and her heart had raced and, somewhere deep inside, she had had a hope he might . . . might what? She didn't know.

Aching inside, Eustacia mutely indicated they were to turn into the new path. Silently she strolled beside him to the house where he told her good night and waited while she entered, closing the door behind herself.

Inside, where he could not hear her, Eustacia pushed aside the drapery and stared out the window. *Why,* she wondered, *does he just stand there? And with such a grim look about his mouth.*

What is wrong?

Jason stood exactly where Eustacia left him for so long Sahib settled at his feet. Obviously, his lordship was deep in thought, but what did he think *about?* What had disturbed him so greatly?

And why did he neither come in nor continue his walk? A sudden sharp stab of concern drove into Eustacia's mind: When he *did* wish to move, would he remember where he was? Or would his thoughts have been so dark, so engrossing, he'd have become disoriented?

But what could *she* do? He didn't want her. He had rid himself of her and she could not bring herself to court rebuff by rejoining him. Still, he might harm himself if he were unable to recall where he was, what direction he faced!

What should she do?

An instant later Lord Renwick swung his cane out before him, hitting the door. Sahib moved agilely out of his way when his lordship stepped forward, touched the door, and fumbled for the latch.

Eustacia pressed back into the corner, berating herself

for a fool. She froze, fearing discovery, wondering what she could possibly say to excuse herself for spying on him.

Sahib trailed after Lord Renwick, who stalked down the dim hall as if it were the brightest day. The tiger paused, swung his head to look back at her. "Sahib," said his lordship sharply. "Come."

The tiger opened his mouth and Eustacia could not tell if it were his nearly silent roar of recognition or if, on this occasion, he snarled. She felt the shivery trail of icy fingers up and down her spine and relaxed only when Sahib turned and padded after his master who had disappeared into his study.

The door shut just as Sahib reached it. Eustacia stared, utterly astounded, as the tiger lifted himself up, set one paw against the wall, and pressed down on the door latch with his other. Silently, on well oiled hinges, the door swung inward. The tiger, dropping to all fours, entered the room.

"Now, you great beast," muttered Eustacia, "if you learn to *close* a door once you pass through, we will never know where to find you!"

She heard Lord Renwick's chair squeak, informing her he was seated at his desk, and, taking her nerve in hand, she tiptoed down the long hall. Glancing in the open door, she saw the tiger's great golden eyes staring at her. She held her breath, once again expecting Sahib to reveal her presence.

He did not. He didn't move, only stared. And this time he didn't even open his mouth.

Eustacia lay in her bed that night wondering at the depth of her unhappiness. Why, she asked over and over, had Lord Renwick suddenly found her company distasteful? Would he cease escorting her on those lovely evening strolls? She had found great pleasure in talking to his lordship while walking with him. She had felt needed and respected and had thought he found their discussions equally agreeable.

So *why?*

She tossed from one side to the other and, dragging her braid from under her shoulder, she chewed on the end as she stared out her uncovered window. She saw the constellations she had described to Lord Renwick. Perhaps he had a book among those in his library which would picture the heavens and show her where there were others?

But remembering that first evening when they'd been so very much in agreement, when they'd shared that closeness she craved, was no more than an attempt to forget how terrible she felt *this* evening.

Lord Renwick had wished her elsewhere. Was he tiring of her company? Might he want her gone?

Gone. Really gone? Should she inform Lady Blackburne it was time she returned home?

Eustacia rolled onto her back and sat up when a sudden and unwanted realization burst into her mind like a great flash of hot light. *She didn't want to go home.* She *never* wanted to go home. She didn't wish to leave his lordship. Ever. *She was*—Eustacia, her strength leaving her in a rush, fell against her pillows—*in love with him.*

Pain stabbed into her head. How had it happened? How had she fallen deeply, hopelessly, forever in love with him? With a man who did not want her? *When* did it happened? How had the need to help him, what she'd believed a gentle pity for his blindness, turned into this wonderfully fearful, strangely powerful love?

Perhaps when pity changed to respect for his mind? Perhaps when she realized he was coping in new ways, ways it had not occurred to her he would try to cope? Or perhaps when she saw how their strengths meshed, how well they worked together?

She smiled softly, sadly, visualizing his handsome features, his tall strong body. That, too, might have had something to do with it, might it not? Even the faint scarring on the right side of his face and the even fainter lines on the left distracted not at all from his excellent looks.

Or perhaps, originally, it was that darkness in him, that brooding look he wore so often? Perhaps his melancholy expression had attracted her attention initially?

She recalled her spirits had lightened along with his. Only rarely now did one see him frowning . . . like tonight.

Even with no more than the amber light from the outdoor lamp she could not miss the scowl distorting his forehead. Eustacia frowned herself at the memory. Just how sensitive was Sahib to his master's moods? Would the beast give Lord Renwick extra attention tonight? Press close as she had sometimes seen him do? Would the great tiger give his lordship the warmth of his presence?

Another sharp pang speared into her head, a pain she reluctantly recognized was jealousy. Sahib had the right to press close to his lordship. The right to share his pain and his worry. The right to support and help and . . . to love? Could the beast love the man? As she could and did?

Never. Not as she did.

A breeze came through her slightly open window. Eustacia felt coolness on her face and when she touched her cheek it came away wet. She was crying.

Oh, how empty she felt. How alone . . .

For a long moment her reluctance to leave Tiger's Lair faded and she wished she *might* go home. Home where she knew each nook and cranny. Knew each tree and shrub—*knew her stepmother and Mr. Weaver!*

Eustacia shuddered at the thought that they would live in the same house, share her days. Forever. But *was* that

We'd Like to Invite You to Subscribe to Zebra's Regency Romance Book Club and Give You a Gift of 4 Free Books as Your Introduction! (Worth $19.96!)

If you're a Regency lover, imagine the joy of getting **4 FREE Zebra Regency Romances** and then the chance to have these lovely stories delivered to your home each month at the lowest prices available! Well, that's our offer to you and here's how you benefit by becoming a Zebra Home Subscription Service subscriber:

- **4 FREE** Introductory Regency Romances are delivered to your doorstep
- **4 BRAND NEW** Regencies are then delivered each month (usually before they're available in bookstores)
- Subscribers save almost $4.00 every month
- Home delivery is always **FREE**
- You also receive a **FREE** monthly newsletter, *Zebra/ Pinnacle Romance News* which features author profiles, contests, subscriber benefits, book previews and more
- No risks or obligations...in other words you can cancel whenever you wish with no questions asked

Join the thousands of readers who enjoy the savings and convenience offered to Regency Romance subscribers. After your initial introductory shipment, you receive 4 brand-new Zebra Regency Romances each month to examine for 10 days. Then, if you decide to keep the books, you'll pay the preferred subscriber's price of just $4.00 per title. That's only $16.00 for all 4 books and there's never an extra charge for shipping and handling.

It's a no-lose proposition, so return the FREE BOOK CERTIFICATE today!

Say Yes to 4 Free Books!
Complete and return the order card to receive this $19.96 value, ABSOLUTELY FREE!

(If the certificate is missing below, write to:)
Zebra Home Subscription Service, Inc.,
120 Brighton Road, P.O. Box 5214, Clifton, New Jersey 07015-5214
or call TOLL-FREE 1-888-345-BOOK

Check out our website at www.Kensingtonbooks.com.

FREE BOOK CERTIFICATE

YES! Please rush me 4 Zebra Regency Romances without cost or obligation. I understand that each month thereafter I will be able to preview 4 brand-new Regency Romances FREE for 10 days. Then, if I should decide to keep them, I will pay the money-saving preferred subscriber's price of just $16.00 for all 4...that's a savings of almost $4 off the publisher's price with no additional charge for shipping and handling. I may return any shipment within 10 days and owe nothing, and I may cancel this subscription at any time. My 4 FREE books will be mine to keep in any case.

Name _____

Address _____ Apt. _____

City _____ State _____ Zip _____

Telephone ( ) _____

Signature _____

(If under 18, parent or guardian must sign.)

RN129A

Terms and prices subject to change. Orders subject to acceptance by Zebra Home Subscription Service, Inc. Offer valid in U.S. only.

worse than staying here where her every contact with his lordship would feed her love for him? *Her* love would grow while *he* could never love her such as she was. Her hand crept up to cover the birthmark at the side of her face.

Eustacia sighed a huge soul-searing sigh, accepting it was impossible that his lordship ever want her for his baroness. The daughter of an obscure country vicar could not fill such a position. The pain of knowing she was unsuitable, unworthy to wed him . . . would that eat into her? Would the pain turn her bitter? Eventually, would it make her unfit to act as his secretary?

No! Never. Eustacia vowed that for so long as he wished her to work with him, then for that long she would stay.

While Eustacia tossed and turned in her comfortable bed, Jason sat in his study, staring moodily into the blackness which was his life. His mind ran along channels very similar to those Eustacia's mind trod. His conclusion that he had fallen desperately, deeply, *hopelessly,* in love with his aunt's guest sent him spiraling down into a deeper pit of depression than he'd experienced for weeks.

In fact, not since they'd returned from his visit to his dying godfather. This particular memory brought a brief flickering smile to Jason's lips. It seemed his godfather was not dying after all. Or so said the letter he'd received that morning which his aunt had read to him. Both memory and smile faded as his mind circled back to his current problem. What, he wondered, did a maimed man do when he loved a woman?

What *could* he do? Jason heaved a sigh so deep it brought Sahib to his feet and to his side. The animal pressed his heavy head against Jason's thigh and Jason dropped a hand to the lush fur.

Absently he dug fingers into supple skin as Sahib liked

him to do. There was, he concluded, no way an honorable
man could burden a young woman with his half-manhood.
Any woman. That must be accepted. Therefore he could
not ask Miss Coleson to wed him. He sighed again as he
accepted that fact which would never change.

What he *could* do was continue to enjoy her presence
for so long as she remained with his aunt. And he *would*.
Jason vowed that, for so long as she was there, he would
find every possible excuse to have her at his side.

He could and would store away every memory, collect
them for the long days and weeks and *years* when he
would, once again, be alone in his dark world with no
Miss Coleson to paint word pictures onto the blankness
of his mind, drawing up memories which, on his own,
did not come.

Gradually, as Jason made some decisions, his depression lightened. Still, if he were to have time with Miss
Coleson, then he must find more ways to occupy the boy.
Which meant at least one of his friends had better know
of some young man in need of a position! A properly
strong-minded sporting man who could also act as tutor
for the prince's English and mathematics. How soon,
wondered Jason, might he receive responses to his inquiries?

And what, he wondered, might he do in the meantime?

Could the boy ride? He must asked Bahadur.

Could the boy swim? He would ask about that as well.

Archery . . . hmm. New equipment must be ordered
since Reeves informed him the old, that which he himself
used as a boy, was beyond salvaging. He scribbled on the
pad kept on his desk, tearing off the page and stacking
it with others which Reeves would collect, decipher, and
act upon.

Croquet.

That his aunt could teach. Aunt Luce would never admit it, but she was quite proud of her way with a croquet mallet!

What else had Miss Coleson suggested? Fishing. And pick-nicks.

His lordship sighed. Miss Coleson would teach the boy while he stood aside, waiting as patiently as he could for her to finish and return to him. He smiled, a tight little smile at his next thought: Once the lad learned the sport, however, and assuming he enjoyed it, the shikari and some of his guards could attend the prince whenever he fished.

And perhaps, if he *truly* enjoyed it, then later, it might be arranged for the boy to visit up north where he could go salmon fishing. His friend, Ian McMurrey, had several younger brothers, the youngest, he believed, not *too* much older than the prince.

Ah! That was for the future. Tomorrow, assuming the weather cooperated, they would have a pick-nick out along the river. He would stumble his way to the summer house his grandfather built on the bank of one of the deeper and more pleasant stretches of the Ouse. A muscle jumped in his jaw at the thought of the inevitable humiliation.

Unfortunately Miss Coleson would spend time with the boy rather than with himself. Still, the mere fact a woman could do the thing would give the lad incentive to show he could best her. His young charge, Lord Renwick had discovered, was nothing if not arrogantly superior toward females! The prince would not like the notion a woman could do better than he did himself.

Jason scribbled *pick-nick* across the pad . . . then decided that, since this message involved Cook, it should be passed on at the earliest possible moment. Cook did not like surprises.

Lord Renwick rose to his feet. "Come, Sahib." He found a footman in the front hall and informed the man a pick-nick would be required on the morrow if the day looked suitable. Appropriate orders should be given accordingly.

"Yes, my lord."

"Also someone must look for whatever fishing rods are around and about. Miss Coleson wishes to fish and the prince wishes to learn."

"Fish? . . . Er, yes, my lord."

"That is all."

Lord Renwick turned on his heel, felt with his cane for the edge of the carpet. He felt a faint pressure against his leg, Sahib's cue he needed to alter his direction slightly, and did so. His lordship would have been surprised if a stranger told him that one could not tell, by the way he moved, that he was blind, but it was true. Between his determination to live a more active life, the help of the new cane, and his knowledge of his own home, Lord Renwick moved with very nearly the surety of a sighted person.

If he *had* realized how much he'd improved in this respect, he would have given thanks for that, too, to Miss Coleson. After all, it was she who had inspired him in so many ways, encouraging him to find a life for himself in a black world. And very gradually, picking and choosing, he was beginning to discover what he could and what he could not do.

He'd been rather surprised, actually, at how long the list of things he *could* do had become.

The next morning, Miss Coleson was forced to take her courage in her hands in order to compel herself down the stairs and along the hall to the breakfast room. Arriving there she hesitated, shyness engulfing her. The thought of facing his lordship so soon after realizing how deeply she loved him frightened her. The faint jangle of serving dishes against a tray caught her attention and a blush rose up her throat. She would be caught hovering in the hall when she should have entered the breakfast room the moment she reached it!

Luckily the footman seemed occupied with some item which appeared to be badly placed and, with luck, had not noticed her. Eustacia whisked herself into the room . . . and again hesitated. Lady Blackburne, of course, had her back to the door. But his lordship glanced up and smiled a welcome at the sound of her silver bells and Sahib rose to his feet, politely opening his mouth in greeting.

"Good morning, everyone," said Miss Coleson, finding her voice. She moved away from the door when the footman tapped on it, walking on toward her place at the side of the table. She noticed, without thinking about it, that Lady Blackburne was reading letters, and, for the first time ever, was glad of Lord Renwick's blindness. He could not see how longingly she stared at him.

But she must control herself. Firming her jaw, she turned to the sideboard where she chose the modest breakfast she found quite satisfying after the depravation resulting from her stepmother's inability to control her spending. How, wondered Eustacia fleetingly, had her father controlled it? But that was unimportant just now. Just now she must force herself to act naturally so that she did not give away her emotions.

"You have a letter, Miss Coleson," said Lady Blackburne, handing the missive to the footman who laid it beside Eustacia's plate.

"Why"—Eustacia's eyes widened in surprise—"it is from my father's lawyer!"

"My solicitor must have contacted him about the will. You recall I said I would ask him to look into things for you?"

"Hmm . . ." Eustacia broke the seal and frowned over her correspondent's long involuted sentences.

"Jason, you have one as well." Lady Blackburne held it up. "It is from Lord Wendover. Shall I read it?"

"Later," he said shortly, his face turned toward their guest. "Miss Coleson? Your letter disturbs you?"

"It is," said Eustacia slowly, "that I am uncertain I understand it. There is something about my stepmother's portion here that does not make sense. Something about the estate and reversions and about her remarriage making it necessary to bring the estate to conclusion? Whatever that means? *I* thought it concluded when the solicitor read my father's will. Was it *not* settled then?"

Lord Renwick chuckled. "Probably not. Lawyers love to make everything as complicated as possible. They remain necessary, you see. I suspect your stepmother's portion reverted to the estate upon her marriage to Mr. Weaver. Does your lawyer explain whether *you* benefit or whether your father set those funds aside for charity? Is there nothing which says what happens to the money?"

"Is that what he means?" Eustacia frowned. "Why does he not simply say so instead of using odd phrases and still odder *phrasing*. I *think* he asks if I wish the interest to accumulate or if I wish to receive the income."

"You must decide and write him your decision."

"Yes . . ."

"Something else troubles you?"

"He asks," responded Eustacia slowly, "if the new Mrs. Weaver means to continue living in my house and, if so, should he collect rent."

"It is a sensible question."

"How can I ask *my stepmother* to pay rent?"

"You needn't," said his lordship, mischievously. "You need only to ask that *Mr. Weaver* pay you rent!"

Eustacia chuckled obediently at his mild jest, but quickly sobered. "Oh dear, I don't know what to do."

"Ah!" inserted Lady Blackburne. "I missed this letter when I went through the pile. A second letter for you, Miss Coleson."

Eustacia, staring at the handwriting on the front, sighed.

"From your stepmother?" asked Lord Renwick sympathetically.

"Yes."

"Presumably she, too, has heard from your lawyer."

"Very likely," said Eustacia in a colorless voice. She slit the garish pink wax sealing the back and opened it. "Oh, dear."

"Is she very angry?" asked Lord Renwick.

"It is not she at all. It is from *Mr.* Weaver. He demands that I return home. At once. He says it is important. Imperative, even. That something requires my presence."

Lady Blackburne had, unashamedly, listened. She asked, "He does not explain what that might be?"

"No."

"Then," ordered her ladyship, "you will put him off. The outside was addressed by your stepmother so she cannot be ill and I see no other reason why you should rush off at Mr. Weaver's behest. In fact, from what we know of that man, I would not so much as turn myself around at his request!"

Eustacia smiled. "He is as awful as I painted him, is he not?"

"Worse," said Lady Blackburne in sepulchral tones.

Lord Renwick chuckled at his aunt's dramatics. "The real point, Miss Coleson, is that he has no authority over you. You need not obey him. But you must respond to your solicitor." He nodded in her general direction. "After breakfast we will go to my study where you may read to me the parts you do not understand. Perhaps I can

elucidate them. If I, too, find them written in a language
so intricate as to be indecipherable, then we will have the
carriage out and go into Lewes where my local solicitor
will explain. Now, Aunt, if you would read the letter from
Lord Wendover, please. We shall see if he has the information I require."

The letter was brief. Wendover had not known Renwick
was returned to England. *When did you arrive and why did
you not instantly inform your friends? I will give myself the
pleasure,* wrote his lordship, *of stopping in on my way to
Brighton where I mean to spend the summer.*

"Blast the man!"

"Jason!"

"I did not invite him." Lord Renwick scowled. "How
dare he take it upon himself to decide to come?"

"You know very well that, under normal circumstances,
you would expect him to do so."

Jason's mouth compressed tightly. He pounded the table lightly with his fist, hitting a spoon which bounced.
"I don't want him here."

"What you mean," said Eustacia, "is that you will be
embarrassed by his pity. But why should he feel pity?"

Jason pushed up from the table and leaned on it, his
hands resting flat against it. "I am blind," he said harshly.
"In case you have not noticed, I can no longer do the
things we once did together." He growled, a sound echoed by Sahib. "How the devil—"

"Jason!"

"Am I supposed to entertain a man who can see, does
the things I no longer do?" Jason reached for his cane
which he found without faltering and stomped from the
room, Sahib following.

"Oh, dear." Lady Blackburne sighed.

"A true friend will understand," Eustacia said softly.

"Yes, but Wendover . . . I do not know him at all well.
What if this visit pushes Jason back into his black moods?

Miss Coleson, my nephew has been doing so well. You do not know how frightening those moods can be since"—Lady Blackburne bit her lip, accepting her young friend's role in the change—"he has not fallen into one since you came to us."

Eustacia nodded toward the letter. "What exactly does he say? Does he mean to stop in for tea and go on or is it his intention to stay a few days?

"I imagine he will expect to stay."

"Then we must think of entertainments which involve Lord Renwick in ways he *can* manage. For one thing, I believe this would be an excellent opportunity for your nephew to test his writing abilities. Lord Wendover can, for instance, be astounded by the first chapter of the book!"

"Yes, and there is the fishing. Reeves informed me we are to have a pick-nick today and take the prince fishing. I must ask Jason if Lord Wendover fishes. And if there is any possibility the man would have the patience to teach the boy a few tricks. If you have taught him the basics, then he will like for a man to show him something special, will he not?"

"I believe you understand our prince quite well, Lady Blackburne."

Her ladyship preened in an exaggerated fashion. "Oh, I have lived long enough to know a point or two more than the devil!"

Miss Coleson chuckled as she was meant to do and then, when Lady Blackburne opened still another letter, reread the one from her father's lawyer. She must answer it and the other, but the letter to her stepmother's husband would not be easy.

She could, perhaps, repeat that she would return home when her visit ended and had no notion when that would be. She frowned. Perhaps she should mention that they were free to live in her house?

Or perhaps not. Simply let things go on as they were, telling her lawyer he was not to collect rent, but was, for the time being, to add the income from the widow's portion to what he sent from her inheritance. Assuming Mr. Weaver had *not*, she *must* pay her stepmother's bills and she could not do so without it! It then occurred to her to wonder if Mr. Weaver *had* an income on which he and his wife were living. If not . . .

But just then the prince and the shikari arrived in the breakfast room. The boy was making progress in learning proper manners and bowed first to Lady Blackburne and then, a nicely calculated lesser bow, to Miss Coleson. He seated himself and put his own napkin in his lap, something he once expected the shikari to do for him. Within minutes, a tray covered with small bowls in several sizes and shapes, each tightly covered, arrived at the door and was taken in by the old man who set it on the sideboard.

As usual, Eustacia was enthralled by the exotic odors. She had tried some of the various breads and had liked most of them, but still found most dishes too highly spiced. Every so often the prince offered her something he thought she might like and she, after determining she had enough tea for emergencies, would taste it. Today it was two thin layers of an odd kind of bread with a mildly spiced vegetable filling pressed between them.

Eustacia's eyes widened in surprise when she found that, for once, she enjoyed what she ate.

"You like it," said the prince unnecessarily when she finished off the whole thing. "You begin to understand my country's cooking?"

"I certainly enjoyed that." She turned a rueful look his way. "I doubt, however, I will ever be comfortable eating the spicy curries you and Lord Renwick enjoy so much."

"Savior, Lord and Protector Now and Forever said you are to teach me to fish. Why should I learn to fish?"

"Because it is fun."

"Is it?" he asked, suspicious.

"I learned when I was about your age and enjoy it very much. I pit my wits against a wily fish. Sometimes he wins. Sometimes I do. And I do not know why it is, but when I eat a fish I myself have caught, it tastes ever so much better."

"Do you *always* catch fish?"

Eustacia sighed mournfully. Dramatically. "No. It is the worst part of fishing. One cannot know in advance if one will catch a thing. But then, when one does, it is very exciting."

"I do not think I will like it."

"Why? You think the fish are smarter than you?"

"I think they will not be hungry," he said with young dignity. "Then they will not wish to take my hook. And if they do not, that would be boring, would it not?"

Eustacia looked surprised. "I suppose it *should* be, but somehow, when I am out along a river with a pole in my hands and the world is bright and the day is fine . . . well, somehow I cannot be bored."

"Even when you do not catch a fish?"

"Even then."

Absently, the prince handed her a second of the vegetable-filled pancakes. He munched around the edges of still another.

Eustacia waited.

"I," he said grandly, once he'd made careful scallops all the way around it, "will try."

Eustacia, fingering her letters, was torn between amusement at the boy and her inability to decide what to do about her stepmother. *If only,* she thought, *I could discuss it thoroughly with Lord Renwick.*

Nine

Lord Renwick sat with the shikari in the shade of the little summer house. A breeze, flowing through the open sides, made it very pleasant and achieving his present comfortable position had, he'd discovered, been far less difficult than he'd feared. First of all, with a cry of "Hang on," Lady Blackburne had driven the dogcart off the road and across the grass to a position very near their destination.

Actually, there had been a road of sorts. A lane might better describe it. Or a track? Lord Renwick told himself to remember to ask Miss Coleson who had bounced on her seat and laughed so hard she was unable to say anything. His lordship smiled. It had been good to hear her laugh. She had been all too quiet when she joined the others at the front of the house for the drive to the river. He had taken her aside and asked what troubled her.

"I am always surprised, my lord, that you know another's feelings. I must use visual cues to tell me such things. I have no notion how *you* guess."

"Which is your way of saying you do not mean to tell me what is wrong?"

For another moment she hesitated. "It is merely silliness. I disliked informing my stepmother I would not obey her husband's command that I return home."

"Some parents do not care to admit their children have reached an age of common sense."

"I suppose that might be part of it," said Eustacia doubtfully.

"Part of it?"

"My stepmother has never reacted well to being crossed." Eustacia gasped. "Oh, do not regard that. I should not have said it. Let us say that, whatever the cause, I found it a difficult letter to compose. I did not wish to insult her, of course," she went on quickly, "but felt it necessary to inform her she is no longer responsible for my comings and goings and that, at the moment, I am where I wish to be."

So, knowing she felt low due to her letter, he'd been happy to put up with the discomfort of the short journey from the road to the river when it gave her such pleasure. Or, if *pleasure* was not quite the right word, that she found *humor* in the situation.

Nor had she allowed her mood to darken. Once she'd descended from the cart, she'd described everything. From the way the sun glinted on the water beyond the railing where he sat to each and every dish supplied for their alfresco feast.

And she had gone off cheerfully with the prince, taking him upstream well away from the others so their talk and casting would bother no one. Lord Renwick remembered this area of his estate very well. He had, when much younger, spent many hours here. When his grandfather still lived, the old man had taught him to fish as Miss Coleson now taught the prince. His lordship mused over recollections of a time in his life he had not thought of in years. Precious hours when he stood near the river-bank, a rod in his hands, casting and casting and casting again. He had, he remembered, enjoyed it very much.

It was not the best place for fishing, of course. The water just here was too deep and fast for the best sort of fishing, but, since there were no trees, it was an excellent place for learning and for practicing.

"Miss! Miss! A fish!"

He glanced upstream toward the boy's voice. He could, even at such a distance, hear the excitement in it.

"You have caught a fish!"

"Why, so I have!"

Lord Renwick smiled at the surprise in Miss Coleson's voice. She, too, had known this was not a stretch of river for serious fishing!

"Bring it in, Miss Coleson," ordered the prince. "Bring it in!"

"I am. You see how I reel in a bit and then let the fish run a bit? If I pull too hard I will break the line. Or perhaps pull the hook from the fish. In either case I would lose him."

Renwick heard the faint whine of a furiously turned reel.

"There. You see? I have brought him in quite a bit that time. Now—"

"Miss Coleson. Don't!" The prince's words were lost in a scream and a splash. "Miss Coleson! Miss Coleson!"

There was panic in the high young voice. Lord Renwick rose at the first warning note. He heeled off low boots, ripping off his coat at the same time.

"My lord," said the shikari quietly as Jason climbed to the railing. "I will try to guide you if you will listen for my voice."

"Right. Where is she now?"

"The air in her skirts holds her up. She is the length of six tall men upstream."

Lord Renwick dove. The water hit him like a blast and sooner than he expected. Cursing his blindness, he curved up, breaking free.

"Out another yard, Jason," called his aunt, tension in her voice.

"There, my lord," said Bahadur in a firm tone. "She is a man's length upstream."

"A yard, Jason," shouted Lady Blackburne.

"*Now,* my lord," ordered the shikari.

As those on shore called instructions, Jason listened to Miss Coleson's surprisingly calm voice.

"Here, my lord," she finished, grabbing his arm and then, a moment later, holding him still more tightly while coughing and sputtering. "How foolish," she said when she could speak, "to go under just then when all was well."

"My lord," called the shikari, "you drift downstream at an overly rapid pace."

"We must make for shore, Miss Coleson. If you will trust me, I will put my hands under your arms and lie back and pull you with me as I kick."

"Very well, my lord."

He arranged them while listening to the shikari's instructions and began the return journey to the riverbank. "You are surprisingly calm," he said.

"Not before I saw you prepare to dive in, my lord! Then I knew you would rescue me and I could not see where panic would help either of us." She gasped and sputtered and laughed softly. "Oh, this water! I wonder if I will ever again like water!"

They heard a splash behind them. "I have got you," said the old man.

Lord Renwick felt a hand grasp a handful of cloth at his neck. He lowered his feet, hoping the seams would hold. Unfortunately, he could not find bottom and kicked again, pushing against his rescuer.

"The bank is quite high just here, my lord," said the shikari. "I believe that if you were to allow me to hold one of Miss Coleson's arms while you use your free arm to hold my shoulder? Yes, like that. Now, my lord. On three if we lift her."

"And I will scramble onto the bank."

"Put your foot on a shoulder, Miss Coleson," ordered Lord Renwick. "Whichever of us you . . . ah! Yes, just th—" This time Lord Renwick came up sputtering, the pressure of Miss Coleson's foot sending him under. "And now, my friend," he asked Bahadur when he could speak, "how do you and I return to shore?"

"I hold a footman's arm, my lord. Lady Blackburne, I believe, sits on his back. If you kick and I lift, perhaps you can scramble onto the grass?"

Lord Renwick swore softly. "If only I could see!"

The shikari chuckled. "My lord, so far as *I* could see, your blindness slowed you not a whit!"

Jason sobered. Softly, he admitted, "She . . . is important to me. I could not let her come to harm." He drew in a deep breath. "How high is the bank?"

"The footman has his elbow bent over the edge and I am clasping his wrist. I fear it is something of a stretch."

"I am ready."

They failed the first time. The second time Jason managed to grab a clump of scraggly grass and felt his arm grasped, held by two soft hands. The shikari moved his grip and heaved from low down his back. Jason squirmed forward until he lay from the waist up on the bank. He took two deep breaths and finished clambering up.

Immediately he reversed himself to lay alongside the footman, extending his arms over the edge. A hand grasped him above the elbow. Jason heard the footman grunt and suspected Bahadur had moved his grip higher up the footman's arm, perhaps pinching a muscle.

"We'll inch back and pull him up," said Jason to the footman. He felt hands at his ankles, guiding his progress. Gradually, the old man came up out of the water and over the bank.

In all this the prince had been strangely silent. Now he burst into loud sobs and ran off.

"What was that all about?" asked Jason, pushing his hands through his hair and shaking off the water.

"I had to push him away, my lord," said the old man, panting. "He tried to stop me from entering the water. I do not know why."

"Because he was afraid for you, sir," said Lady Blackburne.

"Afraid for me? What nonsense." But then the old man's teeth began chattering.

With a cluck of dismay, Lady Blackburne ordered the footman out of his coat which she gave the shikari, ordering him to put it on instantly.

"And you, Miss Coleson," said Lord Renwick. "My jacket must be somewhere around?"

"The sun has warmed me and nearly dried me as well. You need it yourself, my lord."

He felt her pressing his coat about his shoulders and pushed wet shirtsleeves into coat sleeves.

"Men wear such heavy cloth," said Eustacia as she helped him. "It does not dry so easily as a woman's dress."

"Come," said Lady Blackburne. "I will drive us back in the cart. Yes, you, too, Marcus. There will be a bonus for you for your help just now. Miss Coleson and I alone could not have gotten the men out of the water."

Except for Bahadur, there were no ill effects of their watery adventure. The prince, awakened in the middle of the night by the shikari's babbling and moaning, ran to wake Jason who immediately sent the lad to wake his aunt. Lady Blackburne had the footmen move the old gentleman from the trundle in the prince's room to a room with a real bed where she and the housekeeper instantly set to work to bring down his fever.

"Do you know if he has ever been ill like this before?" she asked the prince sternly.

"It is the ague," cried the prince. "I knew he should

not go into the water. I knew it." His voice rose, becoming shrill. "He will die. He will die!"

Lady Blackburne ignored the boy, watching the housekeeper wash down the old man, wring out her rag, and do so again. "Jason, do you know how to treat this particular ague?"

"No," said Jason shortly. "We must send a groom for the doctor."

Sometime later the doctor studied the situation and dug deep into his bag. "I haven't much, but perhaps it will suffice until more is sent me."

"What is it?" asked Jason.

"Military doctors call it 'bark.' I know of no reason why it eases this particular illness but it appears to do so." He explained to Lady Blackburne how it was to be administered and left, mumbling about the inconsiderateness of servants who hounded one from one's warm bed on a cold night and merely for another servant.

Since it was not at all cold Jason didn't bother to apologize. He did, however, explain that the man the doctor called a servant had not only saved two lives that afternoon, but had a position and reputation in his own country very near that of a good general in England.

The grouchy old doctor was not appeased. Indeed, only the generous payment Lord Renwick ordered Reeves to give the man went any way at all toward soothing the excess of irritability.

The next days were filled with concern. Although his hair was fully white, the shikari was an active and agile man. One tended to think of him as middle-aged, but it was not so. The medicine appeared to relieve his symptoms, but he did not recover with any quickness, the resiliency of youth long gone from his lean, muscular, body.

One night nearly a week after their disastrous pick-nick, when Miss Coleson sat dozing in her chair, she heard the click of the sickroom door latch. She opened one eye and watched the prince slip through the narrowest possible opening.

For a long moment he stood there, his body rigid and his eyes round with stress. The boy had been forbidden to visit his shikari after a first visit which left the lad in tears, very nearly hysterical. Now he never took his eyes off the old man as he crept stiffly across the carpet.

Miss Coleson, knowing the boy's fear, the depth of his despair, felt that it would not hurt him to see that his servant was much improved. She guessed that once he saw that was so he would creep away just as silently. She would pretend she did not know he was there so as not to embarrass him.

Then, suddenly, she wished she *had.*

"Old man! Old man!" The boy reached for the sick man's shoulder.

The shikari moaned.

"Wake up. I, your prince, order you. Wake up."

Miss Coleson rose to her feet.

"Prince . . . ?" mumbled the shikari.

"I order you to get well. Do you hear me? You are to get well. Immediately. I will not have you die. You *will* not."

The sick man ran his tongue around his teeth. "Water."

Miss Coleson came instantly to his other side. She helped him drink.

"You will not die. Do you hear me?"

"Prince!" began Eustacia.

The old man lifted two fingers in silent demand. He made a great effort, lifting himself to his elbows. "I do not believe I will die. Not this time, my prince," he said. He sighed, fell back, and his eyes fluttered closed.

"Go!" ordered Eustacia in a whisper. She glared at the boy. "You will kill him yourself, demanding so much of him! He needs his rest and you must not wake him."

"Must not? Must not? He is my servant!"

"He is also a very sick old man who needs consideration from those who owe him so much." Miss Coleson
sighed. "Prince Ravi, return to your bed and cease worrying about Bahadur. I, too, think the man will recover.
But *not* if his rest is disturbed!"

"He will recover. That is good. He will take me back
to my country, to my father," said the boy complacently.
"I will not be left alone with strangers, with men I am
uncertain I may trust."

"He will . . . !" Horrified, Miss Coleson stared and
then thrust the boy into the hall. "You self-centered brat!
How unspeakably cruel! I thought you worried about him
because you loved him and did not wish to lose him and
all the time you thought only of yourself! You are . . . !"

The boy straightened to his full height, his features
settling into a cold hard beauty, evidence of how he would
look when mature. "I am his prince. He is merely a servant. One does not love a servant."

Eustacia's eyes narrowed. "Do you not?"

The boy flushed so deeply that even in the poor light
in the hall one noticed it. "One does not love a servant,"
he repeated.

Miss Coleson returned to her charge and found him
awake. "You should sleep," she scolded.

"You must not scold the prince. He is who he is. You
must understand that he will need every bit of that . . .
that . . ." Bahadur frowned.

"Hauteur?"

Bahadur's frown deepened. "I do not know this word.
He will need pride. Pride in his past and in the future."
He breathed heavily for a moment and then continued.
"When he is maharaja, I mean. It is not easy, being ma-
haraja."

"I will remember, but I cannot see why he will not
admit he is worried about *you*, not just himself. You are
special. Now I must give you another drink and then you

will sleep so that you may obey your prince and get well again," scolded Miss Coleson.

The shikari chuckled weakly. "Lord Renwick is a lucky man," he said when he had drunk.

Miss Coleson blushed. "I do not know what you mean."

The old man's bushy brows rose. "Ah, well. If you do not . . ." He yawned. "I will sleep now." And he did. Instantly. Just like *that,* he fell into a deep and restful sleep.

Miss Coleson stared. After frantic thought, she found the explanation for his words: Lord Renwick was lucky she could decipher his writing, that she had an odd memory so she could write out his words after he spoke them. He was lucky he had found such as she to help him with his book.

That was what the old man meant.

"Or did he?" she muttered. "Perhaps he has seen what I've hoped to keep secret?" Then, blushing even more rosily, she returned to her chair where she remained, wide awake, until a maid came at dawn to relieve her.

The shikari recovered but was far more frail than before. Lady Blackburne found an old and overly large wool shawl, a bright plaid, in which he would wrap himself and sit, his eyes closed, in the warmest corners he could find. The boy would look at him, frown, and turn away. Only to come back and stare at him again.

"You are wrong, Prince Ravi, that it is *always* bad to love those who love you, even though they are beneath you socially," said Miss Coleson one day. "You will be a very lonely man if you cannot admit that there are some you love. The thing you must remember is that they will be no less human just because you love them. Even those you love and who love you back can occasionally disappoint." She stared at the boy, thoughtfully. "I guess what I would say is that you must not love blindly."

"Yes. I have had to admit in my heart that I love the stupid old man. But it was wrong of him to make himself ill. It was wrong of him to grow weak and—and unable to care for me properly."

"You mean he was to allow Lord Renwick and myself drown?" asked Eustacia, her voice a trifle stern. "You know how very brave it was of him to lower himself into the water when he cannot swim."

The boy frowned. "He should rescue you, yes, but not become ill."

"Can you always prevent yourself from becoming ill?"

The boy's eyes widened in surprise. "I think so for I have never been ill. And the old man is the only man here who can see to me."

"You would say you cannot see to yourself?"

"Not always," admitted the lad with dignity. "I do not know how to take myself and my servants home again. There is no one but the old man to find a safe ship, no one but he to know who may be trusted and who may not."

"If your only reason for being angry with Bahadur," said Miss Coleson, losing patience, "is because you fear he'll not be able to return you to your home, then cease worrying. Lord Renwick will not send you off on your own. I doubt he will allow _any of you_ to return without someone to care for _Bahadur._ His lordship has a proper understanding of what is due the man who saved his life, the man who once helped save yours and who would, himself, be blind had he not closed his eyes when he shot at that tiger."

"When his old gun exploded."

"Yes. When Lord Renwick was blinded _in your service._"

The boy sighed. "It is difficult sometimes."

"What is difficult?"

"One may not feel special feelings for those of lesser rank. It is not proper." Again that surprising dignity was revealed. "Yet one does feel them. How does one go on?"

"One admits to such feelings and one holds them in balance with one's duty, I would suppose."

"Ah. Duty comes first?"

"Duty tempered with compassion and what is best for those to whom one is responsible."

"You once said I am responsible to my people. That is wrong. They are responsible to me."

"Is it not possible that you have responsibilities, each to the other?"

"Bah!" The prince stamped his foot. "You make things difficult. You allow nothing to be black and white but shade every rule, every thought, so nothing is true just in itself!"

"But is that not good sense? The world is *not* a simple place. It is very complicated. And the more responsibility one has, the more complicated it becomes."

The boy thought about that for a moment and then, again, shouted his favorite oath before stalking from the room.

"Poor lad," murmured Miss Coleson.

"I would rather say poor lady," said Lord Renwick, rising from the chair in which he had been sitting. Neither the prince nor Miss Coleson had noticed his presence because the chair had been turned to the windows, the bright light falling on the eye which could still discern it. Now Jason oriented himself and walked toward her. "He is a great burden not only to us but to himself, is he not?"

"It is mostly, I think, that he is young, my lord." Eustacia felt her heartbeat speed up. How good he looked, so tall and straight.

But it was the first time since her rescue that she had been alone with him. She drew in a deep breath, meaning

to say the piece she had worked on so hard and had
memorized for this moment.

His lordship raised a hand and her breath escaped.
"You would give me thanks for saving you from a watery
death. Do not. I could not have done it without the help
of those on shore. My damnable blindness! I would not
have found you. I would have been in the wrong place
or something equally stupid and utterly helpless, had we
been by ourselves. You must thank those others who led
me to you."

"I have thanked them. But they, my lord, could not
swim." Daringly, she lay her hand on his arm. "Without
you, *they* could not have rescued me. Therefore, I thank
you as well, my lord. From the bottom of my heart."

They were not the words she had meant to speak, the
long careful speech she had composed in the long night
hours when she had watched by the shikari's bed. Still,
his lordship seemed to accept them in the spirit offered.
And he seemed to lose some of the bitterness which his
words to her had revealed.

"You are generous to a man who finds himself, more
often than not, helpless and angry and unhappy."

"Nonsense. Every man and woman has limitations. And
strengths. In the current instance it is that no one but
you could swim. Not many blind men would have the
courage to dive in as you did. You are a very special man,
Lord Renwick." She smiled to see the spots of color touch
his cheeks. "I do not wish to embarrass you, my lord, but
you put too much emphasis on your lack of sight. You
have so many strengths. Strengths which make you worthy
of any man's respect."

The color deepened, reddening not only his cheeks
but his neck and ears. "In the word of our young prince,
I say 'bah.' You spout a great deal of humbug, my dear."
It was his turn to draw in a breath. "Do you think we

might spend an hour in the study now? If you are not too tired?"

"And why would I be tired? I have done nothing."

"My aunt says otherwise. You have spent long hours, most of them night hours, nursing Bahadur."

"Oh, well, recently he has not needed a night nurse and before, when he did, I dozed, off and on, each night." She studied Lord Renwick, not glad he was blind but glad that his blindness gave her the freedom to do so. "I think perhaps *you* are tired, my lord. Do you truly wish to dictate to me?"

"Yes."

He held out his arm. She accepted it and they strolled from the room and along the halls to his study where they found Sahib awaiting them. The tiger stood upon their entry and roared softly.

Lord Renwick stopped short. "Who has had the temerity to bring Sahib from his feeding room?"

Ten

"Miss Coleson, you do not answer! But you know, do you not, whom it is that Sahib willingly obeys?"

"What I suspect," she said with a sigh, "is that Sahib brought himself."

"Do not make up tales to protect the guilty or make jokes about something so important."

"I tell no taradiddles, my lord, nor do I jest. I have seen him open the door to this room."

Lord Renwick was silent for a long moment. "Late the night we last walked in the garden is the only time I have found that door open as it was just now. How can you know that when you returned to the house before I did?"

Eustacia bit her lip.

"You spied on me."

"No! Well . . . yes. I worried you would become disoriented and lose your way. When you did move, it was so quickly I'd no time to move away. Then you shut the door to the study before Sahib entered. He opened it and went in. I thought at the time that, if he also learns to shut a door, we will never know where to find him!"

Lord Renwick smiled, but it was not an entirely pleasant smile. "I do not care to be spied upon, Miss Coleson. In future you will not do so."

Again she was silent.

"Miss Coleson," he said, sharply.

"I will not promise anything so foolish, my lord. There are occasions when it is important that someone knows what you do!"

"So that I do myself no injury." His lordship growled, which roused Sahib who looked from one to the other and then lay down again. "Not ten minutes ago," snarled Lord Renwick, "you told me I place too much importance on my inability to see. You contradict yourself."

"What I said was that you have strengths which are more important, talents you can and will develop. It is unlikely, under normal circumstances, that you would have done a thing with your ability to put words together, for instance. If you were *not* blind you'd not produce the books you'll now write, and, frankly, that would have been a shame. Your writing will give many readers great pleasure."

"You would say my blindness is a boon?" he sneered. "You go too far, Miss Coleson!"

A soft tap and Reeves opened the door, announcing, "Lord Wendover, my lord."

"Damn!"

"What a way to greet an old friend you've not seen in a donkey's age!" laughed the cheerful and mischievous-looking gentleman who rushed in. "Or," he stopped nearly in midstride, looking from a blushing Miss Coleson to a glowering Lord Renwick, "did I, perhaps, interrupt something?"

"You did."

Lord Wendover moved toward Renwick and held out his hand. Unseen, it was ignored and, now, it was *his* face which turned bright red. Then it turned white when Sahib, sensing new tension in the room rose and stepped between Jason and the stranger. Wendover backed cautiously. "My God, a—a *tiger?*"

"Sahib. Down." The beast swung his head up to look

up at Jason and then back toward Wendover. "Friend," said his lordship sternly.

Keeping an eye on Sahib who did not move away, but subsided between the two, Wendover asked bluntly, *"Am* I still your friend, Jase? I do not feel particularly welcome which is something of a settler, when I was so very glad to learn you had returned to England."

Both his lordship and Miss Coleson could hear the hurt in the man's tone. Lord Renwick clenched his fists. "I do welcome you, Tony. It is just that . . ." He turned aside.

"My lord," said Eustacia softly, "you must tell him. Your friend imagines all sorts of things and none are true."

"I am blind," said Lord Renwick, the words gritty on his tongue.

"Blind! Truly?"

Renwick turned back, a crooked grin on his face. "Truly."

"But how, when, what happened?" Lord Wendover shook his head. "No, let us begin again. And this time, give me your hand to shake, Jase, old friend!"

Jason held out his hand and Wendover, reaching across Sahib, grasped it. The tiger moved aside and Wendover stepped nearer, giving Lord Renwick a quick masculine hug. "Lord, it is good to see you again. I thought you were in India, old boy." He glanced at the tiger. "And I was quite right, was I not? That beast doesn't bite, does he?" he finished with only a trifling unease.

Miss Coleson chuckled softly. "Sahib has yet to bite anyone, my lord, but we await the first time."

Sahib padded over to her and pushed his nose into her hand which, she noticed shook as, for the first time, she ran it over the animal's head and behind his ears as she had seen Lord Renwick do.

"Why Sahib, are you telling me you won't bite me?"

The tiger bounced her hand a trifle, seeming to nod

his head and she laughed, Lord Wendover's deeper chuckle joining in.

"Tell me," ordered Lord Renwick, irritated the others could enjoy a jest he could not understand.

Eustacia explained. "I will leave you now," she finished, "and see that Reeves has ordered a room for you, Lord Wendover. And," she added as Prince Ravi entered the room, "I will take this young man away so he will not disturb your talk."

"But it is time for my mathematics," protested the boy.

"You," said Eustacia firmly, "are to have a holiday. Come along and help me . . . oh, help me choose flowers for Lord Wendover's room." She pushed the still protesting boy from the room. Sahib helped her along by roaring. The boy eyed the animal with distrustful eyes. "It is not polite," said Miss Coleson firmly as she closed the door with the prince and herself in the hall, "to push yourself in where you are not wanted."

"Not wanted . . ."

She heard the hurt that the boy, with his pride, would deny. "Just at the moment, Prince, when Lord Wendover has only just arrived, *no one* is wanted. The men are close friends and have not seen each other for years. They will have much catching up to do, and it is not for us to interfere."

"I," said the boy drawing himself up, "am the prince."

"Yes. You are also a boy. And a guest. You are obliged—"

"Never."

"To show proper courtesy. It is a princely thing to do, to know when to show courtesy to others."

"Bah!" The boy turned on his heel and raced off down the hall.

Miss Coleson shook her head and, more sedately, followed.

Inside the study Lord Wendover was telling Lord Renwick he had a delightful wife.

"*Not* my wife. She is my aunt's guest, the daughter of Aunt Luce's old friend."

"Ah." Wendover eyed Renwick. "But you *were* arguing, were you not? I was not wrong about that? Thought you *must* be married, you see. Arguing, you know. Must apologize for bursting in on you that way!"

Renwick chuckled a trifle sourly. "Miss Coleson is determined to prove to me that I am no less a man because of my lack of sight. I wish I could believe her," he added bitterly. He drew in a deep breath. "Tony, there are decanters on the table there." He gestured. "And glasses. Will you do the honors and bring our wine to the window? We've a lot of catching up to do."

For an hour Lord Renwick managed to keep Wendover talking about himself and mutual friends, telling the news for several years back.

Finally though, Wendover would not be put off. "Tell me, Jase. How did it happen?"

Jason made a brief story of it.

"There is more." When Jason didn't answer, Wendover asked, "And that rude boy your Miss Coleson pushed from the room?"

"He is the lad I wrote about, the one for whom I need a tutor. Also the boy in my story. He's a royal prince in his homeland."

"A royal brat, you mean."

Jason chuckled with true humor. "Yes, but he hasn't a notion what it means to be crossed, you see. Miss Coleson gets away with it occasionally. He rarely falls into a tantrum with her as he does when anyone else tells him he may not do exactly as he wishes exactly when he wishes." Jason sipped his wine. "Although, now I think of it, he is doing better. Ever since we nearly lost his Indian mentor to the fever. I think he finally realized he cannot always order life as he wishes, that there are occasions when life orders itself!"

"And this is the lad for whom you need a tutor. I wish you luck!"

"I need it. I teach him myself at the moment, but there is much I cannot do. Gentlemanly sports, for instance. My head groom is teaching him to ride and my coachman tried to give him a driving lesson. The groom has got around the boy, but my coach complained the lad was disobedient and likely to cause himself or someone else harm. I need a young man of good family who likes boys but is old enough to have a firm hand. One needs both tact and, frankly, great strength of will!"

"As I said in my letter I don't know anyone. I'm out of touch with the sort of young man you have in mind." Wendover shrugged. "I'll ask around, though. Now Jase," he turned the subject, "tell me, what is India truly like? I mean other than the heat and the snakes which everyone talks about?"

Jason laughed. "And you want the answer in fifty words or, better, in less? *You* along with everyone else must await the book I am writing. Assuming," he said, sobering and sighing, "it is ever finished."

"Why should it not be?"

"Miss Coleson is my good angel in my attempt to produce it. She not only has the amazing ability that she can decipher my handwriting." He glanced toward Tony when his friend sputtered into his drink. "Yes, you know how bad it is, do you not? I kept detailed journals in India, however difficult to read now. But she *can* read them and has a talent for organizing the disorganized. She marks all she finds on a given subject and reads it to me. Then I think about it and compose paragraphs while she listens. She has another necessary talent in that she remembers my words and later writes them down." He shrugged.

"So why, with such a paragon, should you *not* finish your book?"

"She is a guest. I cannot ask her to spend hours at work. Then, too, there is the prince. He takes up much of my time."

"The real reason for finding a proper tutor."

"I need someone to teach him the things I cannot."

"Irrelevant that you would have more time with your Miss Coleson?" Wendover cast his friend a mischievous look. "To work on your book, of course."

Jason sobered. A bleak look appeared around his blind eyes. "What else would a young woman do with a blind man?"

"Fall in love with him?" asked Tony in innocent tones.

"With half a man?" Jason shifted uncomfortably. "Don't talk nonsense, Tony."

"Surely, Jase, you did no damage to the half which counts."

"You will keep a clean tongue in your mouth when speaking of Miss Coleson. I'll not have anyone making nasty jests about her."

"Which didn't answer my question."

Jason felt his ears go hot. "I assume that to which you refer is in working order."

"You *assume*?" Wendover cast Jason an astounded look. "My boy," he asked, "do you mean you've not had a woman since before you were blinded?"

"I . . . no."

"You don't admit it or you have not?"

"Blast it, Tony, change the subject!"

"You cannot?"

"I don't know," said Renwick crossly. "Oh, yes," he continued, "of course I could. If I would. But I have not."

Tony eyed him. "Ah! You prefer to know what sort of woman you put a leg across, is that it? And haven't wished to take a chance? Perhaps I can help with *this* if I cannot with finding you a tutor!"

Jason grimaced. "Perhaps someday, Tony," he said, not

wishing to admit there was only one woman who interested him in that way and that she was one he could not have. Nor that it made not a whit of difference what she looked like! He sighed. "Tell me . . ." he ordered, dredging up the name of still another acquaintance about whom he could ask.

Lord Wendover stayed for three days. Before he departed he became well acquainted with Miss Coleson. He admired her greatly but knew he would never have a chance, even if he wanted it, with the young lady who was, although she tried to hide it, deeply in love with Jason. He wondered how long it would be before Jase admitted he returned that love.

And how soon thereafter he would act on it.

But perhaps he never would. Wendover grimaced. He'd always thought Jason too honorable by half!

"Still another demanding letter from your stepmother, Miss Coleson?" asked Lady Blackburne, noticing how her young guest ignored her morning egg.

"She seems nearly hysterical, ranting on about a letter from my father's solicitor which arrived in place of her quarterly widow's portion. She says it is intolerable, that the shopkeepers demand payment, that some will not supply her with necessary goods and that it is all my fault."

"But surely Mr. Weaver—"

"He says it is her place to pay for daily household necessaries but then, she says, he uses up wax candles as if they were supplied by the fairies for nothing!"

"It is usually the gentleman who supports his household," suggested Lady Blackburne smoothly, "is it not?"

"It certainly is," said Lord Renwick from his end of the table. "Mr. Weaver is a scoundrel. Perhaps, in a mild way, he is a fortune hunter who has fallen into his own trap, thinking the widow worth more than she was! You, my dear Miss Coleson, have had a lucky escape, in that you were not there for him to wed."

"I don't believe I *would* have wed him," she muttered, rereading a paragraph which bothered her.

"What is it?" asked Jason, staring very nearly at her.

"You are doing it again, my lord, and I will never understand how."

"How I know you are upset? Unhappy? I hear it, Miss Coleson. Or I feel it. I cannot tell you. But you have not said what bothers you."

She sighed. "My stepmother appears to have found it necessary to give over some of the silver in payment for debts. Not that there was much to give, of course."

"Surely it was not hers *to* give!" exclaimed Lady Blackburne.

"No. I do not believe it was," agreed Miss Coleson, speaking quietly.

"Send the soldiers after her," suggested the prince who was, this morning, eating English food and disliking every bite—except for the bacon which he ate greedily. "They will know what to do with a thief."

"She is my stepmother, Prince Ravi. I cannot do that."

"Why not?"

"It is not done."

"Bah!"

"For once I agree with *you*, Prince," said Lord Renwick. "My dear Miss Coleson, this must not be allowed. It is theft."

"But how will she live?" Miss Coleson drew in a deep breath. "If Mr. Weaver cannot support them, someone must, must they not?" After a moment and speaking slowly, she said, "Perhaps . . . I should send her her money . . . when it arrives."

"But it is *not* her money, Miss Coleson," said her ladyship. Lady Blackburne rose to her feet. "And you must do no such thing! They can go to debtor's prison as does anyone who runs up debts they cannot pay!" Without another word, her ladyship departed.

Eustacia could not agree that she'd no responsibility for her father's second wife. Yet she could not see where she had a duty to support Mr. Weaver which forwarding the funds to her stepmother would do. Her ambivalent feelings made her unhappy. She, too, left the room and without her usual wishes that the others have a pleasant day.

"I," said the prince fiercely, "will send my soldiers to kill that person so that Miss Coleson need not concern herself."

Lord Renwick choked on his tea. When he ceased coughing, he told the boy that, whatever could be done in his homeland, things were *not* accomplished that way here in England. There were laws all must obey, *even foreign visitors.*

"Bah!" said the boy, but then sighed. "So . . . how can we help Miss Coleson?"

"Not easily if she will not agree she needs help."

"Can you not write these people a strong letter telling them to go away and leave her alone?"

"An excellent notion, Prince. I will discuss the idea with Miss Coleson. If she agrees, *my solicitor* will write a warning of what will happen if they persist in such behavior. Perhaps that will be sufficient."

"Why must you ask Miss Coleson?"

"Because it is her business."

"She is a woman."

"You would say she has no rights?"

"She is merely a woman," repeated the boy and rose.

The prince nearly forgot the manners taught him for leaving a room politely, but, just before exiting, he turned and bowed stiffly. The properly prim words issued from the lad's arrogant mouth left Lord Renwick smiling. The boy, decided his lordship, might learn proper English modes, as his father wished him to do, but he would always use them in his own style, giving words and actions entirely new meanings!

"Well, Sahib, we are alone. Shall we too depart?"

Sahib growled agreement and the two left for the outdoors where Sahib entered his cage. There he would stay while Lord Renwick discussed business with his agent, the man having told Lord Renwick in the bluntest of fashions he would resign if required to have anything to do with the beast.

That day, among other things, the agent reluctantly admitted that his lordship's plan for allowing the younger servants short periods of amusement twice a day was succeeding far beyond his dreams!

After the first letter from the Weavers which caused Miss Coleson such distress, a flood of letters arrived for her. Perforce, she agreed to Lord Renwick's suggestion that he order his solicitor to send a warning. They'd no knowledge of what, exactly, the solicitor said, but it was unsuccessful and soon became obvious the couple believed Miss Coleson had a moral obligation to support them.

There were even hints in the latest letter that there was no reason why she should *not* and that she could *easily* do so, if only she were to come home. Which made not a jot of sense. And, in each letter, the continued insistence she was needed.

Torn between her ever growing desire to help Lord Renwick in every way and a nagging conscience rubbing at her for her stepmother's problems, Miss Coleson withdrew into herself. Surprisingly, the more nervous and unhappy she grew the more attention Sahib paid her.

He would come to her and nudge her or lay his huge head in her lap and stare up at her. Then, one day, the tiger and Lord Renwick came upon her in the garden where she had taken her latest missive. They found her alone and, although Lord Renwick could not see them, he guessed tears ran down her cheeks.

Sahib put his paws on the bench on either side of her and allowed Eustacia to put her arms around his neck, hug him, and, *almost* silently, cry into his fur. A low rumbling noise of commiseration came from his great throat. Lord Renwick cursed his blindness even more than usual. Something was wrong, but he could not ascertain what.

"I am so sorry," she said, releasing her clutch on the great cat. Sahib leaned back, looked at her, and backed away, settling close to her skirts.

"Something has happened? Something new?"

"Oh, no. Only more of the same. Another demand from my stepmother. She says, again, there is a problem, that it is essential that I return, that nothing can be done without me."

"What is this problem?"

"That, my lord, she does *not* say." A mild anger replaced her agitation of nerves. "I have asked. She will only insist that I can easily solve everything if only I would return home."

"Tell her that only if she describes to you the problem can you decide whether or not to return."

Eustacia sighed. She recalled her last two letters in which she had done just that. "Yes, my lord."

He chuckled. "So submissive."

She didn't respond, but the tinkle of tiny bells as she shifted about revealed her renewed agitation. He frowned, staring thoughtfully in her direction.

"You *have* asked?" he suggested.

"Twice," she admitted.

"Then," he soothed, "there is no problem of a very serious nature."

"Do you think it possible?"

"Nothing which cannot be put off. If it were indeed something urgent she would respond to your demand for an explanation, would she not? For instance, if the roof had developed a leak or if the well had gone dry?"

"One would certainly think so, but she is so unlike herself, my lord. I mean, she has always been a bit of a scold, but her words in these last two letters have nearly threatened me. And don't ask, *threatened what* because I cannot tell you."

"Would it be an imposition if I asked you to read this one aloud?"

Eustacia immediately complied, finishing, *"and at once. There. You see? Nothing one can put a finger on, but still, a strange sort of—"*

"Emotion? Mood?" he supplied when she trailed off.

"Hmm. I was foolish to cry." She leaned down and rubbed the tiger's head. "Sahib must think me an imbecile."

"I doubt Sahib thinks any such thing, Miss Coleson. I certainly do not and, for the most part, Sahib thinks as I do."

"You jest."

"Well"—he smiled gently—"perhaps a trifle." Then he sobered. "Miss Coleson, would it help if we traveled to your home and, together, discovered what this is about? Aunt Luce would agree to it and, once you have verified it is nothing more than selfishness, you could return here with a quiet mind."

"I cannot ask such a thing of Lady Blackburne. Or of you and Sahib. I know you dislike travel and besides I am simply acting a great silly." She drew in a deep breath. "I will not allow my stepmother to overset me." She made an effort and turned the conversation. "Have not you and the prince finished rather early this morning?"

For a moment it seemed that Lord Renwick would not follow her lead, but then, politely, he did so. "The prince seemed more than a trifle restless. Unsettled. He would not concentrate and I finally gave it up as a bad job. I wish I would hear of a proper young man who could take on the boy's training out of doors."

"You had already departed the breakfast room when I arrived this morning." Eustacia remembered that that had upset her even before she knew there was another letter from her stepmother! "I believe," she added, "your aunt mentioned you'd a letter when she gave me mine. Should we see if it is the one you await?"

"A very good notion, Miss Coleson. And if it is nothing, then perhaps we may use this extra time to continue work on the chapter on Indian snakes."

Miss Coleson shuddered. "I fear I would not like India after all. I do not care for snakes, I think."

Lord Renwick chuckled. "You would especially dislike the king cobras although they are not the most dangerous. The krait, fast and aggressive, is the worst, but the cobra can grow to a monstrous size. When it rears up before one and lifts that hood at one it can frighten a grown man. A woman would not be considered cowardly for fearing it!"

The letter was from his lordship's Scottish friend, Ian McMurrey, and, rather diffidently, suggested his youngest brother might be suitable. The brother had been at university until an illness forced his withdrawal. He was recovered now but not yet returned to his college. McMurrey proceeded to list the young man's accomplishments, a list which ran very close to Lord Renwick's thoughts on what was needed.

The letter ended with the information that McMurrey planned to come to London no more than a week after the letter. He would give himself, he added, the pleasure of visiting Renwick Towers.

He would bring Aaron, too, so Jason could judge for himself, but would not, he wrote, tell the young man of the possibility of a position so that if Lord Renwick decided against him there would be no disappointment and no embarrassment. McMurrey, however, was more than half certain that Aaron would prove satisfactory.

"Does he say when they arrive, Miss Coleson?" Lord Renwick scowled.

"There is a postscript to the effect they should be here toward the end of the month." She looked up, noted his expression, and laughed. "You will soon rid yourself of all friends if you scowl that way at even the *thought* of one. I feared Lord Wendover would turn tail and run when he saw you frown at *him* in that particularly nasty fashion!"

Lord Renwick grimaced. "Can you not understand how difficult it is to be with men who knew me before, men with whom I rode, fished, and hunted? All those things I can no longer do?"

"Did you never talk to them?"

"Oh, hours on end," he admitted, and then chuckled ruefully. "And that, you would say, is something I may still do?"

"Yes."

"*All* I can do." Lord Renwick sighed and then was quiet for a moment. He sighed again. "I suppose I must send Wendover a message that McMurrey comes. We three were half of a sextet of boys who met and became friends at school. We remained close until maturity sent us our different ways."

"I have now heard of Mr. McMurrey and I met Lord Wendover. Where are the others, my lord?"

"Jack Princeton, Wendover told me, is in the Peninsula, a dashing cavalry officer; Lord Merwin inherited his father's title and took his seat in the House of Lords. He was, by far, the most politically minded of us. And the last, Miles Seward . . ." He frowned. "I haven't a notion where Miles might be." His mood lightened and he chuckled. "Two traits, Miss Coleson, describe the man. An insatiable curiosity and an enviable talent for learning new languages. He ran off with gypsies when a boy and he had already taken a journey up the Nile disguised as a native before I joined the army and went to India. That was years ago, of course. Since? For all I could tell you, he has been adopted into a wild Indian tribe in the forests of Canada or gone to visit those islands still farther east than where I was on which cannibals are said to reside!"

"When your book is published, perhaps he will read it and write you. At least, is it not the sort of book he might read?"

"Miles hadn't the patience to sit still long enough to read anything. But that is neither here nor there since I have yet to produce a book which *anyone* would wish to read." Before she could demur at this self-castigation, he added, "Miss Coleson, will you do me the favor of penning my letter to Wendover?"

"Yes, of course."

The days counted themselves out as did the pages of the manuscript. Much to the surprise of everyone including himself, the prince took to riding as if he were born to it. He spent long afternoon hours with the head groom, obeying the man to the letter. Miss Coleson wished to know why he obeyed this man and no other.

His lordship chuckled.

"Well?" asked Lady Blackburne. They were drinking their evening tea and she, too, was curious.

"I admit that I wished the answer to that myself."

"I have no doubt you *asked,*" retorted Lady Blackburne.

"Aunt Luce, you know me well. Yes, I asked. Old Riggs, the first time Prince Ravi reacted in one of his bratty ways, plucked the boy from his saddle, took the reins, and walked off. He didn't say one word, merely would have nothing to do with our guest. The prince held out for two days and then, not quite knowing the way of it, apologized. Riggs told him, sternly, he could have *one more chance*, but that he, Riggs, had far too much respect for my horses to allow anyone to harm them and one chance was *all* the lad would get." Lord Renwick smiled. "Our prince appears to believe him."

"A very good thing, too, since I believe you and Miss Coleson are managing to get through quite a bit of work, are you not?"

"We seem to be proceeding reasonably well."

"Yes, and for the last few days there have been none of those nasty letters to upset you, have there, Miss Coleson?"

Eustacia was startled. She was unaware Lady Blackburne had noticed her distress. "Nothing since Monday, my lady. And that no more than a note."

"And a very good thing it is if, finally, they have accepted you have a mind and a life of your own." She turned back to her nephew. "Jason, do you think we might plan another pick-nick for when your friends are here? Could you bear it?"

"There would be someone to rescue Miss Coleson when she becomes overly excited when catching a fish, so there is no reason why we should not."

"You malign me, my lord," said Eustacia, half laughing and half irritated. "As if I became a silly ninny over nothing more than a fish! I was not excited by *that*, my lord! It was a rock. Almost a boulder."

"A *rock* excited you?" teased his lordship.

"No, no, my lord, *it threw me in the river.*"

His lordship blinked and Sahib, feeling a sudden tension in him, gathered himself to rise. Lord Renwick dropped a hand to the tiger's nape. "I believe rocks have changed a great deal while I was in India," he said in a bland tone. "I do not recall that they were so, hmm, *aggressive* in the past."

Lady Blackburne laughed and Miss Coleson smiled. The memory was still too near for her to find humor in the situation. "I believe," she explained, "the water had eaten at the bank beneath it, my lord. When I stepped onto it, trying to achieve a trifle more height in my battle with the fish, my weight tipped it and it threw me in."

"Hmm. I see. Miss Coleson, may I request that, in future, you stay away from potentially aggressive boulders when fishing? I do not care for the notion that a second may attempt to emulate the first's triumph."

"Nor do I. It was not pleasant, finding myself in the water. It would have been a great deal more unpleasant if I had not seen you dive in. Knowing you would rescue me," she finished in a prosaic tone, "kept me from experiencing true horror, my lord."

Lord Renwick felt his skin heating. "I fear my rescue was more luck than planning, Miss Coleson. Do not count on my doing so again."

"It required cooperation, my lord, not luck."

"Then perhaps my difficulty is merely that I cannot adjust from a certain independence in action to the necessity for cooperation," he said in a dry tone. He turned his shoulder toward her and spoke to Lady Blackburne. "Aunt, are we prepared for company?"

"More or less. I have thought of a few entertainments. Perhaps you would not mind if they took guns out for rabbit, for instance, as there have been complaints from the farmers that, due to their increased numbers, the creatures have grown too brave. The crops suffer."

"An excellent notion. We will make use of my friends to do work I should but cannot do." It seemed impossible, but his tone was still more arid. "And . . . ?"

Lady Blackburne drew in a breath and cast a pleading look toward Eustacia. "A dinner party."

"*No.*" Jason exploded from his chair, hands clenched.

"And why not?" blustered his aunt. She glared at him.

"You know very well why not. I will not sit at table entertaining my guests with my inability to keep peas on my fork long enough to get them from plate to mouth!"

Lady Blackburne sighed. "I am not so stupid I had not thought of that, Jason. Believe me, I planned the menu carefully. There is nothing which will give you difficulty."

"No roast impossible to cut up?" he asked, the faintest of sneers curling his lip. "Our local squire, with his love of roast beef, will find that exceedingly strange, will he not?"

"Reeves will see you are not served those few dishes I must include for the reason they will be expected. Jason, you must—"

"Must learn to make a fool of myself in public or become the complete hermit, is that what you would say?" A muscle rolled over his clenched jaw. "Very well. Since fool I must be, I will have Eric order me a motley suit and a cap with bells on it." He stalked from the room, Sahib on his heels.

"Oh, dear."

"But you have the right of it, my lady. The time has come for him to go into society. He is, for instance, lonely for male conversation. Just think about those few days Lord Wendover visited! The two talked incessantly and although he has not said so, I believe he liked riding about the estate in Wendover's curricle. I know Lord Wendover described to him several things to which his agent should attend and that, rather than resenting the information, Lord Renwick was happy to get it."

"He will like associating with his neighbors again, too," said Lady Blackburne firmly, obviously trying to convince herself.

"Of course he will."

"I also plan that we attend the Assembly in Lewes." Her ladyship's eyes widened slightly. "Ah! I am forgetting! We must order you a gown, Miss Coleson. At once. There is nothing in your wardrobe suitable for the Assembly."

"Dancing, my lady?" asked Miss Coleson, doubtfully. "My father did not allow me to learn."

"He *what?*"

"He . . ."

"I heard but did not believe you! Now what do we do?" Lady Blackburne frowned. "I could play on the pianoforte, but could Jason manage the steps?"

"I do not mind sitting with the chaperons, Lady Blackburne," said Miss Coleson. She had repeated the phrase for so many years she had *very nearly* convinced herself of it, but now, suddenly and for no reason, she no longer believed it.

Lady Blackburne didn't, either. "I am very sure you *do* mind. And *I* mind. Aha! *Wendover* will teach you. He is an ornament to the drawing room and ballroom and will know exactly how to go about it."

Having reached that decision, Lady Blackburne turned back to her stitching. She had reached the point she must roll the fabric and set about undoing the frame. Miss Coleson, seeing what she was about, went to help, and they studied the work Lady Blackburne had completed and reset the material into the frame until it was time for bed.

No more was said about dancing and Eustacia went upstairs torn between a desire to respect her father's wishes and an even stronger longing to join other young people in the ballroom! Then she recalled Lord Renwick would not attempt to dance.

All desire to dance, herself, was instantly dampened and she easily convinced herself she must respect her father's wishes.

Eleven

Even though Miss Coleson managed to convince Lady Blackburne she would not learn to dance, her ladyship still insisted that they must travel into Lewes for new gowns. They did so, and, since her ladyship knew exactly what she wanted both for herself and her protege, their business was soon finished.

"Would you find it a great bore to climb up to the castle, my lady?" asked Eustacia as they approached a narrow street which led up toward it.

"I have not done so in years. Yes. Do let us go. Marcus," she said to the footman, "go on to the carriage and deposit our purchases and then return to us. It is not a large castle, Miss Coleson. Marcus will have no difficulty finding us."

They turned into the dim street, the buildings on either side preventing much sun from reaching the dangerously rounded cobbles. The way was steep but, as Lady Blackburne said, not far. Then, near the top, they found their way partially blocked by a crude barricade on which a sign read: DANGER—NO ADMITTANCE.

"Fiddle," said her ladyship, scowling in vexation.

"If it is dangerous," said Miss Coleson, hesitantly, "then perhaps it is well we are informed of it so we do not go in?"

"I have set my heart on our little adventure, Miss Coleson, and I will have it." Her ladyship studied the situation. "Do you not think that, if we are careful, we can get beyond the barricade just there with no damage to our gowns?"

"Oh, but . . ."

"No, no. The sign is a warning to the adventuresome sort. We will not clamber on walls. Nor will we explore a dungeon! We will simply enter and look around. Do come." She glanced behind them. "And hurry. Someone is climbing toward us and I've no wish be polite."

Lady Blackburne slipped around the edge of the barricade which, standing ajar, made it quite simple to gain access to the courtyard beyond the ruined walls. Once they achieved that, the rest was simple, the ancient stone paving preventing the growth of the sort of greenery which surrounded the outer walls.

In places, however, tree trunks had pushed in the low defensive wall, leaving tumbled piles of stone and brick. The women, avoiding such areas, and the strangers who explored not far away, rambled through the roofless rooms. They came to what must have been, by the shape of the remaining window, a chapel. On the whole, they thought it in worse condition than the rest.

"I am glad we explored," said Eustacia. "Thank you for indulging me."

"I believe we may also indulge ourselves in a light repast, do not you?" asked Lady Blackburne as she ducked her head under the low lintel. Suddenly a hand covered her mouth, another going around her and pulling her away from the door. Miss Coleson screamed but was, almost instantly, treated in a like fashion. She was blindfolded before she recognized either man and, willy-nilly, forced away from the chapel and toward the gate.

Eustacia heard Marcus swear an oath, heard him rush toward them, . . . and heard him groan as he was felled. "You have hurt him!"

"Shut your mummer," growled one man. "I'll gag you iffen you make any trouble."

"What do you want? Why have you done this?"

"Silence," said a second voice, one she almost recognized.

"I—"

Suddenly she was pushed against stone and a dose of something awful-tasting tipped into her mouth. The promised gag followed and a shawl or something of the sort wrapped around her.

Stumbling between the men, she felt herself rushed down the steep lane. "Mad," she heard the second voice tell a curious passerby. "Quite mad. Escaped us but we found her. Sad case, don't you know?"

Weaver!

But Eustacia felt her head swirling and could not think, could not plan. In fact, just as they reached the bottom of the hill and turned onto the high street, she felt her knees buckle.

"About time," said the first voice laconically.

Someone lifted her and that was the last she knew for a very long time.

"She once told me there was something frightening about those letters," said Jason, raising a haggard-looking face toward his aunt.

"Thank heaven Marcus recognized Weaver," responded her ladyship. "But Jason, what are we to do?"

"*You* will do nothing. I leave immediately for her home. I can afford to travel far more quickly than Weaver. I may even arrive before him."

"But Jason . . ."

"No. My blindness will not interfere with my tongue, Aunt Luce. And I have Sahib. Sahib is a great deterrent! To anything."

"But—"

"I must do this." A muscle jumped in his jaw. "Can you not understand?"

"That you must attempt to rescue her by yourself? No, I do not! Jason, at least take a footman."

"You will take me, my lord," said the old shikari with great dignity. The old man had entered quietly sometime during their talk. "I cannot perhaps be of much use to you if strength is required, but I do know how to use words to describe that which will help you."

"Thank you, Bahadur. I will appreciate your help."

"But not mine!"

"Aunt, you must understand—"

"Oh, I do. What *you* have not thought on is what you are to do with Miss Coleson once you have rescued her!"

Lord Renwick's eyes widened. Then he chuckled softly. "You are correct. I had thought no farther than her rescue." He turned over options. "Aunt, I cannot have you with me. There may be dangers of which I know nothing. After all, you and Marcus were knocked out which indicates a willingness to violence and our villain may be desperate to retain that which he's gained. You follow after, Aunt. In the smaller carriage. There will be a decent sort of inn in Handcross. We will return there once we have Miss Coleson safe."

"Or use one of my prince's carriages, my lady," suggested Bahadur. "They are well sprung and built for travel."

There was a knock at the door and Reeves entered. "The carriage is at the door and all is as you ordered, my lord."

"Excellent. Take time, Aunt, to pack. You require little, but that little will, I think, be appreciated."

"Oh, dear me, *yes*," said his aunt. "That poor girl. She'll have nothing but what she wore when she was . . . was . . ."

"Aunt"—Jason spoke sternly to hide his own agitation—"do not dissolve into tears. You have done well up to now, but there is more for you to do." He heard her draw in a deep breath.

"I am all right, Jason."

"Very well. Now I must go."

Lady Blackburne followed Jason, Sahib, and the old man to the front door. She watched Sahib climb in his fluid fashion into the specially designed carriage and take his place on his ledge. Lord Renwick and Bahadur entered and, moments later, the rig disappeared beyond the gate.

For several long minutes which Lady Blackburne could ill afford to waste she stared along the empty drive. Finally she realized what she had seen, what had bothered her: For a moment, not quite hidden by the roof edge, brightly colored silks, such as the prince wore, had fluttered into view. Swearing softly, her ladyship started out the door, only to realize there was nothing she could do. She turned toward the door, but the sound of carriage wheels drew her attention and she turned still again.

Unfortunately, the carriage bowling up the drive was not the one which had departed moments earlier. She had never seen this lightly built traveling carriage, but recalled that Mr. McMurrey was due soon. Although she'd not expected him for a day or two, could this be he?

It was he and Aaron, his youngest brother. Lady Blackburne gave quiet directions to Reeves who passed on her directions to suitable maids concerning the packing of two portmanteaus. Then she explained to the McMurreys the situation, including her fears for her blind nephew!

"Blind! But why did he never say?" asked the outraged Scot.

"When he first returned from India"—she interrupted herself to explain that that was some time ago—"he was so depressed he wanted nothing more than to crawl into a hole and allow the world to forget his existence." Lady Blackburne continued with a touch of acid, "So, although I did not approve, he contacted none of his old friends. I could not, however, bring myself to go against his wishes. Besides," she added in some sort of justification, "he had much to learn."

"Blind," repeated Ian, "and he means to rescue the lady?"

"Well," said her ladyship, bridling slightly, "I said he had much to learn. I did not say how much he *has* learned! I must follow him."

"We will join you," decided Ian McMurrey. "If it is unnecessary for us to help, all well and good, but if we *are* needed . . ." A grim look filled the arctic blue eyes set deep under brushy brows. "Aaron, return that portmanteau and the small bag to the carriage. My lady," he said, "the horses are tired. Can you supply a fresh team?"

"We will use the prince's horses."

"Prinny is visiting?" Ian shook his head. "No, of course not. You may explain once we are on our way. Aaron?" The young man had just reentered the house. "We must be on our way immediately."

"Verra well," said the younger man softly. "My lady? Is there luggage I should see to?"

"Marcu—" She recalled that Marcus was suffering a severe headache. *"Jenkins* will see to it."

Once they were in the carriage, a maid seated beside Aaron on the back facing seat, Lady Blackburne explained the whole history of her meeting with Miss Coleson and how the young lady had become not only indispensable, but that she had also somehow wormed her way into her ladyship's heart so that she often forgot the girl was *not* the daughter of an old friend!

"I think she has become . . . important to Jason, as well," finished Lady Blackburne. She was unable to completely hide the fact that that bothered her.

"You say she is helping him write a book?"

"The first of two or three, assuming she continues her work with him. There is this ridiculous situation with her stepmother, whatever it may be. I wish the woman would take that awful man and disappear!"

His aunt's wishes would be satisfied by the plan Lord Renwick formed as the miles disappeared under his carriage wheels. It would require a bribe, very likely an annuity which would be paid only so long as the couple stayed out of England, but the loss of such funds would be well worthwhile if they assured Miss Coleson's peace of mind.

He devised the scheme in the hopes it would satisfy Miss Coleson. What he *wished* to do was to take Weaver and his friend before a magistrate and see they were sent to Botany Bay for as long as a judge saw fit. But Miss Coleson's feelings *must* be considered and she would not approve disgracing her stepmother.

Jason sighed, shoved one foot against Sahib's side of the carriage, and settled as well as he could into his corner. The old man settled into his and soon fell into one of the easy sleeps which had become a habit with him since his illness. It was not until they reached the posting house where Lord Renwick meant to change horses for the first time that they discovered the presence of the prince who, boy fashion, had rather enjoyed his ride hidden away on top of the carriage! Jason did not look forward to hours spent enclosed in the carriage with the boy, but would not take time to return to Tiger's Lair.

Hours later he had changed his mind: The boy's questions and wild speculations not only distracted him from his concerns, but on one occasion made him laugh. Still, he was exceedingly pleased when his driver pulled up in the village in which Miss Coleson's house was situated. A word with a loiterer leaning against a wall and enjoying the sun, told them which one it was. They arrived before

it and Lord Renwick stepped down from the carriage,
Sahib flowing down behind.

"Describe the house," said Jason to the shikari who
followed after.

"A low stone fence, a short path, a two-story house
about the size of your carriage house, my lord," said the
man softly.

"Any sign of life?"

A touch of humor lightened Bahadur's words. "The
curtain to a window to the left of the door just twitched,
my lord."

"Good. Sahib."

The tiger moved to Jason's side. His fingers touching
the big cat's head, Jason stepped forward.

"One step to the left for the gate," he heard softly,
this advice coming from the prince.

Jason stopped. "You are to return to the carriage," he
told the boy.

"I won't."

"You will or we all will. Boy, think. If anything happened to you, how could I ever explain it to your father?"

"My father," said the boy with dignity, "would expect
me to show courage in the face of danger."

"He would, my lord," said the shikari. "You may come,
my prince, if you promise to stay behind Sahib."

Sahib turned his great head and looked at the boy, a
long slow look. The lad paled slightly, nodded, and took
his place at the cat's flank.

"Now," said Jason, drawing in a breath and starting
forward again. Again he stopped when the sound of clat-
tering hoofs and iron shod wheels caught everyone's attention. A second carriage drew up. "Now what? Surely
it cannot be Aunt Luce?"

"Jase!" rumbled a deep voice. "Wait!"

"This becomes a farce," said Jason, rolling his eyes.
"Come on, you blasted Scot," he called, recognizing the

bass tones. "But don't get in my way." This time when he started forward he didn't stop.

"One step up, my lord."

His cane finding the step, he next touched the door and searched for the knob. Not bothering to knock, he opened it and entered.

"A woman stands before you," said Bahadur softly. "She looks nervous."

"I have come for Miss Coleson," said Lord Renwick coldly.

"My stepdaughter? Why . . . why . . . why would you think her here?" asked Mrs. Weaver plaintively.

"Not?" For half a moment Jason hesitated. "I think she is." He touched the tiger. "Sahib. Find Miss Coleson."

The beast surged forward rousing a scream from Mrs. Weaver who then fainted dead away. The top of a steep flight of stairs was guarded by a ratty-looking little man who also took one look at the tiger and discovered an intense desire to be elsewhere. He disappeared—out a window it was later discovered.

Following the shikari's words, Jason climbed the stairs and followed Sahib who padded to a closed door at the end of a short hall. The tiger turned to Jason, his mouth opening in something a trifle more than the silent growl one usually saw. It was a snarl, actually.

"There is a closed door, my lord," said the shikari, continuing to speak quietly, his hand on the prince's shoulder.

"Shall I break it down?" asked McMurrey, his voice like ice.

"I'll see if it is locked," said his brother and, only a trifle hesitantly, eased beyond the tiger. Unsurprised, he discovered it was.

"Miss Coleson," called Jason.

There was a smothered sound and Sahib roared.

"Miss Coleson, we mean to break down the door."

A low-toned, vicious-sounding voice muttered something.

"My lord," said Miss Coleson, "I have been ordered to tell you that if you do any such thing I'll have a knife in me. I think you should do so awaywmf."

Jason smiled wryly. "That's my girl! But, Miss Coleson, to begin with, I believe we will try negotiation." He tugged his big Scottish friend toward the steps. "Check the house from the outside. See if that room can be reached."

"Excellent notion." Despite his size, Ian went silently down to the ground floor.

"Now Mr. Weaver, perhaps you would tell me what this is all about," said Jason to the blank door.

"Go away. I got business with m'daughter. Don't need you."

"Business which involves knives, Mr. Weaver? The magistrate would find that exceedingly interesting, would he not? Especially since it involves the daughter of a much-beloved vicar."

Jason tipped his head toward the stairs. Aaron, correctly interpreting the silent order, gave Jason a quick pat on his back and headed off to find a magistrate.

"Magist—" Soft swearing came from behind the door. "None o' that now. And none o' your business, I say!"

"You have yet to say what the business is."

Renewed and earthier oaths resulted in a roar from Sahib—and then instant silence. "Wha-a-at was that?"

"My tiger."

A long moment's silence. "Gammon! Why are you nodding your head, you little fool!" Jason and the shikari looked at each other. Disbelief was next heard: "Yes? A tiger? A *real* tiger."

"Sahib will tear you limb from limb if you harm me," those in the hall heard distinctly.

"Damn you to hell and back! All you had to do was sign the papers and you could have gone back to your dratted lord and his unspeakable tiger."

Jason heard steps on the stairs and turned that way, moving nearer to them when Ian called to him in a soft voice. "Jase. I climbed a tree. He's got her in a one-armed grip and a knife in his other hand. The room is tiny. There's a table and a narrow bed and that is about it. Not much room to maneuver."

"I'll kill the bastard."

"I'm damned if I'll lose you to the gibbet now I know you're home again!"

Jason barked a laugh. "Do you have a better suggestion?"

"He'll grow hungry," suggested the Scot.

"Yes, and so will Miss Coleson."

"Better hungry than dead, Jase."

Jason winced. "There must be another way." He mind worked furiously. "Ah! You know these old houses. Often the key to one room works for all. Do you see any keys?"

"Excellent thought." Ian looked at the other doors in the hallway. "Here's one. Let me see if you are correct." He moved to the nearest door, tried the key, moved to the next, and tried it again. "The key works. So . . . ?"

Jason sighed. "You'll have to do it, Ian. I'd make too much noise trying to find the keyhole. Wait until I get a grip on Sahib and then open the door."

"A grip?"

"I hope I can control him if he thinks Miss Coleson is in danger. He *likes* Miss Coleson."

Ian glanced at the tiger who snarled again. "Well, tell him I'm on her side, will you?"

Jason smiled, then quietly introduced Sahib to his friend. They faced the door and he took a good grip on a fold of skin at the back of the tiger's neck. Ian McMurrey turned the key and threw open the door. With a roar, the tiger burst from Jason's hold, into the room, and, his paws on Mr. Weaver's shoulders, pushed the villain against the wall.

The attack was so fast the villain dropped his knife which was a good thing since the big cat would have been even more dangerous if it had been wounded.

Miss Coleson, freed in the tiger's rush, ran from the room straight into Jason's arms, burrowing her head into his shoulder. "Oh, Jason, I've been so frightened."

"You are safe," he said cuddling her close and burying his face in her hair. For a long moment he stood that way, wishing he could do more, could tell her all that was in his heart. His arms tightened as he heard Bahadur speaking softly to the prince and Ian. He lifted his head but didn't release her. "What is happening?" he asked.

"Your beast has the villain under control," said Ian with satisfaction.

Reluctantly, Eustacia turned, remaining in Jason's arm. "Sahib has his paws against Mr. Weaver's chest and has him pressed against the wall. Sahib is staring Mr. Weaver in the eye. Oh, my lord, I *wish* Sahib could talk. I would very much like to know what he is thinking!"

"Get him away," whispered the villain. *"Get him away!"*

"Not until you tell me what you want with Miss Coleson."

"Get him away and I'll tell!"

Jason thought about it. "Miss Coleson, are the papers he wished you to sign somewhere nearby?"

"Yes."

"Ian, get them. Look through them. Quickly, please. Sahib may get ideas if I allow him to stay as he is much longer."

"Get him away from me!"

"Give me one good reason why I should?"

"Married her ma. I'm her pa."

"Mrs. Weaver is her stepmother. You are no relation, Mr. Weaver. None whatsoever."

"Don't let 'im bite me!"

"I cannot think why I should not."

"Jase," said McMurrey, shuffling from one paper to the next, "if I understand them correctly, these papers give the man the right to take over Miss Coleson's inheritance."

"Inheritance? But my father had so little. . . ."

"It doesn't mention your father, Miss Coleson. These concern Lord Hayworth's estate and are addressed to his lordship's solicitors."

"Lord Hayworth? But that is my *grandfather.*"

"Hayworth was your grandfather?" asked Ian, looking up.

"Was?"

"He died something over a month ago," said the Scot gently. "I read of his funeral in an old copy of *The Edinburgh Review.*"

"Get this blasted tiger off me," howled Mr. Weaver.

"Sahib," ordered Miss Coleson softly, "come here."

The tiger looked over his shoulder. Then, after a warning snarl right into Mr. Weaver's face, the tiger dropped his front paws to the floor. He turned and padded over to Jason and Miss Coleson, winding around them.

Mr. Weaver, his legs buckling, slid down the wall to the floor. He mopped his brow and panted.

"Now, then," said a new and very cross voice from the lower hall. "What is all this, then?"

"I suppose that is the magistrate." Jason frowned. "Now I wish I had not sent for him!"

Eustacia watched Mr. Weaver's skin turn pasty white. "I don't believe Mr. Weaver wishes to see the man, Lord Renwi—" Her eyes widened as she realized she had, when rescued, actually used his lordship's name! And here she was, still in his embrace. *Oh dear, what will everyone think?*

she wondered as, gently, she removed herself from his arms.

"The question," said Lord Renwick, reluctantly allowing her her freedom, "is not what he wants, but what *you* want."

"I want to know what this is all about. I want to know why he wanted me to sign those papers which he would not let me read and I want to know what any of this has to do with my grandfather's death. His lordship disowned my mother, my lord. Surely that means I, too . . ." Eustacia frowned. Would not she, too, be disinherited as a result? "Or does it?"

"A man can leave his estate where he wishes, Miss Coleson, assuming it isn't under entail," said McMurrey. "Shall we lock this fellow in and discuss it with the magistrate?"

"The prince and I will remain on guard," said Bahadur who had held the boy in front of him for some time now. "We will not let him escape, will we, my prince?"

McMurrey looked from the boy in his brightly colored silks to the old man and back again. He turned to Jason who grinned.

"Prince Ravi," said Renwick, "I entrust this important duty to you. Will you accept the responsibility?"

"I am not allowed to kill the villain?" asked the scowling prince.

A gurgle of protest came from Mr. Weaver's throat.

"Be still, villain," ordered the boy, an unmistakably royal arrogance in the order which must have been copied from his father.

"You cannot kill him unless he tries to escape. Mr. Weaver, the boy is young, but he is, in his own land, an absolute ruler. He will not hesitate to kill you, or if he cannot do so himself, to order his shikari to do so for him. Or perhaps Sahib will only savage you." Jason touched his pet's head and the tiger roared.

Mr. Weaver's face contorted into a vicious grimace which turned to a look of hopelessness. "Don't see why *she* needs a fortune. Don't see why she deserves one. Not fair—"

"A fortune? How very interesting. I wonder when *you* first learned of it."

Mr. Weaver, his eyes unfocused, admitted, "I was the earl's solicitor's clerk. Copied out the new will."

"Copied it out, quit your job, and came to see if you could not worm your way into the heiress's pocket. When you lost your chance to wed *her*, you wed her stepmother instead, hoping Miss Coleson would be too stupid to know you were up to tricks when you asked her to sign those papers giving you power over her inheritance! A nice little plot, Mr. Weaver. The problem, of course, is that Miss Coleson is neither stupid nor lacking courage."

"Jase, I think we better talk to the magistrate. As you can hear, he isn't at all happy." McMurrey closed and locked the door, solemnly handed the prince the key, and, carefully skirting the tiger, followed his friend and Miss Coleson down the stairs.

Sahib watched Jason disappear and then, with something which sounded suspiciously like a sigh, flopped down on the floor outside the makeshift prison. Then, from time to time, he roared—as if to remind the man inside of his presence.

Two days later all was settled and the Renwick party had returned to Tiger's Lair. "Do you think it will serve?" Ian asked. He leaned back and warmed a brandy snifter between his palms. He looked around the study in which he and Wendover, who had arrived only that afternoon, sat with their old friend. Hard to believe, he thought, that Jase is blind.

"Sending Mr. and Mrs. Weaver out of the country as

we did?" Jason shrugged. "Only so long as they stay abroad will they receive the damned annuity I granted them. They know it."

"I can understand," said Wendover, "why Miss Coleson didn't wish her stepmother prosecuted, but why did she object to Mr. Weaver facing judgment?"

"It appears Mrs. Weaver is genuinely fond of her despicable husband. She does not see why it was so wrong to wish to have enough money to live right up to the knocker, as she expressed it!" said Jason bitingly. He ran his glass under his nose, sniffing delicately.

"And it never occurred to her," said Eustacia sadly, from the open doorway in which she stood, "that I would have given her a sum to live on if I had known of the inheritance and she had only asked."

Wendover raised his glass to her. "You are generous, Miss Coleson. Very generous."

Eustacia chuckled. "Oh, no. Not at all. You see, she would have gone away. To Bath or Brighton. *Somewhere.* I would have paid for her absence!"

"But surely," objected Wendover, "you yourself wish to go to Brighton. Or, come the Season, up to London, where you will enjoy the social round."

"No."

The three men were silent for a moment. Then, softly, "No, Miss Coleson?" asked Jason.

"I do not believe I *would* enjoy it. Oh, yes, the occasional concert or perhaps the opera, but what I hear of the balls, the soirees . . . no." She shook her head. "That life is not for me. Perhaps it is because I am no more than a country mouse, but I think it more likely that my father instilled a desire for a different sort of life. And, too," she added slowly, "my stepmother may have prejudiced me against people who *do* enjoy a *tonnish* life."

"Here now!" began Wendover, who enjoyed such things very much indeed.

"As I remember it," interrupted Jason, "from before I went to India, there is as much good as bad in a London Season. I think, under the proper tutelage, you *would* enjoy it. Perhaps you will go with my aunt when the time comes and find out for yourself?"

"At the moment I've no desire to even think of such things. Actually," she added, startled she had forgotten her errand, "I came to ask if you would not join Lady Blackburne and a few neighbors in a game of croquet? The prince is there and doing very well. My lord?" she asked, turning to Jason who sat, his features rigid and his sightless eyes staring.

"Come on, Jase," said Wendover, rising to his feet. "I'm a dab hand at croquet. I'll show your guests how it's done!"

"Jase?" asked McMurrey, more sensitive to Renwick's feelings.

"Must I?"

Miss Coleson waved the two men away and, looking at her in perplexity, they left. "Your friends are wondering what is in your mind, my lord."

"They have gone?"

"Yes."

"The first thing in my mind is the desire to wring my aunt's neck," he said harshly. "Why did she do it?"

"Very likely you have forgotten that, besides yourself, there are two more exceedingly eligible bachelors under your roof. Your neighbors," said Eustacia dryly, "appear to have a plethora of unmarried daughters and would have arrived, willy-nilly, if she had not invited them."

"You mean two eligibles."

"Three," said Eustacia firmly.

Half a moment's silence and Jason barked a laugh. "I would be selfish, you think, to discourage their hopes?"

"You know you would. My lord, chairs have been moved out near the croquet ground. May I not take you there?"

"Where I must, a blind man, fend off any young female

aspiring to become Lady Renwick? Miss Coleson, I will go on one condition. You will not leave my side and you will warn me whenever I am in danger!"

"Agreed," she said promptly. And then she wondered if she had agreed too hastily. Perhaps he would guess *her* feelings, that she did not wish any of those lovely and suitable young women to wed him.

Jason emptied his glass, set it down, and rose to his feet. "Very well, Miss Coleson. But remember I rely on you to keep me safe!"

"How can I do otherwise," she said lightly, "when *you* just rescued *me*?"

"Not I alone."

"If you will recall the heroic myths you read in your youth, my lord, you will remember that most heroes have help. If not a god or goddess, dropping by for a last minute rescue, it was a band of friends. In this case, the band of friends played their part, did they not?"

They strolled toward the croquet grounds as they spoke, Sahib prowling at their heels. Eustacia's words struck Jason as humorous and his sudden merriment called attention to them. Therefore, the first sight his guests had of the reclusive Lord Renwick was with his head back and laughter issuing from his throat—and the tiger, about which they had heard so much, sitting up on his haunches to stare at his master.

Jason, his mood lighter for Miss Coleson's teasing, allowed her to place his hand on the back of a chair, and, after settling Sahib, proceeded to enjoy himself. In fact, he enjoyed himself very much indeed, which surprised his aunt, of course, but surprised *him* still more!

Twelve

"Aunt," said Jason later that evening, "I apologize. You were quite right and it is not so impossible to enjoy my neighbors as I'd thought it would be." He grinned wickedly. "Thanks to Sahib."

"Thanks to that *beast*? Whatever do you mean?" asked his bemused aunt.

"Very simple. Sahib scared away anyone he thought bothered me. You have no idea how intimidating he can be when he wishes."

Wendover amended Jason's comment. "Even when he doesn't wish it, hmm, Sahib?"

Sahib opened his mouth and roared softly in seeming agreement and everyone chuckled. Jason laid a hand on the tiger's head and the animal subsided.

"I was glad of his assistance," said Jason. "And yours, Miss Coleson. You dealt tactfully with the young women who dared approach. Not that many did." Again he grinned. "Most, I think, were satisfied with *two* bachelors and didn't need a third. Ian? Would you agree or were you not hounded and harassed as I remember from when we went the pace together during the season?"

"Wendover drew their fire, Jase," said McMurrey in his deep rumbling voice. "His title you know." He paused slightly. "Which is just as well."

"I hear a frown in your voice, my old friend. Is there trouble with which we might help?"

"No. Not really. Well, if you must have it, my next younger brother is worrying me a trifle which leaves me with no interest in dalliance!"

"How so?"

"You recall how wild James can be, do you not?"

Jason nodded. "What has he done now?"

"It is all nonsense of course, but, for the *second* time, he has come up with an excuse to postpone his marriage to the daughter of a friend of our father's. The marriage was, in the old way, arranged when both were quite young. It became," said Ian in a dry tone, "of much *more* interest to my father when the young lady inherited a fortune from her godmother. Da is not about to let that prize escape and is angry with James. Jamie, that is. At school he was called the Prince which he disliked. Our family, you see, did not support the Pretender so he felt the nickname an insult. Bad enough, he always thought, that he'd the *name,* but the *title!* Well, verra wretched it made him."

"Can one blame him?" asked Eustacia, sympathy in her voice. "Parents do terrible things to the young, giving them names without remembering how cruel other children can be. There was a girl in our village named Cherry. I never understood why the boys found her name hilarious, but they did and made life a misery for her until she wed. Her husband calls her Cherryl which I've never heard before, but it sounds quite pleasant."

Wendover hummed a few bars of music which had Lord Renwick choking back a laugh and McMurrey's deep voice half singing, "Cherry ripe!" And then, through his laughter, demanded that Wendover, "Give over. At once!"

Eustacia, frowned. "Lady Blackburne, why have the gentlemen succumbed to hysterics?"

"My dear," said her ladyship who was, herself, fighting

giggles, "you have said it. Men find the name humorous. You must allow them their little peculiarities."

"But you, too . . ."

Lady Blackburne interrupted. "Never mind, Miss Coleson. I will explain, if you insist, some other time."

Eustacia's frown deepened. Then her eyes widened. Her color rose and she ducked her head. Sahib, sensitive creature that he was, lifted himself and padded to her side. He laid his head in her lap and she petted him. He helped her get beyond the realization there must be something of a not very nice nature involved, and that, inadvertently, she had embarrassed herself and, perhaps, the company.

Lady Blackburne changed the subject. "Miss Coleson, our modiste sent a note that we must drive into Lewes for a fitting. We go tomorrow. Gentlemen? Will you join us?"

They would not. They meant to fish. Jason had agreed to try sailing and they meant to go to a particularly good spot along the coast.

Jason had concluded some weeks earlier that he must discover more of what he could and could not do. Who better to help him make such discoveries than old friends? But, even aware Wendover and McMurrey would do all they could to ease things for him, he was experiencing a trifling reluctance. Perhaps a storm would arise or a sudden gust of wind would bring the boom across. Or any of the other multitude of things which could go wrong when sailing.

And he unable to see!

"Unless, my lady," McMurrey's grumbling voice broke into Jason's thoughts, "you are nervous, given your experience the last time you visited Lewes? In that case, of course you will have our escort."

"Thank you, but I believe neither Miss Coleson nor I are so much a ninny as all that. Weaver cannot repeat his attack since he is well out on the high seas, on his way to our colonies across the Atlantic. There will be no danger from him!"

"In that case, Aunt Luce, we will try our hand at sea fishing," said Jason. A part of him wished Ian had guessed correctly and that his aunt *had* required one or all of them to accompany her. That way he need not, yet, find *another* way of making a fool of himself! But why not? It would be one among many.

Jason scowled. The Assembly in Lewes was the next torture devised for him by his aunt. That would be amusing, would it not? Sitting on the sidelines with the chaperons and available to every matchmaking mother in the county since he would be nicely trapped. Worse, he'd not have Sahib to protect him!

He rose to his feet. "I am tired. Please excuse me. Sahib? Bed?" The tiger took his place at Jason's side and the two left the room.

"That was sudden. What did we do? Or *not* do that led to his departure?" wondered Lady Blackburne, staring after him.

"Exactly what he said, perhaps?" suggested Miss Coleson. "It was, I would guess, a tiring day for him. I find being polite to so many strangers exhausting, and I see those cues which help one understand or anticipate or . . . well, surely you know what I mean?"

"Hmm. Perhaps."

"Or perhaps he is thinking ahead," suggested Wendover, tipping his quizzing glass to one side and then the other. "He agreed to our jaunt tomorrow, but I think it worries him."

"Every new attempt must fret a blind man," rumbled Ian. "But he has done so much. He'll find there is more he can do if he will only try. He agrees. In theory. If one thing does not work, then we attempt another. We have discussed it, you see."

Lady Blackburne blinked. "He talked about his blindness?"

Wendover laughed softly. "Not exactly. Ian and I sat him down and *we* discussed it. A problem to be solved. Solutions to be found. Things to try and things to avoid. Finally he came out of the sulks and grew interested enough to add his bit. We have made a list." He shrugged.

Lady Blackburne bit her lip. She looked at Miss Coleson, read approval in her face, and sighed. She rose to her feet. "I see. Very well. But"—a fierce expression matched her scolding tone—"do have a care for him. I cannot help but worry. He is *blind* and do not forget it!" She stalked from the room forgetting to say good night.

"Do not regard her. It is her love for him which makes her scold so," said Eustacia softly. "Your plan is admirable. If even one or two things among those you try become new ways of entertaining his lordship then it will have been worth all the worry and the inevitable failures."

"You expect failure, Miss Coleson?" asked Wendover, his brows arching high onto his smooth forehead.

"In some cases. Do not you? However he tries, there are things he'll never accomplish. I've no notion what you have on your list, but weigh them and try the things you believe he's a chance of mastering in between ones you are less sure will have a happy ending." She looked from one man to the other and smiled wryly. "I, too, you see, worry about him! Good evening, gentlemen. Lady Blackburne did not say when we leave for Lewes, but, knowing her ladyship, it will be early."

The men stood. Wendover bowed slightly. "We rise early ourselves, so perhaps it is best to end the evening now. And Miss Coleson—"

She paused, glancing at him.

"We, too, want the best for Jase. He himself pointed

out activities where he believes he'll have little or no success, but he is willing, now, to try. Should we let our desire to protect him push him back from what well may be good for him?"

"Wrap him in cotton wool?" Eustacia felt heat in her throat. "I have, on at least one occasion, scolded Lady Blackburne for that very thing. I must not, myself, fall into the same error. Is that what you would say?"

"Yes."

"Very well. And I know from my own experience that his lordship is an excellent swimmer, so I will worry less than I might about this sailing adventure!" She departed, leaving a pair of bemused men behind.

"What," asked McMurrey, "did she mean by that?"

"From her own experience?" Wendover bounced his quizzing glass against his chin. *"What* experience?"

"I believe we must ask the shikari. He will tell us where Jason is very likely to put us off, being embarrassed or modest or both. Depending. Come along. Bahadur is quite addicted to billiards. We are likely to find him playing against himself. Unless Aaron is giving him a game, of course."

When told the story of Jase's rescue of Miss Coleson, both men were stunned into silence. "Well!" said Wendover, finally.

"Very well done of him," applauded McMurrey.

"But not to be mentioned," insisted Bahadur, warningly. "I was not to tell you and I have broken my word. Please do not tell him!"

The next day proceeded peacefully. The women had their fitting and Lord Renwick discovered that, on a day when the wind blew softly, he enjoyed sailing, liked being on the water, and was still able to catch a fish or two. And the chimes attached to the spar helped keep him informed of its movement! That "invention" had been Miss Coleson's suggestion and worked very well on a day when the wind behaved itself, indulging in no sudden shifts!

"There is nothing," said Lady Blackburne that evening at dinner, "like freshly caught fish." She took a second serving. "Jason, I must thank your friends for taking you out."

"So must I, Aunt Luce. Tomorrow's plans are less appealing, but we shall endeavor."

"What have you in mind?" asked Miss Coleson.

Wendover eyed the platter of scallops of veal offered to him. He shook his head. "We mean to ride over Jason's acres," he said, accepting a portion of the mulligatawny stew presented by the next footman.

Lady Blackburne's silverware clattered onto her plate. "Ride!"

"With a rider on either side of me, I doubt I'll come a cropper, Aunt," said Jason. His tone suggested further objections would not be appreciated. "Miss Coleson, do you ride?"

"I had no opportunity to learn, my lord. And, no," she added when he opened his mouth, "I do not care to do so now. I can, if the horse is a placid beast, handle a cart or gig. That is sufficient."

"Did your father teach you to drive?" asked Wendover.

"Yes. When he thought me old enough to take on certain pastoral duties. My stepmother disliked visiting the old and the ill."

Lord Renwick nodded. "I will tell Georgie to take you driving so he may judge which rig and horse may be made available for your use."

Miss Coleson cast his lordship a startled look. "For *my* use, my lord? For what purpose would I need a gig?"

"To go into the village. Or to visit neighbors. Perhaps to drive me to visit a tenant if a problem arises. How should I know? But if you need a rig, then Georgie will know what to supply. Tomorrow, perhaps?"

"Very well, my lord."

Eustacia sighed as she wondered when he and she would return to his writing. Before the kidnapping and the arrival of Lord Renwick's friends, she had looked forward to his words on the rites surrounding an Indian marriage. He'd been a guest at a marriage in a wealthy family and had observed more than one wedding among the poor. It would be an interesting chapter.

"The day after tomorrow we go to the Assembly," said Lady Blackburne, interrupting Miss Coleson's thoughts. "I ordered rooms held for us at the inn so we've a place to change and a meal will be served in the adjoining parlor."

"Well thought of, Aunt Luce. Wendover has offered his carriage. Since Sahib must remain home and we need a forward seat, it seems a good notion. Then, too," he continued, "I thought perhaps the prince, Bahadur, and Aaron might attend for a time. The prince is too young, really, but the Assembly illustrates a common way in which the English disport themselves. They may use the smaller carriage and leave at an early hour." Jason cast a look around the table, his unseeing gaze settling very nearly on Miss Coleson. "Have I forgotten anything?"

"I think not," she responded, wishing he and she could remain at home and sit cozily together in his study. Just the two of them.

How she missed there being just the two of them.

Eustacia sighed again ever so softly. Dancing, since she could not participate, held no interest and she would be forced to deal with a mild jealousy of young women who *did* join the sets! Still, for a time it would be interesting to watch the color and the patterns of movement and hear the music. In the past she enjoyed conversing with friends who would spend the duration of a set beside her. Perhaps one or two whom she had met at the croquet party would be kind enough to sit with her?

"Miss Coleson?"

It registered that Lord Wendover had said her name.
"Yes, my lord?"

"Will you save me the first dance?"

"Here now!" said Ian, pretending outrage. "I meant
to ask Miss Coleson for that dance."

"But you did not and I have done so. I will have the
delightful duty of leading her out first!"

"You were always a pirate, Tony." Ian pretended to
pout.

"May I speak?" asked Eustacia, who found it rather
pleasant to be the object of such rivalry even when the
competition was in jest. The men turned to her and she
said, "Mr. McMurrey, you need not call your friend
names, because he will not be burdened with the duty of
leading me out!"

"You reject me? But this is terrible. Lady Blackburne,
inform your charming friend that I dance excellently well,
that I will not step on her toes more than once or twice!"

"But, my lord," said Eustacia firmly, "it is quite otherwise. If you were so foolish as to partner me, *I* would step
on *yours. Often.*" She shrugged. "I do not dance." Silence
followed her confession, except for the clink of Lady
Blackburne's fork against her plate.

"Do-not-dance?" asked Wendover, finally.

"You have never learned to . . ." began McMurrey.

"Did your father disapprove?" interrupted Renwick.

"You have guessed it, my lord. And I cannot feel it
right to go against his wishes now he is gone. I am a
wallflower by choice when, on rare occasions, I attend a
ball."

"Then," said Lord Renwick, "if you would not find it
burdensome, will you sit with me?" He drew in a deep
breath, let it out. "You would do me a great favor by
agreeing. I will not have Sahib to protect me and, frankly,
I dread the matchmaking mamas. You," he added, "will

not deter them from *descending* on us, but your presence may keep their behavior within bounds!" he finished darkly.

His friends chuckled. "We will join you when we can," said Wendover.

"When-you-can! Ha!" Jason pointed his knife toward Wendover. "And when, you great butterfly, will that be?"

"I can think of *one* occasion," said his lordship smugly. "When the musicians put down their instruments and supper is served!"

"Ha! You might manage that, but you will have a lady on your arm even then, so I am unconvinced you will remember I need protecting!"

"Enough nonsense," said Lady Blackburne, glancing around the table. "My dear?" she said to Eustacia. "Have you finished?"

They left the men to their port and cigars and adjourned to the blue salon where her ladyship sat biting her lip and frowning and staring into the small fire Reeves had built in the fireplace.

Finally, a decision made, her ladyship looked up. "Miss Coleson, I believe I must think seriously about providing Jason with a wife."

"A wife, my lady?" Eustacia had been hemming a handkerchief but her hands stilled . . . and then began to tremble slightly. "Have you someone in mind?" she asked.

"No."

Eustacia found she could breathe again.

"But it is obvious he will do nothing, himself, to promote a match and he *must* wed. I'd not thought it necessary quite so soon, but if he is to behave in the rash manner he is indulging while with his friends, then he must see to the succession."

"Rash, my lady?"

"This sailing. And that he would even think of riding!

He is behaving irresponsibly." She paused. "You do not agree," she added.

"I've no idea what he can and cannot do. But now, surely"—Eustacia knew she trod on treacherous ground—"while he has friends to see he does not come to grief, it makes sense that he try!"

"Thank you," said Jason from the doorway. "Aunt Luce? Are you again thinking you must watch my every step?" Jason's friends followed him into the room.

Spots of color marred her ladyship's fine complexion. "I was unaware you knew I did that, Jason. I have not for a long time now, so it is unkind of you to remind me."

"Even when you need reminding?" he asked whimsically.

"It is because she loves you, my lord," said Eustacia, looking from one to the other.

"I am aware, but I will not be coddled and cradled and made to act the invalid when there is nothing the matter with my health. Aunt, please understand that I need to discover some method of exercise, other than walking in the garden. Something which will keep me fit."

"Understanding with my head and understanding in my heart are two entirely different things, Jason," said his aunt with dignity. "My *head* is in agreement with what you would do!"

The others chuckled. "Would you, my lady, care to ride with us," rumbled McMurrey's deep tones. "You may see for yourself how Jase fares."

"I will ride with Jason later if he discovers it is an activity he enjoys," she said and returned to her stitching.

"Miss Coleson," asked Jason, as he sat down and laid his head against the back of his chair, "would you be agreeable to reading to us? I believe a new packet of books arrived today, and I miss your reading."

"Reeves must bring them so we may choose," she said, sunnily.

The evening passed quickly once Eustacia opened the covers of a travel book detailing a journey with a tribe of proud Saharan warriors who painted themselves blue. With them the author had crossed the great desert. Occasionally the writer indulged in overly ornate phrasing, but the subject, a society about which no one knew the least bit, was exotic in the extreme and interested all.

The tea tray arrived and Lady Blackburne suggested Miss Coleson pour out. Once the tray was removed, Eustacia removed herself as well. How, she wondered as she climbed the stairs, had she contained herself? A wife. Lady Blackburne would find her nephew a wife!

Lord Renwick, *married*. A new mistress for the household. A lady who would not want an extra woman around while she fitted into the family and found her way with his lordship. Especially not an unwed guest who was in love with that woman's husband!

So. There was no question now as to when she would leave. When Lady Blackburne settled on a wife for Lord Renwick, then she herself must go, must return to her own little house. Alone.

Except—horror filled her—she could *not* live alone. *It was not done.*

Ah well, perhaps the monies that awful Weaver man claimed she'd inherited from her grandfather, when added to her own, would give sufficient extra income she could hire a companion, some older lady who would lend her consequence. For the very first time, Eustacia wondered how much she'd inherited.

The next day a coach and six pulled up to the house. It carried two men. One, conservatively dressed, carried a leather folder. The second was a foppish sort of gentleman. The dandy handed Reeves his card, the corner turned down, and asked if Miss Coleson might be available.

Reeves glanced at the card, took a second quick look

at his lordship and, with appropriately deferential graciousness, settled the two men in a salon opening off the blue salon. Reeves hurried to the stillroom where, swathed in protective aprons, Lady Blackburne was taking inventory with Miss Coleson's help.

"My lady, Miss Coleson?" asked Reeves, extending the tray and card. "His lordship asks for you, miss. I put them in the ivory salon, my lady." He bowed.

Eustacia handed the card to Lady Blackburne. Reminded by the bit of pasteboard, she recalled that, before her death although only on rare occasions, her mother had spoken of a much younger brother. She herself had forgotten his existence. What if he objected to his father leaving her an inheritance? What if he wished to interfere? What would she do? *She needed it.* If it did no more than double her current income, it would make possible a genteel life lived with propriety.

"Lord Hayworth?" mused Lady Blackburne. "Ah, the new Lord Hayworth!" Her lips twitched and her eyes sparkled. "Eustacia, you are in for a rare treat. Now," she added, pretending a sternness her twinkling eyes denied, "I want your promise that you will not laugh at the poor gentleman. He is your uncle and you must show appropriate respect!"

"My lady? I do not understand?"

Lady Blackburne chuckled. "My dear, Augustus Henley is a fop of the most extraordinary variety! He adopts all the most outrageous styles and does his best to invent his own. Unfortunately, he has yet to come up with a notion which does not provide a great deal of amusement for the *ton!*"

"Oh, dear."

"Do not worry. He is an amiable man and you will like him excessively. Very likely he will invite you to live with himself and his aunt and we will lose you, which would be a great shame. Come along now."

Her ladyship took off the enveloping apron she had donned to protect her gown. After ridding herself of her own apron, Eustacia trailed after her ladyship who breezed into the salon talking even before the door was fully open, welcoming the man who sprang to his feet to peer around her.

"And this, Lord Hayworth, is your niece, Eustacia Coleson," finished Lady Blackburne, drawing Eustacia forward.

His lordship said all that was proper and Eustacia must, she thought, have responded, although she could not, later, recall exactly what she said. She was much too startled to remember!

Her uncle was overly tall and exceedingly thin. His long legs were encased in slim trousers cut from a striped material, alternating green and brown. His waistcoat was closed by only one oversized button. A bright green shirt showed between it and a meager neckcloth, which was embroidered all over with brown and green birds. A triangle of the shirt also showed below the vest and above the trousers. His coat was made of both colors, the right half green and the left brown. He was, to say the least, a startling sight.

"Most unaccountable, that I forgot I had a niece," said his lordship when the other gentleman, a solicitor, had been introduced. "Remember m'sister. I think." He frowned hugely. "Half-sister, of course. Much older, you know. But then she ran off in that silly way. The Pater never forgave her. Too bad of him. Or maybe he did?" His lordship turned a beaming face toward Eustacia. "Left you a tidy little inheritance to make up for his curmudgeonly behavior to your mother, you see." When Eustacia looked bewildered, he added, "Or you *will* see as soon as George here explains. George?"

He turned to the solicitor who cleared his throat.

"George knows all about it, right and tight," continued

Lord Hayworth. "Not a *fortune,* you know," he warned, frowning. The frown faded. "But not too stingy. Considering. Lady Blackburne," he said, turning slightly and excluding Eustacia and George from his conversation, "haven't seen you for a donkey's age."

The solicitor cleared his throat again and, softly, suggested Miss Coleson might oblige him by coming to the table near the windows. He needed, it seemed, a surface on which to lay out his papers.

"Lord Renwick sent a message to us, my dear young lady. Such a terrible experience for you! Stepparents, I fear, do not always have the best interests of their children at heart." He put aside all further discussion of the Weavers. "Now, I will read you his lordship's will."

"Sir! Mr. George . . ."

"Mr. Tullet, my dear," said the solicitor, looking over the tops of the square lenses perched on his nose. "His lordship calls all solicitors George."

"Mr. Tullet, then. I remember when my father's will was read and how difficult it was to understand. I would prefer that you summarize the portion of this one which is relevant to myself. If you would not object to proceeding in such a way, that is."

"An excellent notion. My dear, you are a lucky young lady. His lordship left you an annuity of a thousand pounds a year so long as you remain unwed and, if you marry, you are to have a dowry of six thousand pounds. Here now"—his brows arched and he peered over his lenses—"my dear! You are not about to swoon, are you?"

Eustacia drew in several deep breaths. "A thousand pou . . ."

"Yes. And six outright if you wed." He nodded several times, smiling in a fatherly fashion. "Now," he added in a more businesslike tone, "if you will sign these papers . . . oh dear." He blinked. "We need ink and a pen, do we not?" Mr. Tullet looked around the salon in a rather bewildered fashion as if the desired objects might appear by magic.

"I will ask Reeves to supply what is needed." Eustacia, on her way to the hall, paused by Lady Blackburne and asked quietly if she should order refreshments as well.

"Please do. Our guests will remain a few nights and go with us to Lewes tomorrow evening. Is that not delightful?"

"Quite delightful," said Eustacia solemnly.

She wondered if Mr. Tullet would agree. When she returned from giving orders that rooms be prepared and a tray as well as the writing implements brought in, she discovered he had not. Mr. Tullet would be glad of refreshment, but then, if his lordship had no further need of him, he would beg the use of his lordship's carriage to take himself to Barcombe Cross where he would catch a coach to London.

"Nonsense. Coachy will take you to London and return in a day or three. Want to get to know my niece." Lord Hayworth beamed at Eustacia who murmured some soothing but meaningless reply. "Maybe she'll agree to visit my aunt and myself so we can really get to know her? Hmmm?"

The papers were soon signed, it was explained to Eustacia how she might gain control of her first quarter's funds, and, after complimenting Lady Blackburne on the tastiness of the ginger biscuits to say nothing of a sponge cake soaked in sherry and covered in custard, the solicitor departed.

Eustacia realized Lady Blackburne already had had enough of her guest and that she must, herself, entertain her uncle. She suggested a stroll in the rose garden.

He frowned. "The paths? Hasn't rained, has it?" he asked sharply. "Won't get m' new boots scuffed, will I?" He extended one leg so that the women could admire the low-topped boots. They were brown with a green leather bow where most men sported a tassel. Very quickly, his lordship became lost in admiring them himself.

When Eustacia felt she might regain his attention, she told him that not only had it not rained, but the paths were raked each morning. He would find them in excellent condition and unlikely to do his boots any damage whatsoever. After a trifle hemming and hawing, he agreed, bowed to Lady Blackburne and they departed through windows designed to allow exit from the room to the paved terrace.

"Didn't like to say anything," he said once they left the house, "but rather hoped your chaperon would take herself off and leave us alone. Your uncle, after all. Don't need a chaperon, do you?" He frowned. "Don't much care for the outdoors, you see?"

"At my age, I surely don't need chaperoning, my lord, even if you were not my uncle," said Eustacia. "If we merely stroll back and forth here for a bit, perhaps she will go elsewhere and we may return to the salon."

Pleased by the suggestion, he darted a look into the salon every time they passed the windows, and finally said, "Aha! She has gone." Once reseated inside, his lordship sighed gustily. "Much better, my dear. Now, Niece, you sit yourself right there." He pointed a bony finger. "And we'll indulge in a regular old coze!"

Which they did. Lord Hayworth asked a multitude of questions, some of which Eustacia found impertinent until finally leaning forward and patting her hand, he asked, diffidently, that if it would not upset her too badly, would she please explain what had happened, that Lord Renwick's letter had not explained, exactly, the problem with her stepparents.

"Didn't quite understand it all," finished Lord Hayworth. "Seemed a bit strange, you know, when your stepmother wrote George she hadn't a notion where you were. Rather bothersome that, when we needed to settle everything and were unable to find you to sign the papers and all."

Eustacia explained that her direction *was* known, but that her stepfather had hoped to feather his nest and had wanted her to sign over her funds to his use, but to do so he had to get her home first and she had refused to go.

"In the end, the man kidnapped me and carried me off, but it was all right. Lord Renwick rescued me."

"Kidnapped you?" Lord Hayworth's brows arched. "Rescued? Why it's a tale for a Minerva Press novel, is it not?"

Eustacia smiled, her eyes sparkling. "Complete with a tiger, an east Indian prince, and other bits and pieces a novelist would have liked very much indeed!"

"A *tiger*?"

Keeping her features as bland as possible, she said, "Lord Renwick was given a white tiger by an Indian maharaja, my lord."

"By jove. A tiger, you say." Hayworth blinked rapidly. "And the *tiger* helped rescue you?"

Eustacia described the scene where the tiger pushed Weaver into the wall, knocking the knife from the villain's hand and allowing her to escape.

"By jove! Enough excitement to last a lifetime, is my guess," said Lord Hayworth with more insight than he'd so far revealed. "And this tiger? He is your friend?"

"Sahib and I get along very well, my lord."

"Glad to hear it, but," Lord Hayworth's brows drew in, "that's the third or fourth time you've m'lorded me. Can't have that. My niece, after all. Do you think," he asked, suddenly shy, "you might call me Uncle Gus? No one has called me Gus since my school days. Always liked it, don't you know? Cozy. That's what it is."

"Very well, Uncle Gus. And I, of course, am Eustacia.

Or," she added, "my mother called me Stacy which no one else ever does."

"Stacy. Just in private then," he said, beaming. "Don't want every Tom, Dick, and Harry calling you that! Just for me, hmmm?" He invited her to come for a long visit to Hayworth Hall which was situated in Devon a bit south of Ashburton.

"I would like to visit, Uncle Gus, but," she hesitated, frowning, "just for the moment, I think I must remain here. If you would keep the invitation open?"

"Gladly. Very much like to have you, my dear," he said so sincerely, she could not disbelieve him.

She smiled. "It is nice having a new relative, Uncle Gus. I had thought myself completely alone in the world, you see."

"Never was, you know. Had a grandfather. And an uncle. Suppose my aunt's a mere connection. M' mother's sister, you see, but, not alone!"

Eustacia decided that acquiring a new relative was somewhat heavy going, but she persisted, taking it in turn to ask him questions, which kept him talking until it was time to change for dinner. Only then did she remember to wonder how the riding went, and if Lord Renwick had enjoyed it or merely endured it.

Thirteen

Wendover, arriving in the salon before dinner, stopped short. "Hayworth!"

"That you, Wendover? Ah, yes. Remember now. You and Renwick were school chums, were you not? Remember when you first came on the *ton*."

"Don't talk as if you were a graybeard, Hayworth. You hadn't been down from your college more than a decade, yourself!" Wendover turned. "McMurrey, look who is here."

"Yes, *do* look at him," said McMurrey, walking all around the new guest. "Hayworth, I don't know where you get such notions."

Lord Hayworth twisted his neck to look at McMurrey who was behind him. "Never understood why the ladies should have all the fine feathers," he complained. "I *like* bright colors," he finished defensively and brushed his hand down the front of his canary yellow coat.

"And why should you not, Uncle?" asked Miss Coleson from the doorway. She glared at Renwick's friends who understood they were not to tease her relative. Eustacia, once the two appeared well cowed, turned. "My lord," she said, to Renwick who escorted her, "my uncle arrived today bringing his solicitor who explained my inheritance to me. I told Lord Hayworth about Sahib, but I don't know if he understood your tiger roams free."

Jason's lips twitched but he dropped a hand to Sahib's head. "Shall we introduce Sahib to your uncle?"

Much to the surprise of both Wendover and McMurrey, who were a trifle leery of the beast, Sahib and Lord Hayworth got along very well. Later Eustacia heard Wendover whisper to McMurrey, "It is likely Hayworth hasn't the sense to fear the beast."

"Or perhaps," said Eustacia, breaking into their conversation, "it is that Sahib knows who *is* and who is *not* his friend!"

"He's a wild beast, Miss Coleson," said Wendover a trifle stiffly. "One cannot know what a wild animal will do."

"Very true. But Sahib is a special beast. I'll not have him insulted."

Wendover's eyes widened. "But my dear Miss Coleson! I thought it was that I had insulted your relative!"

"I won't have that, either."

"McMurrey, old friend," said Wendover earnestly, "break my arm, or insult me. Do *something* so that I, too, am deserving of Miss Coleson's sympathy!"

Eustacia laughed. "I do tend to jump to the aid of those who are least likely to defend themselves, do I not? And you, Lord Wendover, are perfectly capable. You've no need of any aid *I* might give."

"I, on the other hand," said McMurrey, "need all the help I can get. Would you believe that not only Wendover, but Renwick as well, beat me in a race this afternoon?"

"Race?"

The sharp voice brought the three around. Lady Blackburne stood stock-still, her skin pale and her eyes wide.

"Not much of a race," said Wendover deprecatingly.

"Not a race at all, really," agreed McMurrey, raising his eyes to the ceiling.

"You allowed my nephew to race?"

"Aunt Luce?" Jason, standing across the room with Hayworth, turned. "What is the difficulty?" He dropped a hand to Sahib's head. "Take me to her," he ordered softly. Sahib pressed against his leg, turning him slightly, and then moved across the room, stopping just short of where Lady Blackburne stood. The beast gave that silent roar.

"Now, Aunt," said Jason looking toward the tinkling chains she wore, "tell me."

"They said you *raced.*" Lady Blackburne's hand rose to cover her throat. "You were so foolish as to *race?*"

Jason smiled a tight smile which grew as he recalled that ride.

"I told her it wasn't much of a race," said McMurrey apologetically.

"But if you had not mentioned it, she'd not have known of it," added Wendover. "Your fault, ol' boy!"

"Perhaps, but I'd no notion she was anywhere near."

"Will you two idiots be still?" demanded Lady Blackburne who was seriously upset.

The two, brows raised, gave each other a well-we-tried look and, simultaneously, turned a hopeful look toward Miss Coleson.

"Perhaps if you told us how your ride went, my lord, it would help?" suggested Eustacia.

"It went well. Very well. Far better than I'd thought possible. I would not wish to go alone, of course, but with friends, or with yourself, Aunt, it is something I will enjoy a great deal."

"I cannot like it. You were so foolish as to *race.* Jason, how could you?"

"Very easily. We went to the exercise oval which, even though we've no longer young horses to train, is in excellent condition. We walked the horses around the trace. We cantered them around. And then, once they had the idea, we raced them around. It was wonderful."

"But—"

"Aunt! Enough. Wendover was to my right and McMurrey slightly behind and to my left. Wendover, blast him, pulled ahead at the end, my horse put on a burst of speed, and poor McMurrey came in last. There you have it. Miss Coleson," he said, turning to her, "how did you and my coachman get along?"

"He did not find my driving too contemptible, I think, but said he'd prefer to give me a lesson or two before allowing me to take out anything larger than a gig. He said I might like to learn to drive a pair."

"Your father must have taught you well if Georgie offered you lessons." He frowned. "Miss Coleson, from what you said, or even more from what you have *not* said, I am surprised your father could afford to keep a gig!"

"Our church had a generous patron who felt the area too extensive for my father to manage properly with no transport. She leant him the gig rather than a riding horse so that he could, as well, take Mother out and about and, later, my stepmother, something he could *not* have done on horseback."

"I see." Jason touched Sahib's ears. "And, Miss Coleson, I apologize for asking impertinent questions!"

"So you should, my boy," said Hayworth. "My dear niece, I'd no notion things were so difficult for you. M' father behaved scabbily to my sister when he refused your father more than a pittance for a dowry. Apologize!"

"Do not concern yourself, Uncle. My father told me they knew your father would disapprove but eloped anyway. We were a very happy family while my mother lived." Eustacia was beginning to feel just a trifle harassed that so much attention was directed her way and was, therefore, more than slightly pleased that Reeves announced dinner.

The Lewes Assembly drew a far larger attendance than usual. Word that three exceedingly eligible bachelors were expected had spread. Every unwed female was escorted there, hopeful mothers, guardians, and brothers arriving from every point of the compass. Discovering a *fourth* eligible among the company was an unexpected bonus!

For a time Lady Blackburne sat with Lord Renwick and Miss Coleson but then saw an old friend across the room. She excused herself. "Just for a moment, Jason. I'll not desert you."

But she did.

Eustacia felt scornful of the hopeful guardians who, with their unmarried charges, approached Lord Renwick. The young ladies introduced to him included all the least lovely, the most ungainly, and older women fated to lead apes in hell.

Worse, there were some who seemed to think that, if one was blind, one could not hear. Jason and Eustacia had a good chuckle over one chit who walked off complaining that to attract Lord Renwick was impossible, for how was one to flirt with a man who could not see?

Another young woman, somewhat older than the others, asked questions about India. Unfortunately, she held strong opinions of her own. When what Jason recounted did not agree with her notions, *she* lectured *him* on what he *should* have observed!

She reluctantly relinquished her chair to an elderly neighbor who rudely poked her once or twice with his cane. The man, who wished words with Lord Renwick, overheard Jason who had bluntly asked Eustacia how anyone could consider themselves more knowledgeable about India than someone who had actually been there.

The neighbor, introducing himself as Sir Litchard, told Lord Renwick he was not to allow Miss Foggert to overset him. Everyone knew she had such a good opinion of herself she would never listen to anyone.

"But our local maidens ain't what I wish to discuss,

Renwick. Don't know if you're aware, but I'm the last of my line. Oh, a few distant cousins, don't you know, but as old a Methuselah. Unlikely to outlive me, don't you know? What I want to know, my boy, is whether you'd be interested in buying some land. That southern meadow and the river land to the east of it which includes riparian rights, of course . . . well, anyway, recently remembered your grandfather expressed an interest. Don't know if you'd feel the same?"

Jason frowned. "You refer to the low-lying land along the Ouse?"

"Oh, yes, that, but more particularly the good meadowland farther west." Sir Litchard cast a shrewd glance toward Renwick. "Might include the oak plantations if that would tempt you." Then the elderly gentleman sighed. "Been remembering my youth, don't you know? My grand tour? Nappy's spoiled most of it. For traveling, you know, but there's still Naples. Ah! Italy! Warm. Lovely women. Beautiful flowers." Litchard barked a sharp laugh. "Getting old, my boy. Can't do much but look at the women. Only look at the flowers for that matter, but *warm*. About froze last winter. Swore I'd not put up with it again. So, if you'd think about it?"

"I'm tempted. Very tempted. Come see me, if you will?"

"Good. Very good. Got rid of the northern part of the estate already. If I sell off the rest I can be off!" The old man rose stiffly to his feet. "Shouldn't have said that," he muttered. "Now the boy will drive me a hard bargain," they heard as he wandered off. "Not," he added, stepping out with a jauntier step, "that it matters. I've plenty to keep me warm for a long, long time!"

Lord Renwick grinned. "If you are nearby when I reach that age, will you poke me if I begin talking to myself?"

"My lord?" asked an amused voice.

Lord Renwick sighed. "Miss Coleson?"

Eustacia touched his arm. "I am here.

"Ah. I thought you spoke to me," said the stranger. "You remember me, I'm certain, from the old days? How well you danced! But you've yet to take the floor tonight. Although it is forward of me, may I request that you partner me in this next set?" She flashed an oddly coy smile. "For old time's sake?"

Lord Renwick opened his mouth. Closed it. Opened it again and then turned, somewhat frantically, toward Miss Coleson. He held out his hand and Eustacia touched it. She rose to her feet. A light hand on the stranger's arm turned the woman and they promenaded away from his lordship.

"Lord Renwick was blinded in India," explained Eustacia softly. "He cannot recognize you, my lady. He does not dance and it embarrasses him to admit to his blindness."

"Blind!" The stranger's eyes narrowed. "How terrible. And how *embarrassing*. For *me*, I mean." The woman, in turn, took Eustacia's arm and walked her on. "And you, my dear? You do not dance?"

"My father felt strongly that it was not the thing. A vicar, my lady."

"Not my lady anything. A mere Mrs. Merriweather, you know. I am visiting relatives who dragged me along this evening."

Married? thought Eustacia. *Somehow she doesn't act like a married lady. Or are these London manners?* "I believe you danced with Lord Wendover?"

"You are acquainted with Wendover? A delightful man but wary." Mrs. Merriweather sighed dramatically. "Wendover will not be caught in Parson's mousetrap any time soon and I do wish to wed again." She looked across the room to where McMurrey stood with several gentlemen laughing at some jest. "Nor will Mr. McMurrey. Do you also know our huge Scotsman?"

"Yes." Eustacia glanced back down the room. "I must return to Lord Renwick now. It is just that he didn't know how to tell you."

"I will come, too, and apologize," said Mrs. Merriweather firmly. On the words she reversed their progress. "That will make it all right," she added with a sly sideways glance accompanied by a quirky smile Eustacia could not help but find amusing. They reached Lord Renwick's side just in time to prevent a young lady from sitting in his lap. "Miss Jane!" said Mrs. Merriweather in a mocking voice. "Your mother will be looking for you," she added, more sternly.

Angry her little plot had been foiled, the red-faced chit hurried off, glaring angrily over her shoulder.

"What is happening?" asked Lord Renwick, frowning.

"Miss Jane, whoever she is, was about to sit with you," said Eustacia shortly. "On your lap, if she could manage it. My lord, Mrs. Merriweather would like to speak to you."

"Mrs. Merriweather . . . oh! *Lucia!*" Lord Renwick actually rose to his feet and extended his hand. When the woman placed her fingers on his, he raised them to his lips. "How have you gone on, my dear?"

"Quite well." The woman laid one finger on his chest just above his vest. "I am sorry to hear life has treated you less gently."

"My eyes?" Jason grimaced. He turned slightly. "Thank you, Miss Coleson, for explaining."

"It was nothing," said Eustacia, feeling exceedingly *de trop*.

"It was more than I can say," said Jason softly. "Lucia," he went on, turning back to the older woman, "do take a seat. I try to keep those beside me empty for just such friends." Seemingly as an afterthought, he extended his hand toward her, but Eustacia avoided it. "Miss Coleson?"

"I must . . . the retiring room," she said on a gasp and escaped.

Jason frowned slightly but turned back to his friend. They discussed the season and her immediate plans. He told her of the prince who was his guest and that Miss Coleson was his aunt's and was continually bemused by the light touches Mrs. Merriweather placed on his arm, his cheek, his hand. He was startled, not to say unsettled, to discover he was *glad* his aunt appeared!

"Mrs. Merriweather," said her ladyship in a chill tone.

"Ah. The inevitable dragon," said Lucia, chuckling. "My lord, now your honor guard has arrived, I will make a strategic retreat! But another time and soon, I hope. I have enjoyed our talk." Bangles on her wrist jangled as she walked off.

"Aunt?" asked Jason.

"I was unaware you knew that . . . woman."

"A friend from long ago. Why do you call her *that woman?*"

"You do not know she has made a byword of herself! You must have nothing to do with her, Jason."

"She is a friend, Aunt Luce," said Jason quietly. "I will not cut her unless you give me better reason than vague talk of scandal."

"She is not invited into better homes."

"Is she not?" He grinned, a brief, rather sardonic, twist to his lips. "If you refer to a stuffy top-of-the-trees sort of personage, I very much doubt she was ever patronized by such!"

"You try my patience, Jason. You know what I mean without my saying it in so many words!"

"Bah, to quote our young prince," said Jason. "If she offends your sensibilities, Aunt, you need have nothing to do with her, of course, but you will not tell me with whom I may and may not associate! Ah, I hear McMurrey's rumbling grumble approaching." He rose to his feet. "Aunt, Miss Coleson retired some little time ago. I would appreciate it if you would see that she is all right. I believe it is time to go in to supper and she will not wish to miss it. You will bring her to our table, will you not?" He turned to his friend. "Ian?"

McMurrey came to his side, a young lady on his arm. "Jase! I don't know about you, but I am sharp set." He made the introductions and then, offering his other arm to Jason, they set off for the dining room.

Lady Blackburne stared after her nephew, her jaw clenched and her mouth a tight line. "Oh, yes, Jason, it is time and more I find you a wife!" she muttered, and continued the thought in her mind, *But not Mrs. Merriweather!*

After supper Lord Renwick claimed exhaustion and, before his aunt knew what he planned, he had left the Assembly with the prince, Bahadur, and Aaron. Lady Blackburne, who meant to introduce him to the eldest daughter of the Lewes vicar, was momentarily furious.

Then, realizing he'd not be flirting with the tarnished widow, she resolved that, since *Jason* had eluded her she would, instead, introduce Eustacia to every eligible man she knew.

Which she did, along with some she did *not.* Know, that is. Unfortunately, all were engaged and unable to sit through a set with a woman who, incomprehensible as it seemed, did not dance.

Eustacia was happy when the evening ended and, settling into a corner of the carriage, pretended to sleep. She was not, however, allowed to escape to her room when they returned to Tiger's Lair, as was her intention.

"His lordship sits in the blue salon, my lady," Reeves said, his eyes trained somewhere over Lady Blackburne's shoulder.

"The *salon?* But . . . how strange. Come along, Miss Coleson. Lord Hayworth? Lord Wendover and Mr. McMurrey? Would you not enjoy a cup of tea before retiring? Reeves, see to it." Her ladyship moved even as she spoke and entered the salon on the last words. "Jason! What is the matter? And why did you leave the Assembly in such a scrambling way?"

"I left because it was time the prince returned home. I did not tell you because you might have insisted you leave as well." His hand dropped to Sahib's head, stilling the animal who stirred at the edge to his voice. "Or alternately, Aunt Luce, you might have insisted I stay because there was a sweet young thing to whom you wished to introduce me and, frankly, I had had quite enough of sweet young things"—a brief humorless smile crossed his face, disappeared—"although their mothers were worse."

"Enough of . . . ! Worse!"

"More than enough. You will oblige me by never again suggesting I attend such an evening. The music was abominably played and pure torture to my ears. The added cacophony of people speaking and moving hither and yon did not amuse me." His hand gripped his pet's nape. "I will not suffer the like again."

It was a warning and his aunt did not misunderstand. Still, her nephew must wed. And wed someone who would not interfere in her plans to continue aiding her nephew!

"You do not speak, Aunt. Hear me and hear me well. I will not be persecuted in that way again."

"*How* can you say you were *persecuted?*" asked his aunt, a faintly dangerous note entering her voice.

"You, I believe, danced most every dance, so, very likely you did not notice how many chaperons brought their daughters to meet me."

"I don't suppose I did. But why would you dislike meeting your neighbor's daughters?" she asked with as much innocence as she could manage.

"Aunt Luce, you are not dense! Do not pretend you've no notion why the local matrons wished to introduce their daughters!"

"Any parent would think it"—she could not suppress a defensive note in her tone—"a great coup if their daughter wedded you. It is perfectly natural so what is wrong with it?"

"Aunt!" The tiger growled. "No, Sahib. You cannot protect me."

His hand on Sahib's shoulder subdued the beast, but Miss Coleson smiled to see the wrinkled forehead Sahib turned up toward his master as the animal only half settled back.

"If, tomorrow night, that creature roars at our guests in that offensive fashion," snapped Lady Blackburne, "I doubt they will stay ten minutes which would be a great shame. Cook has gone to great efforts to provide for their dinner and would be insulted if it were not enjoyed." She turned to the company. "My lord, did you enjoy the Assembly?" she asked Wendover.

"I did. And I believe, when he was not harassed by matchmaking mothers, that Jason did as well."

"True to a small degree," said Jason, feeling a trifle embarrassed. He had been too angry with his aunt to notice others were present when he scolded her or he'd not have done so. Attempting to lighten things with humor, he said, "There is a solution. I shall hold only bachelor parties."

"You will do no such thing," said his aunt, blustering, and then realized her nephew jested. "Ah. I see. Perhaps we can solve the problem." She watched him carefully. "We shall simply arrange your marriage in the old way so that you need not feel it necessary to fend off the husband-hunting multitude?"

"I warn you, Aunt, I will not oblige you in such a project." Once again Jason made a great effort to relax. "I will," he joked, "rely on Sahib and Miss Coleson to keep me safe."

"Sahib, perhaps," said Lady Blackburne. She stared

narrowly at her nephew. "I believe," she said, "that I have been remiss. I must look about me for a husband for Miss Coleson." She was neither surprised nor particularly pleased to see Jason's color fade. It was as she had suspected: He thought of wedding the chit himself . . . and the girl was *not* the sort of woman Lady Blackburne wanted for her nephew. "She will like that."

"I think not. Besides, that would be a rather difficult project, my lady," objected Miss Coleson, keeping her voice steady with difficulty. "Not only am I, at my great age, firmly on the shelf, but you would find it difficult to discover a man willing to sit, year in and year out, across the breakfast cups from one whose face is as flawed as mine is." Her hand rose to her cheek.

"Flawed, Miss Coleson?" asked Lord Wendover, his brows arched high. "If it is to that delightful beauty mark you refer, then you are fair and far off! Who has suggested it is a fault?"

Eustacia's fingers pressed against her birthmark, covering it. "I have known it forever, my lord. You are kind to pretend it does not matter."

"Ha!" barked McMurrey. "That idiotic stepmother told you so? Your Mrs. Weaver?"

Eustacia's reddened cheeks answered him.

"She was very wrong to say the mark is a flaw!" McMurrey bowed. "A beauty mark, as Tony says."

"If you are convinced it will bother a husband who must *look* at it, then you shall marry me, Miss Coleson," said Jason, inserting himself into the conversation. He gave a sharp bark of laughter. "With *my particular flaw,* yours will be none at all!"

Eustacia felt herself blanch and wondered if she would disgrace herself by swooning. "Thank you, my lord, for your very flattering offer, but when you wed you will wish a wife of whom you may be proud. I must decline."

Lord Renwick opened his mouth, closed it with a snap,

and then pretended a yawn. "It is late. I find the concentration necessary when among so many to be very tiring." He rose. "Sahib?"

The big cat walked over to Eustacia and nosed her hand. He looked up at her and opened his mouth in that way he had.

She smiled sadly at the beast. "Good night, Sahib," she said softly.

The cat nudged her again, before placing himself at Lord Renwick's side. Very gently he nudged his master's leg and Jason, after a curt nod, left the room, swinging his long cane lightly ahead of him.

"Blast the boy," muttered Lady Blackburne. A grim look settled about her eyes. "My dear," she said crossly, "I know you could have done no other, but I wish that idiotic scene had not happened. I think your refusal hurt my nephew."

"But he merely jested!"

"Did he?" Lady Blackburne remembered her own plans. "Yes, of course he did." She too yawned. "I think"—she sounded surprised—"that I must have become unused to late hours. The Assembly tired me, too. Miss Coleson, please pour out when the tea comes." She yawned a second time. "Gentlemen? Good night."

The four remaining in the salon were silent for a long moment. Then Miss Coleson rose to her feet. Her head slightly averted, she said, "Lord Wendover? Mr. McMurrey? Uncle Gus? I apologize, but I fear I, too, must leave you to your own devices. Good night." She very nearly ran from the room.

Lord Hayworth, who had been unusually silent throughout, stared after her. Absently he excused himself as well. A thoughtful mien sobered his usual clownish expression.

"Did he jest?" asked Wendover idly, once he and

McMurrey were alone. He swung his quizzing glass on its ribbon.

"What did you think?"

"If I knew, would I ask?"

McMurrey chuckled. "Oh, yes. You will not mention a topic frankly. You approach any serious subject from an angle, pretending surprise. To say, outright, that Jason Renwick has fallen deeply in love with that very interesting young lady is not your way. Tony?"

"Yes?"

"How can we help?"

Wendover sighed. "Damned if I know, Ian. Damned if I know."

"Ha! Asked your question before you could, did I not?"

Wendover grinned. "Caught me nicely, you think?"

"Yes." McMurrey sobered. "Tony, if you think of something, you will tell me?"

"Of course I will." Wendover played with the quizzing glass, dangling it from his fingertips. "I would have to, would I not? Very likely you'll be necessary to any plot I devise."

"You must hurry."

"Why?"

"I am needed in Edinburgh. In fact, I was to return once I took care of a certain problem in London and saw that Aaron was settled here. I'm a week late as it is."

"Put it off as long as you can."

"Hmmm . . ."

The two friends fell into a companionable silence. When the tea tray arrived they looked at it, looked at each other, and told Reeves to take it away.

Then they took themselves to bed.

Fourteen

Deep in the night Sahib stalked to the side of the bed where Lord Renwick turned and twisted. An occasional word escaped the sleeping man and finally a name. "Eustacia . . ." Such pain. Such anguish.

Sahib, sensitive to Jason's every mood, patted the bed. The frame shook slightly and Jason subsided. The tiger watched for a moment before he lay down again, this time beside the bed. When Jason once again moaned the tiger rose to his feet. Like a ghost, he moved across the room, looking back when, once again, he heard, "Eustacia!"

Sahib opened the door and padded down the hall. A pale and silent shadow in the dark and silent night, the tiger climbed the stairs. At the top, he paused to snuffle up the disturbing mixture of human scent. Finding the one he wanted, he followed it and again entered a room. This one was strange to him and he paused, listening. The light breathing of the sleeping woman caught his ear and he moved to her bedside.

Rising up, his paws on the mattress, Sahib growled softly. The sleeping woman shifted position, turning away from him. He nudged her and she, more than half asleep, pushed his head away from her thigh. Sahib grasped her wrist gently in his mouth and pulled.

Eustacia, rudely awakened by the wet maw as much as

the tug, sat up, her heart pounding. "Sahib?" she asked. Gently she pulled her hand back. He didn't release her, tugging harder. "What is it? Does Ja . . . his lordship . . . is he in need?"

The tiger gave that silent roar, allowing Eustacia to have her hand back.

"You want me to come?" It occurred to Eustacia it was silly, having a conversation with a mute beast, but Sahib had never before come to her room. He must want something. "I'll come."

She slid to the side of the bed and searched with her feet for her slippers, finding one only. The other had been pushed beneath the bed by Sahib and, perforce, she abandoned both. She reached for her robe, but when she stood to put it on Sahib got between her and the bed. He pushed her, stumbling, toward the door. Clutching her robe, Eustacia, willy-nilly, exited her room and moved toward the stairs.

"Yes, yes, I'm coming," she whispered. "Don't push or I'll fall." She didn't know if Sahib understood, but he did allow her to clutch the bannister and make a slow, careful way into the deeper darkness of the entry hall.

Once they reached the ground floor, Sahib herded Eustacia toward Jason's wing, her hesitant steps too slow to suit him. Finally, trusting him as she'd seen Jason do, she let him guide her through the dark. Soon she had a hand on the hallway wall. With that to encourage her she moved still more quickly toward his lordship's room. Then, having arrived, she resisted Sahib's efforts to push her in.

"Please . . . not nay," she heard. "Say yes . . . yeesss."

"Lord Renwick?" she whispered, confused.

"Hurt. Such pain . . ."

"My lord!"

Bemused, Eustacia yielded to Sahib's next gentle shove and entered the room. Once inside, she was reluctant either to leave or to proceed. *Perhaps,* she considered as she stood silent, listening, *I should find Lady Blackburne.*

"Eustacia . . ."

Her name! It pulled her toward the bed.

A full moon approached the western horizon and moonlight through the uncovered window eased the darkness. Eustacia saw that his lordship had thrown off his covers, had twisted his nightshirt around his body in such a way it looked extremely uncomfortable. Why did he not get up and rearrange himself?

"Eustacia . . ."

"Yes, my lord?"

"Need . . . love . . ."

Eustacia gasped. What did he mean? Was he speaking of her? *To* her? Did he know she was there? Or did he still sleep? Was this, perhaps, a dream? A *nightmare?*

Sahib nudged her again, this time pushing her tight against the bed. She set her hand on the mattress to steady herself.

"My dear, my love . . ." His lordship thrashed around, twisting a sheet around his leg. And then distinctly, despairingly, "Ah, but who could love a blind man?"

"I could," she whispered. *"I do."*

"Useless . . . failure . . . half a man . . . no good . . ."

"Nonsense," she said a trifle more loudly.

"Need . . . need . . . her love . . ."

Eustacia frowned. Her? Mrs. Merriweather, perhaps? Oh, surely it would be best to wake his aunt.

But Sahib was tired of waiting for Eustacia to know what she should do. He lifted a paw to the middle of her back and shoved. Eustacia found herself sprawling across his lordship's chest. She found herself held in a desperate embrace, kissed, touched as she had not known a man would touch a woman.

"My lord!"

Her heart pounding, she tried, breathlessly, to push

herself away and found, instead, that she was rolled onto her back, his body half over hers. Again his lips found hers. Words became impossible . . . and undesirable.

For a moment, through flooding emotions, Eustacia knew that what she intended was wrong, knew what would happen if she did not, instantly, prevent it. Then, just as quickly, she was aware she did not care. Somewhere in the words she heard, in the anguish and despair, she perceived a need that matched her own.

She could not find it in her heart to deny either of them.

Twice more that night Lord Renwick reached for the woman in his bed. Only the first time had he believed he dreamed. After that he knew what he did, knew it was wrong, knew he was behaving in the most dastardly of fashions and could not care. He might never again know such love so freely given. He might never again feel the trust, the unbelievable presence of intimacy in which he allowed his needy heart to revel, *even while part of him knew it for a sham.*

He didn't want to know anything about the woman his friends had introduced into his bed. That she was skilled in simulating the emotions he needed to feel in the *right* woman, in the woman he loved, well that would have to be enough, would it not?

Because he didn't wish to know her, he had avoided touching her face. He enjoyed his game of giving features and form to his love, but would that *remain* enough? Could he not, perhaps, give *this* face to the woman about whom he dreamed?

Tentatively he touched her throat. Hesitantly he ran his palm up the side of her face. Delicately he trailed his finger tips across high cheekbones, smooth, gently arched brows, down a straight little nose which was, perhaps, very slightly tip-tilted at the end. He outlined her lips, felt them purse against his fingers, smiled to feel it. He traced her chin, along her jaw first one way and then the other and then up that cheek . . . and paused.

An odd roughness. A small area only. A slightly different texture and in the shape of a heart . . . a birthmark.

"My lord?"

Abruptly, Jason sat up, pushed away from her. "Oh, my God!" he muttered.

She sighed. "I told you no man would sit across the breakfast cups from my disfigurement. Even you, who cannot see it, agree."

"Don't be a fool. You know it isn't that. I thought you a . . . I thought Wendover or McMurrey had . . . why did you . . . ?"

Sahib rose and planted his feet on the bed. Leaning he thrust his muzzle into Jason's back, pressing him down onto Eustacia. She giggled as his lordship apologized, pushing up and away, one arm supporting him.

"How," he asked, "can you laugh?"

"But my lord, you asked why I . . . did what I did. You must ask Sahib. It was his idea."

Jason turned, flopped back against his pillow. "Tell me."

"I don't know why he came for me, but he did." Eustacia described how the tiger had awakened her, had seemed to insist she come with him. And then how, when she'd stood undecided beside his lordship's bed, the tiger had pushed her down and across his lordship's chest.

"Undecided?"

Eustacia hesitated. "You . . . were dreaming. Perhaps a nightmare? You must have disturbed Sahib."

"Dreaming . . ." Jason threw an arm up across his forehead. "Yes. Very likely I was dreaming." A wry chuckle escaped him. "Perhaps I dream still!"

A dream. Did he *hope* it was a dream? "It grows late,

my lord. I'd best leave you and return to my room." She rose.

In vain he reached for her. Panicked, he insisted, *"We must talk."*

She put aside the wonder and the glory of their night together. Then, just as she had firmed her spine, she firmed her voice. "My lord, we will pretend this never happened. That will be best, I think."

"Can you?"

"I have discovered, as have you, that it is quite amazing what one can do if one must."

"But . . . must we?"

"My lord?"

"Why must we?" A hint of last night's desperation could be heard. "I know I am no catch for any woman, blind as I am, and you suggested you would never wed because of your face. Perhaps we two *do* belong together."

"Your aunt wishes to see you wed to a proper bride, my lord," said Eustacia quietly. "I do not qualify."

"Do *my* wishes count for nothing?"

"My lord . . ." *How could he sound so sincere?* "I must go."

"We have not finished."

"I must go."

Eustacia heard her name called as she shut the door. For a moment she leaned against it; then she straightened her nightshift and pulled on the gown she'd scooped from the floor on her way across his room. And then, knowing the servants would soon be up and around, she fled down the hall and up the stairs.

And just in time. She heard footsteps on the servant's stairs at the end of the hall just as she scooted into her room and, softly, closed her door.

Again she leaned against a door, this time fighting hot tears which would no longer be denied. He had thought her a *whore,* a gift brought him by one or both of his friends! He would never have touched her as he had if he had known it was she.

She sighed, recognizing that last as a self-pitying bit of inanity. *Of course* he would not have touched her. He was a gentleman and gentlemen did not ravage their aunt's guests. But she had allowed him to do so, had not fought him. Had, in fact, reveled in their lovemaking in an exceedingly unladylike fashion! And *because* she had shown no restraint he would come to believe her the whore he had thought her. He would despise her for allowing him such liberties.

A smile flickered into being: *such wonderful liberties!*

The smile faded. Could she pretend none of it had happened? Would he? There was that gentlemanly streak in him, the honorable man and officer. Would he allow himself to forget?

Or would he feel that, having ruined her, he *must* offer his name to her?

What nonsense. That first time . . .

Eustacia's eyes widened. That first time he had called her by name, called her his love. That first time he had not been wholly awake and had acted without thinking. But . . .

Oh, surely it was impossible. He could not love her.

How could he possibly love her?

Why would he love her?

What, other than the fact she had been under his nose, so to speak, was there about her for a man to love? Or was that enough? She had *been* there, *available*, alone with him day after day, working with him, arguing with him, talking to him, helping him complete work of interest to him.

Was that enough when a man was ready to fall in love? Was it enough for her? Was that why *she* had fallen in love with him?

"No."

Eustacia wandered to the window and stared out. She listed all the reasons she had fallen hopelessly in love with Lord Renwick and they were good reasons, *not* mere propinquity.

"But he was dreaming," she said softly. "He suffered a nightmare, feared losing someone . . . *me?*"

Oh, surely not. There was nothing about her a man would or could *truly* love. Surely that was proven. She was very nearly twenty-five and never once had a man shown the least interest in her! Except Mr. Weaver. She shuddered.

But Lord Renwick had proposed, had he not? Before his friends and her uncle! And she had, of course, turned down his lighthearted teasing proposal, had she not? As was expected of her?

Except . . . he had left the room almost immediately thereafter.

Had he been more serious than she'd thought? Had he believed she rejected *him* rather than that she did her poor best to turn off what she believed a jest? Eustacia bit her lip.

The door opened and a maid brought in a tray with her morning tea on it. Eustacia turned and, for the first time, realized she felt just a trifle sore here and there. Particularly *there*.

"Thank you, Jane. That will be all," she said, wishing to be alone. As the door was closing, Eustacia changed her mind and called the girl back. "I would like a bath this morning. When the early chores are finished, will you arrange for the tub to be brought up?"

The maid nodded and withdrew.

Eustacia chose her morning dress with care before removing her robe and gown. She noticed a smear of blood on the gown and blushed. Very quickly she put the robe back on and went to her washbowl where she rinsed the stain away.

His sheets! Oh, dear. What would his valet see? Would he mention it if he did? Inform Lady Blackburne, perhaps? Or gossip with the servants?

Eustacia sighed.

There was nothing she could do. Pouring herself a cup of tea she wandered back to the window and stood there, sipping, staring unseeingly across the garden until the tub and water arrived and she could bathe.

All of which meant she was very late for breakfast.

Had she meant to avoid his lordship? If she had, she did not succeed. He sat in his usual place, his elbows on the table and his head in his hands, the room's only occupant, unless one counted Sahib.

"You are very late," he said, not looking up.

"Yes." Her hand went to the tinkling bells she'd put on without thinking. He'd not have known she was here if she had not . . .

"Did you sleep late?" he asked politely.

"I . . . had a bath."

"Hmm." A slightly wicked smile quirked his lips. "Yes. So did I. Someday we must arrange to bathe together."

"My lord!"

"After we are wed."

"My lord!"

He sighed. "Eat your breakfast, my dear. We will go to my study where we may be private as soon as you've broken your fast."

He reached for the hand bell, groping irritably when he did not instantly grasp it. Then, achieving his goal, he rang it firmly. Very shortly Eustacia had fresh tea and toast and a plate filled with her favorite foods.

She ate absently, staring at his lordship who sat back and, with well simulated patience, waited for her to finish.

"My lord . . ." she began once but was hushed.

She decided to wait until they were in his study. Until they were private and would not be disturbed. So she ate silently, took his arm in silence once finished, and, in silence, strolled at his side.

Then, finally seated in her usual chair, she said, "Now, my lord—"

"*Now* you will listen to me. I have thought about that scene in the salon last evening. It has occurred to me that you thought I jested when I suggested we wed. It *was* a most maladroit attempt at a proposal, was it not? Not only were we not alone, but, because my blindness makes me ineligible, I tried to protect myself. Which obviously I did. All too well. You turned me down for no other reason than you thought I jested . . . did you not?"

He had begun with seeming confidence, but the tone of the last three words indicated how insecure he felt. He cast a worried look her way and Eustacia very nearly rose from her chair and went to him.

"My lord," she said, hesitantly, "I will not wed you if you believe you should, merely because of . . . what happened. You thought me a woman hired for that purpose. You must not feel *obliged* to wed me."

"Whenever I recall you will someday leave us I despair. I have wondered how I'll survive your absence and wished I dared offer you marriage." His lips firmed and his eyes narrowed slightly. "Miss Coleson, it occurred to me as I lay alone this morning, that a woman raised as you were, a vicar's daughter who will not learn to dance because of his disapproval, such a woman would not lightly do . . . what you did freely and gladly and with, I think"—the slightest of questions tinted his tone—"some joy?"

He drew in a breath and continued before she could think how to reply. "And if you gave me freely what you should carefully guard until properly wed, then you did so for deep and powerful reasons. And," he added, when she would, again, have interrupted, "the only possible reason is that, by some miracle, some grace of God, you love me as much as I love you."

Eustacia stared at him. "You . . . love me? But why?"

"So bewildered, my dear?" He chuckled. "You are a delight in so many ways I don't know where to begin. First, I suppose, is that which originally drew me, the molten gold of your voice, the tones of an angel. Then your generosity. Your wisdom. Your sensitivity. Your willingness to take responsibility where you see a need." He smiled. "I could go on forever, my love, but is that enough for going on with?"

"But I am nothing special."

"That, my dear, sounds like your stepmother speaking!"

Eustacia was silenced for a long moment. "I suppose it does. You would say she was wrong?"

"Very wrong."

Eustacia sighed deeply. "I doubt I will ever manage to believe that."

"It will be my duty, as your husband," he said solemnly, "to spend part of each day convincing you. And you must spend an equal amount of time convincing *me* that I am not so very bad. Which will be difficult, will it not? Because it is far more obvious *I* am no prize."

She laughed as she knew she was meant to do. "Still, even if we each agree the other is wonderful, there is your aunt."

A touch of arrogance lifted his chin. "What has she to do with my marriage?"

"Surely you agree"—Eustacia hesitated only a moment before continuing—"it would be improper to go against her wishes!"

"Do I? I think not. I know the sort of girl my aunt would wish upon me. A meek little mouse who will never learn how to say boo. A chit she can mold into the form she wishes my wife to have. In other words, a woman who will not demand Aunt Luce depart instantly to the dower house or some more distant location!"

Eustacia realized there was a great deal of truth in that. "Still . . . surely . . ."

"You would wish such a meek creature on me? My dear, you have not thought. *Sahib* would *never* approve. And, although I can and will, if necessary, wed against my aunt's wishes, I *cannot* marry to disoblige Sahib. Impossible!"

"You are in a teasing mood, my lord," she responded absently. Her racing thoughts were interrupted when the door opened. She turned and saw a frowning prince standing there. "Prince Ravi?" she asked.

"Lord Renwick is to teach me maths now. He does so each day at this time. So why has he said he is not to be disturbed?" The boy glowered and, arrogantly, he added, "That is nonsense."

"Lord Renwick," said his lordship in a dry tone, "said he was not to be disturbed because he wished he not be disturbed. You will have a holiday, prince, and you will like it."

The boy came further into the study. "I do not wish a holiday. I have had several holidays recently and they do not forward my education. I cannot return home until my education is complete and it is my *desire* that I return home. Therefore we will do my maths now."

"My lord," said Eustacia, "I have a great deal about which I must think. If you feel able, perhaps you will indulge our prince in his desire to forward his education."

"One more thing—"

She turned at the door, the silver bells jingling.

"About which you must think," he said. "Consequences, my dear. There might very well be consequences and I would not like to think you thought I did not realize it."

Eustacia responded, her voice very slightly strangled. "Yes, my lord."

She, after all, until that moment, had had not one single thought of possible . . . consequences!

Eustacia paced her room. She would *not* wed his lordship only to save her good name. She was no longer poverty-stricken. Her grandfather had had a change of heart and her uncle assured her it was true.

I could pretend to be a widow, make up a history about a soldier husband, brave and loyal. I could move to some small community, raise my child if I am lucky and have one, could live . . .

She turned on her heel and, head bowed, stalked in the other direction.

Live. Just live. But to live without Jason? Without his loving, his love?

Again she turned.

Assuming, of course, he does love me. Ah, that is the true question, is it not? The only question? If he loves me . . .

She turned.

Oh, if only he loved me!

And how did one know? How does one distinguish between the love of a good man and a good man's pretense when he must convince a woman of his love?

Eustacia stopped.

"Why can I not believe him? Why not accept that my stepmother, for selfish reasons, convinced me I am unlovable?"

"Miss?"

Eustacia swung around, her skin heating. "Ah! Jane. I thought you had finished here."

"Lady Blackburne wishes you to join her in the blue salon, miss."

Eustacia bit her lip. "The blue salon . . . yes. Of course, Jane. I will go down immediately."

The maid remained for another half moment, then

nodded, and closed the door as silently as she'd opened it. *Maybe his lordship's valet,* thought the chit, *doesn't have rats in his attic after all! Miss Coleson looks as betwattled as a wet hen!*

"There you are," said Lady Blackburne some minutes later. "Jason says I must congratulate you."

Eustacia groaned silently. One did not *congratulate* the woman. One gave her best wishes!

"You have done very well for yourself, have you not?"

"I think not."

Lady Blackburne's eyes narrowed. "Explain yourself."

"I love Lord Renwick deeply, but I do not feel that is sufficient. I have not told him I will wed him. My lady," continued Eustacia before her ladyship could comment, "I have not been reared to such a position." Inspiration struck and she quickly added, "I would not know how to go on in the *ton,* nor have I the training to care for a home such as this. Unless I was assured you would not abandon me, I know I would fail. My lady, I could not bear to be an embarrassment to his lordship."

Lady Blackburne started to speak then closed her mouth. "You love him?"

"Beyond anything, my lady."

"But you do not feel worthy of him?"

"He tells me that is my stepmother speaking and I should not feel that way, but I do." Without thinking she covered the mark on her cheek.

"If you refer to that birthmark, he is correct. That is insignificant, not a thing any man would object to. On the other hand . . . you do *not* know all you should if you were to become his baroness—"

"As I am all too well aware! I have watched you give orders here, watched you check that tasks are properly completed. I think it takes a very long time to learn all one must know to run a household such as this." Eustacia sighed. "And there is his lordship's writing. If I were to continue helping with that, well, you know how time-consuming it can be."

"You would need a great deal of help, would you not?"

"And patience, my lady. I am not a particularly social creature. I dislike crowds and I understand a London entertainment is considered unsuccessful unless it may be called a crush! How would I go on? Or his lordship, for that matter?"

"One need not entertain in that fashion," said Lady Blackburne absently, her mind elsewhere. "There are musicales and dinners and, where there is a sufficiency of space, garden parties or the like. Balls and soirees require a certain style of house. Most do not own such and must entertain in a less ostentatious manner."

"How ridiculously idiotic that I did not see that for myself! My lady, do you think I *could* learn to be a good wife for his lordship?"

"You are intelligent. And there is the problem of the voice . . ."

"Voice?"

Lady Blackburne sighed. "It occurred to me in the night watches that finding another woman with a voice my Jason could tolerate day in and day out might be a trifle difficult. It crossed my mind to promote a match between the two of you, but I had not reached a decision." She scowled. "You can understand, perhaps, why I was more than a trifle surprised to be informed by my nephew that I was to arrange a marriage between the two of you. Worse, that it was to be done by license and before Mr. McMurrey is required to leave us."

"But Mr. McMurrey has indicated he must leave any day now!"

"Exactly."

Eustacia chuckled. "You think it all a trifle havey-cavey, do you not?"

"I see no reason for such haste."

Eustacia hesitated. Then she went to shut the door which, unaccountably, she had left open. When she returned she sat, staring at nothing at all, her lips compressed. Finally, sighing, she reached a decision. "My lady . . ."

"You had best call me Aunt Luce as Jason does."

A quick smile flashed across Eustacia's lips and vanished. "You will pardon me if it takes time to accept your generosity in that respect?"

Lady Blackburne smiled a chilly smile. "I see where I might have made it a trifle difficult. But you've something to say. A confession, I'd guess."

Eustacia nodded. "Last night Sahib came to my room. He insisted I go with him. Fearing something was wrong with his lordship, that he was ill or had lost himself, I followed Sahib."

"That beast came right into your room!" Lady Blackburne looked horrified. "I would have been frightened out of my wits, my dear. I feel for you! And was something wrong?"

"Lord Renwick suffered nightmares, my lady."

Lady Blackburne scowled. "I had thought him done with that. He had them most every night when he first returned from India, but then, gradually, he ceased having them. I allowed his valet to have a room of his own instead of sleeping in Jason's dressing room."

Eustacia gave fleeting thought to how embarrassing it would have been if the valet still slept in that little room! *But then,* she thought, *Sahib would not have come for me. Eric would have heard his lordship, would have awakened him.*

"Do continue. Jason was trapped in a nightmare . . . ?"

Eustacia sighed. "He talks in his sleep, did you know?"

"Eric was ordered to repeat what he heard to me. What was said in English, I mean, but, of course, I had thought Jason long over such things. I wonder what had him in such a bother."

Eustacia sighed. "I believe it was my fault. You will remember, in the salon last night, that Jason made what I
thought a jesting proposal. He assures me he was serious
but pretended he merely bantered in order to protect
himself." In a voice which underlined her lack of understanding, Eustacia said, "For reasons beyond my compre-
hension, he does not feel himself fully a man, a suitable
prospect for any marriage."

"Perhaps he has reason to feel that way. I overheard a
conversation at the Assembly which bothered me. Two
chits discussed Jason. One would not think of marrying
a blind man. The other said of course one would. One
would be Lady Renwick and very rich and, after produc-
ing a son, one could go one's own way."

"How terrible! How could any girl be so cynical?" She
frowned fiercely. "And how could anyone feel that way
about Ja—Lord Renwick?"

"Bravo!" Lord Wendover, standing in the open door,
clapped his hands softly. "You feel just as you ought, Miss
Coleson."

McMurrey, behind Lord Wendover, pushed his friend
into the room at a pace Lord Wendover found at odds
with his dignity. "Here now!" he objected.

"Then," said McMurrey, "stop acting the ass. Miss
Coleson, we need your signature on this paper and then
we are off."

"Off?" asked Lady Blackburne.

"To arrange for a license, my lady. Jason is insistent he
be wed before I depart and, much to my distress, I must
go as soon as may be."

Wendover carried the paper, pen, and ink, to a small
table against the wall. He turned toward Miss Coleson.
"Will you sign?"

"I . . ." She glanced at Lady Blackburne.

"Oh, sign so they may be on their way. You and I, Miss
Coleson, will have a very busy few days."

No sooner were Jason's friends off to beard the nearest bishop in his den, than Lord Hayworth sauntered into the room. The faintest of frown lines marred his usually smooth brow and they deepened when he noticed his niece. "My dear Stacy!" he said in an insistent sort of voice. "Is this *truly* what you wish?"

"Uncle Gus, if you refer to my wedding Lord Renwick, then it is. But I cannot tell if I'm on my head or my heels, the pace the day is going!"

"What I cannot like is the havey-cavey manner of it all! I thought you were to come to me for a visit, my dear. I thought . . ." He sighed. "Well, never mind. I have sent off a letter to my solicitor. George will come instantly and proper arrangements may be made for the widow's portion and all those other things which must be seen to before a young lady weds."

"My nephew insists the wedding be within the week."

"So he told me," said Hayworth in a disapproving tone. He sounded very unlike his normal self which included a sort of vacuousness. "I told him he can insist all he wants, but my niece will not wed until the papers are properly signed!"

Eustacia thought of mentioning she was of age and need not obey him in this or any other respect, but it occurred to her that perhaps a delay would bring his lordship to his senses and he would realize he did not truly wish to wed her.

A bubble of panic rose up to choke her at the thought he might change his mind! Perhaps, instead, she should wed him out of hand? But no. That would be dishonorable. She must allow Jason time to know if this was truly what he wished.

It was, of course, and, over the next few days, Jason spent every possible moment convincing Eustacia of that fact. Lady Blackburne, convinced far more quickly of her nephew's true feelings, resigned herself to the inevitable and worked hard to plan a not totally inadequate wedding. Only gradually did Lord Renwick realize she had ordered a far more elaborate ceremony than he envisaged but she overrode his objections by explaining, in words of one syllable, how Eustacia would be looked down upon if he went ahead with his own hole-in-the-corner plans.

As she'd guessed, he gave in the instant he realized Eustacia might suffer for no other reason than that he had hoped to avoid making a spectacle of himself!

Eustacia went around in a daze, continuing to be uncertain she was right to agree but reluctant to disagree. She wanted this marriage and knew she would be a good wife to Jason. Every time it occurred to her she really should postpone it all, should give Jason more time, she would remember Lady Blackburne's tale of the young woman who would happily be Lady Renwick, but *not* so happily Jason's *wife*.

I will go ahead as planned because I dare not chance his falling into such a trap as that.

Her wedding day arrived and so did Lady Blackburne who supervised her bath and the washing of her hair. She produced a gown Eustacia had never seen and helped her into it.

"But," objected Eustacia, "this is none of mine!" Very gently, she touched the cobwebby lace. "It is far too fine!"

"I had it reconstructed from the gown Jason's mother wore. People are invited who will remember it. It will hurt nothing that Jason asked you to wear his mother's wedding gown! Besides, it is a shame for such lovely lace to languish in a dark attic, gradually deteriorating into uselessness. You will enjoy it."

Eustacia blinked, then chuckled. "Is that an order, Aunt Luce?"

Lady Blackburne's hands, busy with buttons down the bride's back, stilled. "That is the first time you have called me aunt."

"Only a trifle premature," said Eustacia, attempting to cover an emotional moment with a jest.

"Or overly long in the coming," mused Lady Blackburne. "I know not which. You have called your uncle, whom you never before knew, by a diminutive from the very beginning."

"But, my lady," said Eustacia, smiling, "my uncle is not the least little bit intimidating!"

Lady Blackburne chuckled, returning to the long row of buttons. "You, my dearest *fraud,* have never, not once, found me the least little bit intimidating!"

"But only because I knew how much you love Jason. How much you wanted the very best for him." That comment sobered Eustacia. "And how difficult it is for you to accept me, obviously second best, when he might have wed someone much more suitable."

"But I have come to the conclusion that you are not second best. I was forced to understand two things, my dear. My nephew is a very intelligent man who needs a serious-minded and intelligent woman to encourage his writing. And secondly, that *beast* must approve any female allowed near Jason. Can you not imagine the uproar if, every time Jason wished to share his wife's bed, that animal must first be put into his cage?"

Eustacia blushed rosily.

"My dear," said Lady Blackburne gently, her hands once again hesitating, "should I tell you what to expect this night or should I leave that to Jason?"

"I think . . . leave it to Jason?" Eustacia dared not inform Lady Blackburne, to whom she had once been on the verge of confessing, that she needed no telling, that she waited with anticipation, with impatience, for the

coming night and the opportunity to once again be alone
with Jason!

The wedding party left in three carriages. Jason, accompanied by his friends and Sahib, went first. They had
some difficulty convincing the vicar the tiger must be allowed to attend the service. He finally capitulated when
Jason insisted they would find another church if he did
not.

The prince and *his* entourage went in the second carriage, the Indians dressed in their ceremonial best, young
Aaron a drab brown bird against their colorful plumage.
No one knew the prince had, some time earlier that
morning, sent his private army off to the church with his
precise orders. Those silent, well-trained men stood
against the walls from an early hour and were another
thing upsetting the poor vicar!

Finally, in the last carriage, Lady Blackburne, Lord Hayworth, and Eustacia drove up to the church. They heard
several voices coming from inside the sanctuary and
paused in the entry to listen. The four guests nearest the
door vied in a scrambling sort of conversation.

"A wild animal in church!" said one. "Outrageous."

"The chit is a no one," said another querulously.
"Foolish beyond permission."

"First thing *I'd* do is shoot that creature and have his
skin prepared for a rug!" said a third.

"Now, Effie," a man answered the second, "the girl's
more than presentable. Her uncle's an earl!"

"Wild beasts don't belong in church!" insisted the first.

"Where'd you hear that nonsense?" asked the one
called Effie. "She's a vicar's daughter!"

The first voice spoke a trifle more loudly. "No, he's
right, Effie. Lord Hayworth is her uncle."

"That man! A laughingstock, I've heard!"

"Nonsense. Merely an odd sense of humor," said the
man who would have Sahib shot. "Rather reprehensible

of him of course, but he loves to take a rise from the *ton* with his nonsense. Knew the man at school, you see. A bit of an eccentric, perhaps, but *not* to be laughed at!''

Eustacia cast a look at her uncle who, that day, looked very nearly up to the knocker with nothing odd about him. He winked at her and she blushed. Lady Blackburne, along with a burning sidelong glance at his lordship whom she'd never guessed was a jokesmith and always slightly despised, muttered a few words no one wished to distinguish and, nose in the air, sailed down the aisle to the family pew. No one, after all, liked to admit they'd been taken in, her ladyship least of all!

Then, the choir raising its collective voice in song, Eustacia started down the aisle with her hand on her uncle's arm. As they paced along she noticed that the prince's private army had been stationed facing inward, their colorful uniforms bright against the whitewashed walls. And fragments of conversations floated to her ears. *His mother's gown* . . . and . . . Remember that magnificent lace! . . . were two she felt she must remember to tell Lady Blackburne who had guessed correctly about adapting the dress to her needs.

They were halfway down the aisle when Sahib, who had lain quietly at Jason's feet, rose. He stalked up the aisle ignoring squeaks and stifled screeches and, here and there, a muffled, deep-timbered, oath. When he reached Eustacia he paused. Then turned. At a stately pace he led the way to the altar. When Eustacia did not instantly take her place exactly where she was wanted, the tiger moved around her and pushed her into place at Jason's side. Then, after one exceedingly loud and unexpected roar of what sounded very like triumph, Sahib settled himself behind the couple and eyed the congregation as if daring anyone to interfere.

Just as soon as the vicar found his voice, the ceremony proceeded, but at a rather faster pace than the poor man usually performed this particular rite! When the vicar pronounced them man and wife Jason turned, found Eustacia's other arm, and very gently pulled her near. He lowered his face slowly and, just as carefully, Eustacia raised hers.

It was an exceedingly gentle kiss and the crowded church heaved a collective sigh.

Lady Blackburne, against Jason's wishes, had organized a wedding breakfast. The house was crowded and Jason, who had put Sahib in his pen, sat beside Eustacia silent and glowering and not at all welcoming.

Even a scolding from his aunt didn't help.

"But I do not wish to be amiable. I want them to go away."

There was a gasp and an embarrassed titter from a couple who happened to overhear.

Jason sighed. "I was unaware someone was near. I haven't a notion who it is, but I will not apologize. I prefer company in small doses, not in groups where I cannot know who is where or what goes on. Aunt, I and my wife will retire to my study. We will, over the next weeks, invite our neighbors to small parties where we may get to know them again as I once did."

"For now, however," he continued as he rose and held a hand toward Eustacia, "please tell our friends and neighbors that I am tired. It is, after all, nothing but the truth. Public affairs such as this exhaust me as can nothing else. Eustacia?" He offered his arm and with a muttered plea to her that she help him escape, swept from the room, stalking down an open space which formed rapidly as two of the prince's servants, at the prince's command, arrogantly cleared a path for them.

Eustacia described the silk clad Indian servants' behavior once they crossed the hall to Jason's wing where, finally, they had privacy. Jason, relaxing in his usual chair, his head laid back, chuckled.

"I see I must thank the prince for the loan of his servants this day. Can you guess what wonders they have done for my consequence in the neighborhood?"

"They had done that already. Perhaps you are unaware they were at the church, weapons much in evidence? Do you think the prince felt something untoward might happen or did he merely object to the lack of pageantry and add his own touch? He has been frowning most of the day, you know."

Jason groaned. "I thought I settled that! He is, you see, to go off with Aaron and a small retinue including Bahadur and Aunt Luce to see something of London. Wendover will house them all and organize their stay. He also means to introduce Prince Ravi to our Prinny, which should be an interesting experience for the both of them!"

"You sound as if you wished you could be there, my lord." She hesitated only a moment. "We *could*—"

"Not," he interrupted, smiling. "Not when I have gone to such lengths to assure us a week or two alone. Just the two of us."

A gentle grumbling roar turned them to where Sahib stood in the doorway.

"The two of us and Sahib, you mean," said Eustacia.

"How did he get out of his pen?"

"Undoubtedly he grew tired of waiting for you to come and let himself out. We may as well get used to it, Jason. Sahib has a mind of his own."

"So he does." Jason grinned wickedly. "He decided we belong together, did he not? And grew tired of our dithering and havering and making excuses when we each knew, in our hearts, that we loved each other."

"You would say that Sahib is our Cupid?"

"An odd Cupid, wearing fur and claws, but yes. Eros, Amor, Cupid, whatever you would call him, Sahib was our very good angel, was he not?"

Sahib lifted his head and roared a second time. This time far more loudly.

"We are corrected!" added Jason, grinning. "Sahib says he *is* and *will continue to be* our angel!"

Sahib laid himself down, closed his eyes sleepily, and drifted off. A contented tiger, after all, is a drowsy tiger and this tiger was very contented indeed.

Dear Reader,

I found writing Jason's story difficult. He was lucky, I think, to have an aunt who was so managing she even managed to find the proper bride for him!

Ian McMurrey, Jason's Scottish friend, is the hero in *Lady Serena's Surrender* (in bookstores in May 2000). Lady Serena Dixon fought all her life to retain some sense of self-worth. Her monstrous father and uncouth brothers have distorted her view of men and marriage and she would do most anything to avoid matrimony. Her father beats and starves her, but, in the end, forces her agreement to wedding Ian McMurrey by threatening to beat her mother in her place.

Slowly, carefully, Ian wins Serena's trust, her love, and, finally, her surrender. Surrendering, Lady Serena discovers *she* wins as much as Ian does. Her only remaining dissatisfaction is that she cannot help her mother.

But Lady Serena is not one to give up and, since discovering the power of love and loving, she believes *anything* is possible. In the book following *Lady Serena's Surrender* another friend of Jason and Ian, the badly wounded Jack Princeton, discovers life holds something of interest beyond horses and his cavalry regiment. Perhaps Lady Serena's mother can be rescued in that book?

Or perhaps not. Life is not always so perfect as one would like and Jack's story is yet to be written: We'll see what happens.

I love to hear from my readers and may be reached at: Jeanne Savery, P.O. Box 81771, Rochester, MI, 48308. Please include a self-addressed stamped envelope for my response. Or E-mail: JeanneSavery@Juno.com.

Wishing you the best of good reading,

Cheerfully,
Jeanne Savery

BOOK YOUR PLACE ON OUR WEBSITE
AND MAKE THE
READING CONNECTION!

We've created a customized website just for our very special readers, where you can get the inside scoop on everything that's going on with Zebra, Pinnacle and Kensington books.

When you come online, you'll have the exciting opportunity to:

- View covers of upcoming books
- Read sample chapters
- Learn about our future publishing schedule (listed by publication month *and author*)
- Find out when your favorite authors will be visiting a city near you
- Search for and order backlist books from our online catalog
- Check out author bios and background information
- Send e-mail to your favorite authors
- Meet the Kensington staff online
- Join us in weekly chats with authors, readers and other guests
- Get writing guidelines
- AND MUCH MORE!

Visit our website at
http://www.zebrabooks.com

More Zebra Regency Romances

Put a Little Romance in Your Life With
Fern Michaels

__Dear Emily	0-8217-5676-1	$6.99US/$8.50CAN
__Sara's Song	0-8217-5856-X	$6.99US/$8.50CAN
__Wish List	0-8217-5228-6	$6.99US/$7.99CAN
__Vegas Rich	0-8217-5594-3	$6.99US/$8.50CAN
__Vegas Heat	0-8217-5758-X	$6.99US/$8.50CAN
__Vegas Sunrise	1-55817-5983-3	$6.99US/$8.50CAN
__Whitefire	0-8217-5638-9	$6.99US/$8.50CAN